THE LION COM

JIM CHERRY

ALSO BY JIM CHERRY

The Last Stage

Michael Night is an aging professional student looking for a way out of a small town, and away from a loving girlfriend who increasingly wants more from him. And he's also a Doors fan with ambition. But he doesn't know how to act upon it, or even admit them to himself, until, inspired by friends who tell him he looks like Jim Morrison, and a chance meeting with Ray Manzarek he takes a chance on his dream and starts a Doors cover band.

He sidetracks a band on their road to fame, and together they experience the exhilaration of being a Rock n' Roll band on tour, from the long hours, the agents, the travel, the groupies, record company executives and the growing ego of Michael Night, until they're offered the gig of their Rock n' Roll dreams. On the road Michael meets and falls in love with Caitlin Stewart, daughter of legendary guitarist Jerry Osprey, but she doesn't trust his motives, does he truly love her, or is she a career move for Michael? Or even a collectible?

They're carried to the doors of stardom when the band plays in Los Angeles where Michael meets former child star Jimmy Stark who shows him the monster fame, celebrity and stardom can be, crashing studios and parties Michael assembles an entourage of has been's and wanna be's . Then Michael Night and the band meet their destines on the stage of the Whisky a-go-go! And when it's all over Michael Night is afforded the last stage he has.

The Doors Examined

The Doors remain one of the most influential and exciting bands in rock 'n' roll history, and The Doors Examined offers a unique, expressive insight into the history of the band, their influence on culture, and the group's journey following the death of Jim Morrison in Paris in 1971. It starts at the beginning, on a Venice Beach rooftop, and takes the reader on an invigorating journey, from The Whisky a Go-Go to the Dinner Key Auditorium, The Ed Sullivan Show to Père Lachaise Cemetery.

Comprised of selected acclaimed articles from The Doors Examiner, The Doors Examined also serves up original content that assesses seminal albums, how the group's music has influenced other artists, and key people in the band's history; people like Jac Holzman, Paul Rothchild, Bruce Botnick, and Pam Courson.

The Doors Examined is a must read investigation into one of the greatest rock 'n' roll bands of all time.

TABLE OF CONTENTS

The Games Children Play   1

As Good a Name as Any   9

Dawn's Hwy   15

Judgement Night   35

The Seas Have No Stars   53

Father's Son   69

The Christmas Truce   91

Arrival for Duty   101

The Captured Dead   115

Ghosts   133

Godwired   147

Judgement Night—Redemption   161

The Third Day   179

Acknowledgement   213

About the Author   215

PRAISE FOR JIM CHERRY

"Jim Cherry is a writer who has paid his dues and now knows the way around his craft with a hard-earned confidence. His imagination ranges widely, from what seems to be a memory of childhood that then echoes 'An Occurrence at Owl Creek Bridge', to the fictionalised metaphysical and poetic transformation of Jim Morrison. He dives deeply into a gripping science fictional tale that could be the basis of a motion picture but is fortunately rooted more deeply in character than special effects. The title story is a lengthy investigation of a son's relationship with his Hemingway-style father, how the conceits of literary fame and paternal machismo can weigh on the shoulders of a son. There are explorations of common soldiers making their own kind of peace, the shamelessness of politicians in the aftermath of their Armageddon, and General Sherman called to account by the numberless souls that built his fearless reputation. There is little in the tough knots of real life or through inspired speculations on conscience-risen ghosts or even UFOs that Cherry can't turn to compelling prose."

—Jay Jeff Jones, author of
*The Wind Pours by like Destiny: Sylvia Plath,
Asa Benveniste, and the Poetic Afterlife*

"*Godwired* is an evocative story that melds together science and religion, which should have a much bigger place in science fiction. Read it, reflect upon it, and look for it in Jim Cherry's forthcoming anthology of tales that bump into the human condition."

—Paul Levinson, author of
The Silk Code and The Plot to Save Socrates

For,
My Mother

Jason,

I hope you enjoy
the book!

[signature]
11/27/24

THE GAMES CHILDREN PLAY

Kapow! I brought down the arm of the G.I. Joe with the Kung-Fu grip on top of the head of one of the enemy G.I. Joe's who was guarding my G.I. Joe. He made his way out of the Popsicle stick fort Wesley Lemont and I had made, weaving in and out of divisions of plastic soldiers, blue and green armies facing off against each other. It was an epic battle in a miniature backyard war, everything was out of scale, but it was to the scale of our imaginations. We had already played a couple games of Battleship in Wesley's room earlier while we had our Popsicles. When we got bored with that, we grabbed the rest of the Popsicle sticks we had collected over the summer, got a couple more from his sisters and went outside. We had scratched out a trench in the hard dirt of the backyard, it was a river running near the fort. Wesley was driving a jeep up from the jungle while my G.I. Joe escaped from the enemy.

"Do you think it would be more exciting if there was an explosion or if the river was on fire?" I asked. We looked at each other blankly, not sure how to do it, or how much trouble we'd get into if we started a fire. At that moment Mrs. Lemont called out from the screened-in porch above us,

"Come in for lunch boys."

Wesley led me to the dining room where his sisters Andrea and Vicki were already eating. The dining room was darker than at my house, not only were there heavy drapes covering the windows the dining room table

1

was a darker and heavier wood than ours at home. Mrs. Lemont brought out a sandwich and a bowl of tomato soup.

"Have you ever had fried Spam, Jacky?" She asked.

"No, but I'm sure it's very good," I said putting on my best manners. I took a bite of the sandwich, I didn't like it, but I politely ate it knowing that if my mother found out she would disapprove. Wesley's sisters were at the far end of the table. Andrea was the oldest, she was tall and thin, and in eighth grade, and Vicki was only a couple of years older than Wesley and me maybe in the sixth grade. In a few years Vicki would fill out and I'd feel the first flash of sexual attraction, it wasn't even sex, it was just suddenly I became of aware of her and I was more interested in talking with her than Wesley. It would surprise me as much as anyone but something I knew I couldn't tell anyone else. I started coming over to Wesley's house in the hope Vicki would be there. I finished my soup and took the empty bowl to the kitchen.

After lunch. I was bored, Wesley and I had spent most of the morning in his room, and I wanted to go out looking for some other adventure. Mrs. Lemont was very protective of Wesley and wouldn't let him go out, so she shoo'd me out of the house.

I was walking down the neatly manicured street, green lawns, trees, and houses. I grabbed the imaginary machine gun hanging at my side and started spraying the neighborhood with imaginary bullets at the japs, krauts, or gooks that were just over the smallest hill, behind every bush or hiding behind every building. Everybody was familiar with these slurs because we'd heard them regularly, we were a generation born of war. All our fathers had been in a war— my father had been in Korea, some of the other kids' fathers had been in World War II. A lot of my friends' older brothers were in Vietnam, and all this was reinforced by TV shows like *Combat, Rat Patrol* and even comedies like *Hogan's Heroes, McHale's Navy*, or the silly *F-Troop*. The war was in all the morning papers and the ten o'clock news, and the death toll climbed. While our fathers exclaimed with pride at what "good little soldiers" we were, our inheritance was war.

I zig-zagged across the Fieldman's lawn, then the Usher's house. Roger Usher was a classmate of mine at Kellogg Public School. We were acquaintances and would occasionally hang-out. One time Roger Usher and I were out riding bikes together when a car passed us by on the street. Someone in the car threw a soda cup out the window and it hit me in the forehead. Roger laughed and said, "That guy sure had good aim." He wasn't part of today's mission. The Kosinski twins, James and Eddie, lived close by, I'd go over and see if they could come out. I cut across more lawns, storming the beaches of Normandy avoiding a Kraut stronghold or the jungles of Iwo Jima rushing a Jap embankment. I turned up an alley, or was it a bombed-out city, walls falling over, cratered streets. I continued up the alley toward the Kosinski's house. I stopped. On top of a garbage can was an army helmet. I picked it up. It had a ghostly skull painted on it, and it looked cool. I put it on and continued on my mission. At the Kosinski's backyard I threw myself over the fence and ducked into the bushes. I was a commando camouflaged behind leaves and branches, laying-in-wait for them. The Kosinski brothers were known in the neighborhood for their obsession with firecrackers and blowing things up. Last week they had made a cannon out of soda cans and a tennis ball, it was about five or six soda cans with the ends cut off and taped together except the bottom one. A hole was drilled in the bottom can, you poured in a little lighter fluid and it would fire a tennis ball out of it. I don't know where or how they learned to make one, but they could explain all the different parts of it. We had spent an afternoon sitting on the hill in front of my parents' house firing it at passing cars.

Finally, Eddie Kosinski came out the back door and walked down the sidewalk to the backyard, towards the alley. When he was even with me, I sprang out of the bushes, tackling him. We rolled once or twice into the grass and came up laughing.

"I got you! You never even saw me!"

"Jesus, Jacky, you're such a jerk-off."

"Awww, come on, we're just having some fun." The helmet had fallen off in my surprise attack, and was rolling around on the grass, I picked it up and put it back on. We sat there quietly for a moment. Eddie rubbed at the underside of his arm, the skin was melted and folded over, it was a tortured, scalding red where the skin met, which faded quickly to white, but it was a weird white, like I'd seen on a dead fish. It was the absence of color it was a little creepy. He never talked about it, so I never mentioned the healed-over burn. It was probably some failed experiment with making firecrackers. I knew I wasn't supposed to look at it, but I always did.

"What're you doing here?" He asked.

"I'm on a mission. Let's grab your cannon and go shoot it off."

"I can't."

"Why not?"

"I don't have it anymore; my parents took it because James and I shot out some windows."

I was disappointed but determined not to let it get me down. "How about some firecrackers? We could blow something up."

"All gone, my parents took everything, but if you're looking to blow something up, I heard that Jimmy Bowman has some M-80's and he blew up a small tree. It was really cool."

"Let's go see if he can come out!"

Jimmy Bowman was the neighborhood bully. He and Sammy Filson used came over to my house, call me out, "Yo, Jacky! Come out and play!" It was a sing-songy invitation to come out and play that carried up to the kids' room and echoed across the neighborhood on the weekends and when school was out. My mother, wanting me to have friends, would send me out, and they were friendly until we were at the end of the block and out of sight of my house. Sammy would grab me from behind, and hold me, while Jimmy would give me a quick three or four punches to my stomach, and they would send me home sniffling. They had once miscalculated and given me a black eye, and with that evidence, they got in trouble. Jimmy was big, bigger than most other kids our age, but size is all that kids see. It's how they judge either strength or weakness. Jimmy had the attitude of a "tough" kid, his father was an alcoholic, and every Friday, when he got paid, the Bowman's house would be in an uproar and while we never heard what happened, sometimes the police were called. It was common knowledge in our neighborhood, and I guess it had toughened him up. He was the leader of our "gang," his ideas are what we did. If he wanted to go over to Sammy Filson's and watch Godzilla movies in a storage area turned clubhouse or go over to the nearby woods, that's what we did. I don't remember how it happened, it just always was, like the natural order of the neighborhood. There was a definite pecking order in the neighborhood,

Jimmy Bowman, Sammy Filson and me, third out of three. Maybe it was simpler than that and it was just some weird survival instinct on my part—make friends with your enemies. It wasn't quite the law of the jungle, but it was the law of the neighborhood. It's how kids think.

We went over to the Bowman's house. It was in disrepair, paint was peeling off the wooden siding, doors and windows hung off their hinges, the grass was overgrown and brown.

Their garage couldn't hold a car, it was so filled with garbage its walls were askew leaning to the side, as if a strong wind had pushed it off kilter. It looked as if it would fall over if you tried to do anything in it. It looked dangerous even to kids, and we never played in it.

Next door to the Bowman's house was "the prairie" a space where two houses had once been at the end of the block. Now it was all overgrown with trees and weeds. In our exploration of this wilderness, we had found the foundations of the houses, that's how we knew this little bit of neighborhood archaeology. God knows how long ago they had been ruined. Over the years neighborhood kids had tracked a couple of trails through the prairie, and we had dug out a couple of "forts," holes we had dug which were our command centers for "wars" we had in the prairie. One was even pretty sophisticated. It had two rooms connected by a tunnel. We had thrown a piece of plywood over it and covered it with dirt and plants. On one side we cut out a hole to stick out a crude periscope James Kosinski had built.

Eddie yelled out "yo Jimmy!" It sounded hard and flat echoing between the houses. A minute or two later Jimmy came out of the house. The screen door of the back porch screeched open and slammed shut. He was dressed like we were, jeans and a pullover striped shirt, and Keds gym shoes.

"We heard you had some M-80's?" I asked. Jimmy looked back over his shoulder, he looked mad.

"Shut up! Let's get out of here, let's go over to your house." As we walked through his yard, he nodded at the helmet I was wearing, "where'd you get that?" Before I could answer he said, "you better get rid of it."

"Why? I think it looks cool."

"Don't you know what the skull painted on it means?"

"No."

"It means the guy wearing it was killed, it's bad luck to wear it." One of Jimmy's older brothers had been in Vietnam and a lot of stories about the war that flowed through the neighborhood were from him. My mother had explained that he had a lot of problems since coming back from the war, living on and off at his parents' house, and every once in a while, the police came over to their house to arrest him. The Bowmans had a lot of kids. The oldest was thirty, and the youngest was as old as my little brother, so there was a Bowman for just about every age group in the neighborhood.

"Oh," I took the helmet off, my enthusiasm for it lessened. I put it on top of their garbage can as we walked out the back gate.

We walked across the alley and through my backyard all the way to the front of the house, no one said a word until we were standing on the hill in front of my parent's house.

"So, do you really have any M-80's?" I asked.

"Yeah, I have some," he said, pulling three out of his pocket. They didn't look like what I expected them to look like, not that I knew what to expect. They weren't like firecrackers, slim with a fuse coming out the top and had a nice satisfying little *pop* when they exploded. These were short and stubby, they were a thumb sized tube, that gunpowder had been poured into, and the end plugged, with a fuse sticking out of the side, they looked more dangerous than firecrackers.

"Where'd you get them?"

"I stole them from my older brother, and he'd kick the shit out of me if he knew I had them."

"What can we blow up?"

"Anything," Jimmy said, "I already blew up a couple of things, the best was a tree, it just kind of blew it apart."

"That'd be cool to see, let's blow up another tree?"

"Naw, I did that already, we should do something else." We sat down on the hill in front of my house wondering what to blow up. We looked up and down the street for a target. Even though we lived in Chicago it may have well been Mayberry. It was still a simpler time when distance was measured by the number of blocks something is from your house, and time was measured by when the streetlights go on, now we're surrounded by time. Across the street was an apartment building with shops that ran across the front, a barber shop, Dorothy's beauty shop, and at the end of the block Dick's grocery store run by two brothers Dick and Everett. It was a small store but had everything you would find in a supermarket. On our side of the street, houses. On one side of my house the Peterson's, on the other side the Griffith's, then the Hofers' right next to the gas station, a Sinclair with a green brontosaurus on the sign. Then the train tracks, the border of the neighborhood which ran the Rock Island train with passenger cars that looked like they could have been out of the old west. Brown passenger cars that rattled and lurched as the train moved, and if you had to go to the next car there was only a corrugated metal plate over the coupling and a couple of chains that hung loosely at the sides for you to hold onto. Across the tracks a quaint train station with scuffed and dirty floors and wooden benches stripped of any finish. And off to one side, a phone booth. Jimmy had a far-off look in his eye, we knew our target had been chosen.

"C'mon'."

We ran across the tracks to the phone booth to evaluate our target. It was your standard phone booth that Clark Kent would have felt comfortable in, strips of red glass at the top and bottom, clear panes in the middle, and the door folded open and close. The body of the phone looked like it was a solid steel casing, and the coin box was locked and sealed inside the body of the phone.

"It's not going to work," I said, "it's all steel. Maybe we can blow up the receiver it's just plastic."

"And this," Jimmy said, holding up one of the M-80's, "is a quarter of a stick of dynamite. It's simple. We put it here." Jimmy flipped open the coin return and put the M-80 in it. We all looked around one last time to make sure no one was around. The coast was clear, Jimmy took out a Bic lighter and lit the fuse. We ran back across the tracks to the front of Dick's grocery store, not from fear of getting caught, but from the explosion. We had all seen movies and TV shows and knew we shouldn't be standing there when a quarter of a stick of dynamite went off. **BOOM!** It didn't make as big of an explosion as I thought it would. We went back across the tracks. The explosion had blown out two of the glass panels there were small granulated, thick pieces of clear and red glass on the ground. Inside the phone booth, falling from the coinbox, was a river of silver, a frozen waterfall of quarters, dimes and nickels, falling to the floor, which was now a slippery carpet of coins. No one said anything, we were in a state of shock. We had actually blown-up the phone booth! We just stood there admiring our handiwork. Time seemed to stand still. No one was around, nothing was moving, there wasn't even any sound. No one thought of running—all we could do was stare at the damage. We were in awe of what we had done. No one even tried to pick up any of the coins. We weren't trying to steal the money—our goal had been accomplished when the M-80 went off. Suddenly, a car screeched to a stop on the street on the far side of the train station. Time started, and sound returned to the world. A guy in a brown leather jacket got out of the car and was calmly walking towards us.

"Bowman, you part of this?" He asked. I noticed he had a badge clipped to the lapel of his jacket, he was an undercover cop. It was the first time I'd ever seen an undercover cop and he looked like every undercover I'd ever seen on TV. Instinct was gone. We didn't think to run, there was no time. From every street that ran in front of or behind the train station, marked and unmarked cop cars came racing out of nowhere, lights flashing, screeching to a halt. Suddenly it seemed like every cop in the neighborhood was there. We were surrounded by every kind of cop you could think of—undercover cops, uniformed cops, even railroad cops! We were surrounded!

"We're surrounded! Surrounded… Surrounded."

Childhood friends became a shadow of memory.

Where are they now?

Where are they now? I wondered, as light pried at the edge of my consciousness. Water was thrown in my face—I woke up sputtering. I tried getting as much of the water in my mouth as I could, it tasted of the blood and dust that that had dried on my lips. Every part of my body ached, my arms were heavy from supporting my weight, my head hung down, not out of shame or despair but because it was too heavy to hold up. I smiled at the memory of the games I'd played as a child. They'd afforded me an escape. I looked around and remembered where I was. The reality didn't dispel the memories, as the soldiers unchained my limp body and dragged me off to another interrogation.

AS GOOD A NAME AS ANY

(For Chris)

orthern France, September 1918…

The twentieth century was young, but it had seen my aging. I was now an old man, not the lusty youth I'd once been in old London. That was a lifetime ago, almost two lifetimes now, most of which I've spent in a cell wrapped in a strait jacket. My crimes had been bloody and violent and had been the talk of London, a London I'd brought into the twentieth century with a rosy bloom of blood. Since those halcyon days of my youth the bloom has blossomed with the violence of a world war, a war to end all wars. The killing has become mechanized, impersonal, a rolling death that made my crimes seem quaint and old fashioned. Mine were more of an art form than the carnage outside of the trenches, whose contours were gouged from the earth as if some great worm had chewed them out of the landscape. Over the top, a no man's land of mud, barbed wire, and pools of blood. The dead, rag dolls draped over the landscape, a bullet for the soldier unfortunate enough to stick his head over the top, machine guns mowing down men as they charged, poisoned fogs drifting over the battlefield, lumbering machines that were supposed to break the enemy but more often than not became coffins for those inside. Only the mind of man would try to make order from the chaos, this was the philosophy of the factory.

"Johnnie, get ready we're going over the top."

John isn't my given name. That I have forgotten over time. It never seemed that important anyway. I am every man and no one. John is a formalization of my street name, my nom de plume Jack is as good a name as any. The jailers knew who I was, who I am, what my crimes had been. But as the years passed and I've aged, I've watched seasons of jailer's change. I saw generations dying before me, young men became old men. Then like winter into spring, they became younger again and their cruelty increased. They'd forgotten the terror I'd inspired. The memory of my crimes dimmed in their minds. To them my crimes had become history, childhood tales of a bogeyman, an etching in a yellowing newspaper clipping, an oral history passed down from jailer to jailer. They would relieve their boredom and frustrations by beating an aging man in a strait jacket. Maybe they didn't believe who I was, I didn't conform to their idea of what a monster should look like. My hair is long and matted as is my beard. A haircut and shave are among the quarterly cruelties imposed upon me. I'm thin, they've fed me just enough to keep me alive, my clothes hanging off me even more than when I'd been that jungle animal on the prowl. Occasionally, the ancient darkness would burn in my eyes, but either the guards didn't know enough to be afraid of it or, if they noticed the rage, they knew that with my arms tied behind my back, I was as powerless to do anything about it as the dog's threat is made impotent by the fence. They thought my power to act in the world was gone. What they didn't know was that my power would never die out of this world. In my eyes you could see the feral animal. The animal lives in the eyes.

I never thought I'd live to be this old. I thought I'd be shot trying to escape the coppers, that I'd be hung for my crimes, that I'd succumb to the usual maladies of life in Whitechapel, that drink and disease would claim me, or that I'd be worked to death in the slaughterhouse, old before my time. Some very bad planning on my part. Maybe if I'd taken my own life? But I never had the courage, only the courage to take the lives of others. My childhood was not the Eden most look back on as nostalgic reminiscence.

I grew up playing in the streets of Whitechapel knowing every backyard, every shortcut, every cubby-hole or loose board to scramble into or through. I was a street urchin worthy of Dickens. We ran the neighborhood; it was those streets that raised me. I learned cruelty at home so it was out to the streets; and on the streets, I discovered cruelty could be passed along. I wasn't above picking the pockets of a drunk passed out in the gutter or cutting the strings of a "lady's" purse. Those streets were mine long before I claimed them in Jack's name.

When I was a certain age, I had to earn my keep. "It's time to learn a trade," my parents said, and learn one I did. My father in his one besotted act of parental concern got me a job in the slaughterhouse, pushing the offal into the sluice drains. My father made sure he collected a week's wages from me or else I'd be given a good cuffing about the ears. The money went back into the pubs and the prostitutes. It was a decadent circle of life, it was all part of an iron circle, we the guilty pass along the cruelty we've inherited to the innocent. It's what made places like Whitechapel possible, it's the cycle that I later disturbed.

When I was old enough to swing a hammer, they moved me up to the stun line. I'd hit the animals square in the skull with the hammer and saw the uncomprehending look in their eyes, the shock of realization that this was the moment of their death. Everything they knew was no more and I knew they were sentient beings. It was the same look I saw on my victims' faces. The animals were carved up so fast the meat was still warm. The slaughterhouse became an annealing process, awash in offal and blood. It heartened my sanguinary soul. People are afraid of death, they see it as cold and monstrous, but it's warm and inviting, intimate, a friend who walks along with us and easily summoned. When I became broad and strong, my father feared that strength and I was out of his house and into the streets altogether.

It was on the streets of Whitechapel that the darkness found me. If you had seen me, I'd have seemed a lumbering, oddly shaped, awkward beast. I don't know if it was chance or if my native cruelty lifted me above the din of debauchery of Whitechapel, or if there was a purity in my darkness, or if it was just that I was an empty vessel. This darkness, the power, the energy within me, its hard to describe. Maybe I'm too limited in my comprehension to understand its nature, maybe my education too limited to describe it. It's evil but that's too simplistic, too limited a definition of what it is. I don't know where it came from, but it is ancient, it has lived forever, it is a force of nature, chaos. Maybe it has always existed and lived among man, maybe it was cast out of paradise along with man finding refuge in the squalid backstreets of Mesopotamia, Babylon, Sumer, and all the cities

11

through the ages that harbored all the same varieties of life as Whitechapel. It found me in those streets with its whores, drunks, sodomites, degenerates, all species of perverts, thieves, the diseased and disabled, syphilitic artists, the infrequent upper-class tourist slumming so they could feel the plight of the poor souls trapped there, poetes-maudits, and one articulate vivisectionist: myself. When it took refuge in me, it seemed to be fear and rage, something animal yet sentient. It was what lurks out in the night. It was irrational, the unconscious, cold and menacing, yet familiar, darkness seeking darkness, I welcomed it. It gave me power and purpose, it was the unknown that became known, unnamed except for Jack. From the moment it took me over, it consumed me, it was the only true consummation of my life. I was no longer a child of the streets I had been moulded by. Once the killings started, I became the animal I was meant to be—a night stalker, a jungle cat swift and graceful, a creature of the streets, the random element between life and death. There was madness in my method. I remade those London streets.

Like the darkness, war has walked alongside man, the whore of civilization. When the war began, they came to me in that dank dungeon and gave me the choice of rotting away in the cell for what surely would have been only a few more years before madness, death or both overtook me completely. In the cell the darkness was contained, the animal caged, a fire without expression, without a way to exercise its will in the world. It consumed me, a fire trapped, the embers burning red hot, burning from the inside out. Every day I could feel it consuming me more and more. I could feel the dis-ease it created within me. I made the choice for war, not because I chose life—there was no more freedom in the trenches than in the asylum. There was nowhere to run. The war extended to the horizon and beyond, as far as the eye could see, desolation. The rats and the bedlam scurrying around me were the same in the trenches or the asylum. I knew I'd never be free again; I never had any illusions of breathing free air again. They said, "there was always the chance for survival," but that was a fiction. We all understood they wouldn't be sending me anywhere that there was a chance for survival. I did it because I wanted to see terror again in the eyes of those I was killing, to see the knowledge reflected in their eyes that this was their last moment of life. The darkness would again have its moment of expression.

It was in one of my first battles that I made a grim discovery. It started like all the other battles, whistles shrilly blaring, officers' calls to stations. Then we went over the top, running as fast as we could towards the enemy. The officers tried pounding into our heads that the enemy were godless Huns, but I knew that all men in mortal circumstances were in closer communion with a deity than at other times of their lives. With murderous fury I plunged my bayonet deep into the bowels of a German. There was the rending of fabric and flesh I turned the blade, and in the man's eyes I saw nothing—no victory, there was no joy as I had in Whitechapel. I pulled out the bayonet with less ferocity than it had gone in with. I realized I was just an old man waiting for them to tell me when and who to kill. I was their weapon, a plaything of others, a toy soldier moved about by invisible hands, not my own. Killing had become a job as joyless as any job in a factory or slaughterhouse.

I survived many battles, in rare moments, I thought I might survive the war, but I didn't know why. Was the darkness giving me an edge? To what purpose? To continue our work? In war, killing and death is on the factory level. In the trenches I was anonymous. No one remembered Jack, and no one would have believed it anyway.

I witnessed the changing seasons of soldiers in the trenches, as I had each new generation of guards in the asylum. Now, the attrition wasn't because of aging, but death and disease. I was a wizened visage compared to the doughy fresh faces of the conscripts, but they'd seen too much. They would just stare off into the distance—they were already old. I kept to myself. The conscripts sometimes wondered what an old man such as myself was doing here, I smiled enigmatically and said, "I was doing my duty, for God, King and Country." They didn't believe it. In their free time they devised theories and invented stories of why I was there. Their most popular theory was that I had been an officer who had committed some atrocity or had offended a general or even a member of the royal family and had been demoted to private and sent to the trenches to meet my fate. I always smiled to myself, bemused at how close, and yet so far they were from the truth.

"All right boys line up!" The lieutenant yelled, and the order echoed up and down the trench line. We crowded around the nearest ladder that would take us over the top. We all looked alike, grim-faced, dirty men in brown uniforms, rifles at our sides, with bayonets fixed or being affixed to the end of their rifles. Last minute prayers for those who needed them, knowing their fate was only moments away. The order was given, and we quickly climbed the ladders, pushing ourselves over the top, running single file through the lanes between the barbed wire traps towards the German lines. We heard the ratt-a-tat-tat of machine guns as bullets danced around us in a rain of metal, kicking up plumes of dirt. Men fell dead out of the line onto the barbed wire, arms and legs akimbo, bent crucifixions. We finally hit an open area where we spread out and continued rushing towards the German trenches. Germans were coming over the top of their trenches, bayonets fixed and rushing towards us. Some stopped to fire, some fell. Most kept rushing forward until the lines crashed together, rifles fired in close quarters, bayonets slicing air, then the sound of ripping fabric and the puncture of flesh. I felt a sharp jab and saw a little German private too close. I turned my head, a sort of detached insect curiosity came over me, as if I was watching from afar. I'd become an observer. I saw my body, but I was apart from it. I looked down to see a bayonet plunged into the depths of my gut. I felt a surprisingly warm feeling emanating from the wound. I knew the warmth was the internal bleeding of severed organs, blood filling the spaces it hadn't before. But it was a distant thought and not alarming in the least. It was a funny sort of sensation, nothing like I'd imagined. I followed the bayonet down the rifle to the scared, slight, mousy looking private with a bushy mustache holding the rifle. I saw the fear in the little man's eyes, but there was also a slight spark of darkness. I knew my life, this flesh, this identity was ending. I could feel the life ebbing away; this was the moment of my death, but I knew I'd become part of the darkness. I'd left my imprint on it. I was it and it was me, it fed me, and I'd fed it, and it had grown and multiplied within me. I reached out grabbing the little man's arm, contact, skin on skin. It had been a long time since I had touched warm living flesh. I asked, "wie ist ihr name?" The little man looked startled but mumbled, "Adolf Hitler." I smiled; the ancient darkness recognized a kindred soul. I looked into his eyes and saw the feral animal, the cunning and cruelty of his life. "Adolf Hitler, as good a name as any." In that moment the darkness surged into the scared private. The mousy man felt the darkness radiate into him like a jolt of electricity. He pulled the bayonet out of my body with more ferocity than it had gone in with. I slumped into the muck of the battlefield, now nothing more than an empty husk.

DAWN'S HWY

A phone booth stands alone, empty in the Los Angeles night, its dull plastic light an island, in the sea of neon fused darkness. A car pulls up to the curb and a lone figure gets out. The car pulls away, the figure walks to the phone booth closing the door behind him. The inside light pops on illuminating him, a silhouette in relief against the night. He takes a dime out of his black jeans, and picks up the receiver, he puts the dime in the coin slot, and listens as it clinks through the phone's mechanism waiting for the dial tone and dials a number on the rotor and waits as the phone rang on the other end, a woman picks up.

"Yeah, it's me," he said, his voice a soft conspiratorial whisper, "we just got back into town tonight." He listens as the woman asks something, then says, "yeah, we wasted him."

Jim was walking down Sunset Boulevard. He'd been wearing the same clothes for the last couple of days, black jeans, t-shirt, boots, a dark welder's jacket, because in January even Los Angeles is cold. His pants still had some remnants of desert sand in the creases and folds. He had other reminders of the desert as well, the cuts and bruises on his face.

It had only been six months since he'd come down off of Dennis Jacob's roof, where he'd subsisted on acid, Nietzsche and the occasional can of beans. Under the summer sun he came face to face with himself and burned away a lot of old ideas about himself; and while the rest of the city slept, he took notes at a fantastic rock concert in his mind. He wrote down the songs he heard as fast as he could. He had met the spirit of music and it had changed him forever. No one, not even his friends, had understood that. They saw the physical changes. He was lithe, a mere waif, and they thought they saw the change in him, but they only saw the Jim they wanted to see, the Jim they expected.

A police cruiser drove past. One of the cops was looking at him. Suddenly it screeched to a halt and the cops jumped out.

"Are you Jim Morrison?"

"Yeah," Jim said defiantly, "who wants to know?"

"We do wise guy. You're under arrest."

"What for, man?"

"Suspicion of murder." The cops pushed him against the wall of the nearest building and patted him down before handcuffing him and putting him in the back of the cruiser.

The cops hustled him through the police station and booking, then threw him into an interrogation room, his hands still cuffed in front of him. It was a typical interrogation room—bare white walls, sparse cheap furniture, a wooden table with an ashtray on it, a wooden chair on either side of the table. The room was lit by a single bare lightbulb shining right over the table, probably to have it shining in the eyes of the accused, 'make 'em sweat, the third degree, the cops have seen too many cop shows,' Jim thought. He pulled out a chair and sat against a wall, his eyes fixed on the closed door, waiting.

Finally, two plainclothes detectives came in. They looked like cop stereotypes to Jim, two variations on the same theme, crew-cut hair, baggy gray suit pants. One had a white shirt with the sleeves rolled up to the elbow that looked slept in or a little grimy at the edges, a dark tie loosened at the neck. On the other the jacket and tie remained intact. Jim understood the game they were going to run on him and wondered which would play the good cop and which would play the bad cop.

"I'm officer Ellison and this is officer Hanson. We're the investigating officers." The suit-jacketed cop said. "Right now, we have you for assault of Rosalie Munoz, a minor." Jim tilted his head at the cop, a quizzical look on his face. "The girl you kissed. But we don't care about that, we have bigger fish to fry."

"'Bigger fish to fry.' Did you really just say that?"

"Ok, punk, let's cut out the shit! Do you know the whereabouts of one Phillip O'Leno?" Hanson asked, taking the lead. Now, Jim knew which cop was which.

"Um, not really."

"He's missing, we think he may have been killed."

"What makes you think I had anything to do with it?"

"All your friends have said you've been going around telling a story about how you and one Felix Venable killed him." The cop stared at Jim hoping the silence would intimidate him, make him uncomfortable. Jim returned the stare.

"Look son," the other cop, Ellison said, "if you know anything tell us, at least so his father knows what happened."

"Fuck his father."

"How old are you?" Ellison asked.

"Twenty-two."

"That's a bad attitude son, one that's not going to get you very far in life. Do you know his father is a prominent attorney?"

"And mine is a captain in the Navy, so what?"

"Where'd you get all those bruises from?"

"Some greasers didn't like our long hair."

"Serves you right," Hanson said. "What about this Felix Venable?"

"What about him?"

"He's quite a bit older than you." The question hung in the air a moment.

"Yeah." Jim said.

"Where'd you meet him?"

"Film school."

"Film school?"

"He was a graduate student. What're you trying to say?"

"Nothing, nothing at all," Hanson said, with a greasy lasciviousness in his voice.

"Man, with a mind like yours I'd watch what I say. Your mask is slipping, and you're showing your true self, and it ain't too pretty from here."

"If we ran your rap sheet, what do you think we'd find?"

"Just what you want to see, man."

"Do you have a job?" Ellison asked in a softer tone, trying to break through the barriers Jim had up.

"No."

"What do you do for a living son?" Jim thought a moment, considering the audience.

"Nothing you'd understand."

"You're not one of those pretty boys that want to be a star are you?" Hanson sneered, "or with that long hair you wanna' be a starlet?"

"To tell you the truth, son, none of your friends that we've talked to believe you did it. Neither do I, you're not the type."

"What type is that?"

"College boy," Hanson spat out, "but you're not a hard case like your friend Venable. You're acting tough but I bet you're shaking in your boots, so just tell us where Phillip is, and you walk out of here."

"What about the charges?"

"We really don't care about you kissing some Mexican girl," Hanson said with a look of mild distaste on his face. "All Phillip's father wants to know is if his son is, ok?"

"Don't know, man," Jim said, then paused a moment, for effect. "What if we did kill him?"

"Did you?"

"Why don't you just tell us what happened out in the desert son?"

Jim smiled, "what if life is nothing more than an act of remembering?" The cops looked at each other, perplexed by the question.

"What?" Hanson asked.

"What if we're dead already and we're just remembering this?" The two cops just looked at each other. "What if we're just sitting around a campfire in eternity remembering life and telling each other our stories?"

"What're you talking about son?"

"You know, like *Sunset Boulevard, Citizen Kane, Carousel.*" Again, the cops looked at each other.

"This isn't a movie son, this is real."

*

Jim woke up in the backseat of Carol's convertible which he had charmed her into letting him borrow. He looked around; the rising sun was in his eyes.

"Where are we?" He asked.

"The desert," Phil said, "look around, where do you think we are?"

Jim looked around at the highway surrounded by the scrub, cactus and Joshua trees of the desert. His mind flashed on images of dead Indians laying on the highway, blood on the asphalt.

"Oh shit, I'm back." He said.

"Back? Where?"

"Here."

"Here?" Felix asked.

"It looks like it, man."

"What the fuck are you talking about, Jim?" Phil asked, always trying to cut to the heart of a problem.

"When I was a kid, my family was moving to one of my father's new assignments, and one morning, it was like, you know, the time between night and day."

"We know when dawn is, asshole." Felix said, sarcastically.

"Anyway, we drove up to an accident, a truckload of Indians had overturned. There was blood everywhere on the road, and I was really freaking out. I wanted to do something, but I couldn't, I was just a kid, right? My father got out of the car but didn't do anything. My mother told me it was a dream. I don't know if she thought that would make it better or not, but it wavered in strange time between reality and dream since then. I may write a story about it."

"Sounds like you already are."

"Maybe one of the Indians was a shaman, and his soul jumped into mine." Jim posited an idea he liked, a part of the new mythology of himself. He grabbed the notebook next to him on the seat and started writing in it. Felix saw what he was doing and reached into the backseat and grabbed it.

"Morrison, you may have read a lot of philosophy, but you need a philosophy. All great writers have a philosophy."

"What're you going to write about anyway?" Phil asked.

Jim smiled mischievously, "how I lured two dumb motherfuckers into the desert and killed them."

"Fuck you, Morrison! You may get Phil baby here, but I'll take you out first." Felix said, as he looked through the notebook, "Morrison, you're such a pussy! A writer! You stack the deck, choose the circumstances and conditions of a story, so of course the outcome can be anything you want. If you want to be a real artist, you need to do something that is real. A film is real, it records reality, it shows you consciousness, what's really going on." Felix threw the notebook out of the car.

"Hey asshole!" Jim yelled, "that's my notebook!"

"Morrison, you gotta learn to let go of the bullshit. Hell, even that rock band of yours has a better chance of doing something more real than with 'stories.'"

Jim sat back in the seat. That's not what most of his friends thought. Just the opposite, most of his friends thought The Doors were a lark. He thought back to a couple months before. It had been a cool night and he was meeting a couple friends at the UCLA botanical gardens. He walked through the labyrinth of sculpted bushes down the stone path to the grotto in the center, where he was supposed to meet Liz, Katie and Max. They were surrounded by cool green hedges, slick with evening dew, and they were trying to talk him out of being in the band.

"There's too much competition, you'll never make it," Katie said.

"Your film career is going great."

"You don't want to be in a band with those guys Jim, they're not going anywhere." Max said, "Manczarek isn't like you. He isn't a poet, he's a capitalist. He wants fame, money, power."

"That's funny," Jim said. "That's the irony of it, people have told Ray I'm flakey and unreliable." Jim considered it a minor betrayal; it played like a Garden of Gethsemane scene in his mind.

"Hey man, let me drive. I'm bored back here."

"No way, Morrison," Felix said, "you drive like shit. Is there any beer left?"

"Yeah, it's warm," Jim grabbed a can, shook it, and tossed it to Felix. He opened it to a spray of foam, chugged it down and threw the can out of the car after Jim's notebook, the desert claiming both. "Felix, you're one strange cat," Jim said. "Since you're not going to let me drive, wake me when we get somewhere." As he lay down in the backseat, he smiled to himself and wondered if either of them got his joke.

The car pulled up in front of a roadside bar. It was a sun bleached, weather-beaten wooden building with a porch running across the front. There were some motorcycles parked off to the side of the building.

"Wake up, Jim. We're here!"

"Where?"

"Somewhere." Felix said. They went inside.

Inside the bar, it wasn't very big. It was cool, quiet and dark, despite the soft moaning of the jukebox. The bar ran the length of one wall. A little farther in and across from it was a pool table. Sitting at a table were five or six bikers with their girlfriends. All the guys were dressed in leather jackets, white t-shirts, jeans, biker boots, their hair slicked back into DA's. The girls were all dressed in low cut flowery blouses, tight pants, their jackets hanging off their chairs. They all watched as the outsiders came in. Jim was the first to get to the bar.

"What can I get for you?" the bartender asked.

"Beer."

"Beer?"

"Tres cerveza's por favor," Jim said, smiling broadly.

"Tequila with mine," Felix said. 'Always on the road to finding bliss or the end of the night,' Jim thought.

"Excuse me," Phil said timidly as the bartender put a beer in front of him, "can you help us?" The bartender stared at him blankly. "We, we're looking for Senor Reyes." At the mention of the name, the bikers stopped what they were doing, and exchanged looks. One, who Jim took to be the leader, swaggered over to them.

"You sick or something?" he asked menacingly.

"No, why?" Phil asked.

"I thought maybe you're looking for a medicine man."

"No, the shaman, a brujo." The biker looked shocked.

"Where'd gringos like you learn words like that?"

Phil was getting more nervous now, but he was undeterred. "We heard he might have some peyote."

"Peyote? Why don't you just go to church?"

"Because we're looking for a new way to find…"

"It's old, very old."

"We're on a mission of discovery," Jim chimed in smoothly, "looking for a new world."

"A new world?" the biker said, "you mean a new world like when Europeans came here and killed our ancestors, stole our culture and then tried to kill it? Is that what you mean?"

"No, it's like space, but instead of going outwards we want to go inward."

"I thought it was just up and out for you Anglos?"

"The farther I go in, the further I reach out, man." Jim said.

"That's a luxury for us, we only have what was left to us. Now you're coming back for that? They're our beliefs man. You college boys are tourists, slumming, wanting to see what you've read about, but you can leave any time you want. We can't. You're just gringos looking to get high."

"No, no, no," Phil said.

"You may not think you're stealing something…"

"We want to learn those beliefs, to see if it's a way for us."

"Javier, why don't you just tell them where the old man lives?" one of the other bikers said. "He won't see them anyway."

"Sure," the biker said, relenting. "He lives on the outside of town, by a crossroads, the house with all the snakes."

"What does that mean?" Phil asked.

"You'll see," the biker said, as he walked back to the table.

"Cool," Jim said.

Jim, Phil and Felix turned to their beers, Jim looked around taking in the surroundings, trying to memorize everything about the place. He caught the eye of one of the girls. Her blouse was low-cut and there was the undulation of skin across the top of her breasts as she insinuated her way up to the bar. She sidled up next to Jim under the pretense of getting a drink.

"You buy me a drink?" She asked.

"Sure! What do you want?"

"For right now," she said, hesitating, "a beer."

The bikers started to notice Jim flirting with the girl and were getting agitated. The talking amongst themselves grew louder. Phil was the first to notice and leaned over to Jim, "I don't think that's such a good idea, Jim."

"Why not? We're here to have some fun and maybe a few other things that start with f-u."

"Well, for one," Phil said, "you almost got us busted in L.A. when you jumped out of the car and kissed that chick."

"Aww, leave him alone," Felix said, "he's havin' a good time."

"Your egging him on isn't helping any!" Phil snapped.

"Awww, Phil," Jim said with mock innocence, "she was a beautiful angel of womanhood, and I just thought I'd break the ice."

"That's beside the point, Jim. All those guys over there are getting upset."

Jim looked over at them, and roared, "well, fuck them!" The bikers all stopped talking and were glaring at them. Javier, the leader of the gang, walked over to Jim.

"You like my girlfriend, gringo?"

"Who says she's yours?"

"I do."

"We'll see who she leaves with."

"You like girls?"

"Hey man, why don't you fuck off!" Felix yelled. The biker ignored him.

"I thought with your long hair maybe you're a maricón." He looked at Jim to see if he was scared. "You know what a maricón is gringo?"

"Why? You want to fuck me?" Jim said.

"More like fuck you up." The biker punched Jim. Felix jumped up and blindsided the biker, and then there was an explosion of sound as chairs crashed to the floor and the bikers jumped on Jim, Felix, and Phil. The bartender started yelling, "get them out of here! You're not going to break up my bar!" The group scuffled punches were thrown on both sides. They spilled out onto the wooden porch, and the bikers threw Jim, Felix, and

Phil into the desert dust and dirt in front of the bar. The three jumped into the car, tires spinning out a cloud of dust and rock in their wake as the bikers headed back into the bar.

＊

The car pulled up in front of a small shack that seemed to rise out of the desert. It seemed a part of the desert. There was no delineating line between desert and property, no trimmed lawns or neat gardens—just scrub brush, crucifixion bushes and cactus. The shack was made out of sun-bleached wooden planks and a tin roof salvaged from the surrounding desert. A rough fence lined the front. Three pikes stood on either side of the shack's doorway, each with a rattlesnake's head mounted on it, mouths open, fangs bared.

"This must be the place," Phil said.

"How do you know?"

"How many houses are guarded by rattlesnake heads?"

"I hope we can score enough to take back to L.A." Jim said.

"Jim, are you going to take this seriously?" Phil asked. "We're here to find the shaman, to experience the mystical, not to get fucked up." Jim and Felix exchanged knowing looks.

The door to the shack opened and an old man came out. He was darkly complected, his features were more Indian than Spaniard. His body was hard, all sinew, his skin a leathery brown from a lifetime spent working outdoors, hunting, living off the land as though he'd been weathered and preserved by the desert. He was wearing blue jeans, cowboy boots and a blue workers shirt, they looked dusty but not dirty. There was a stiff formality in his demeanor. His age was hard to tell, he could have been anywhere between fifty and a hundred years old.

"Are you Senor Reyes?" Phil asked.

"I am." The man said, speaking softly.

"The shaman?"

"There are some who call me that, but they're all Indian."

"We were told that you're the man to see who we could get peyote from."

"Stop fucking around Phil, just ask him," Felix said.

"Shut-up! I know how to handle this."

"Look, we just came here to score some peyote. We'll pay you for it and split."

"If that's all you're looking for, it's best for you to leave. If you take peyote without knowing how to prepare it or yourselves, all you're going to do is make yourselves sick and wake up with a headache." He spoke very precisely no thought was wasted. Jim looked into his eyes, there was a wisdom from some far-off place, a serene nobility that quietly and gently emanated from him. The shaman noticed Jim and there was a slight jolt to his consciousness.

"Are you an Indian?" He asked, looking straight at Jim.

"No."

"Hmm, strange."

"What is?"

"My soul recognized yours, you have met a spirit before." Jim was startled, it was like the shamans' words had awakened a something in him, a dormant memory, a desire. "Why do you want peyote?"

"To connect with the spiritual," Phil interjected.

Jim was circumspect there was a calculus to consider. Phil and Felix each knew a different side of him, but neither understood both sides of him. Phil would understand, Felix would think him naïve and mock him. Jim didn't know how to answer. Ever since he could remember he knew what answers a teacher was looking for, which buttons to push to impress them. Jim came up with what he thought, a diplomatic answer that would satisfy everyone.

"I want to live a life without regret." Jim said.

"You think that is possible?" The shaman asked. "For every choice you make you may later mourn what you've lost or suffer what you've gained. You may regret this moment. Your life could change by tomorrow. Is that what you're really looking for?" There was a silence, only the moment, "what is the real reason you're here? Don't think I don't know what the reason is."

Jim didn't know what to say.

"Then go!" the shaman said.

"No!" Jim burst out. "There's more, I want more! I met a spirit; I need to understand what it is inside me that makes me different."

The shaman smiled, "maybe more than one?"

"It's something inside that changed me that I haven't been able to find again. I met the spirit of music."

"That is rare, it's like being visited by a god. Not many can handle it."

"What about you?" The shaman asked, turning to Felix.

"What bullshit! Can't you see this guy is running a game on you?" Felix said to Phil and Jim.

The shaman said, "you've been separated from the meaning and purpose of what you're undertaking. Your religions understood this a long time ago. You can't expect knowledge to be given to you."

"Why not? That's what school is, what books are for, imparting knowledge."

"Knowledge is power. You're too used to it being given to you. Knowledge isn't free, there's always a cost. You have to earn it or risk it turning against you. It can destroy you."

Felix was mad, his face flushed, "fine!" He spat out. "I'll be in the car until you boys are done playing and we can get some peyote from a real shaman!" Felix stalked back to the car.

"Peyote isn't something to be taken lightly. It's only for the most serious minded. So far, you've only read about peyote in books, but the forces you're seeking out is a dragon's tail, and if you grab it, it's dangerous and can cost you in spirit and self. The ritual keeps you connected to its purpose and protects you."

"I can assure you," Phil said, in his sincerest voice, "we're only serious minded about this, we're searches in the truest sense."

"What will happen when we take the peyote?" Jim asked.

"It will change the way you see the world. It will change you."

"How?" Phil asked.

"Each of you differently. What you fear is out there, but you will also find the greatest joy."

"And afterwards?" Jim asked.

"You will awake on dawn's highway," the shaman said, pointing to the road, "and you will have true knowledge and power."

"What's at the end of this dawn's highway?"

"No one knows what's at the end of the highway—death, madness or bliss. If you don't take this seriously, it will consume you." Jim looked enthralled, eager for the adventure, while Phil looked hesitant, not sure if this was a trip he really wanted to go on.

"What do we need to do?"

"Wait." the shaman said.

"Wait?"

"Must activity have meaning? Others are coming, they will be here for the ceremony. Now I have to go prepare myself." The shaman went into the house; there was no invitation to follow. Jim and Phil, not knowing what else to do with themselves wandered around before finding refuge sitting in the shadow of the shaman's house close to the porch.

A couple of hours later a truck pulled up in front of the house. Jim knew things would start happening now, and what happened would be important. He watched, making mental note of everything. The truck looked ancient, from the forties or fifties, but he couldn't be sure. Every part of it was caked in dust and rust, and it was stripped of every spare part except for those needed to keep the engine running and the truck usable. The cab was stuffed with three old people. Unlike the shaman, they looked prematurely aged, like they'd had hard lives eking out a living from the desert. A couple of them had hand drums. The shaman came out of the house to greet them.

The elders retired into the shaman's house. In the bed of the truck were a bunch of younger people who jumped out as soon as it stopped. There were a couple of teenagers, between thirteen and fifteen. Jim wondered if it was their fate he was seeing in the faces of their elders. There were a few people in their twenties also. Jim recognized one of them, it was Javier, the biker leader they'd run into at the roadside bar earlier. He'd lost his leather jacket and was now wearing a blue worker's shirt, but still wearing jeans and biker boots. He saw Jim and made his way over to the shaman who was still on the porch. Jim was apprehensive, he walked over to them.

"Senor Reyes," the biker said. Gone was the roar and arrogance of earlier.

"Yes?"

"Are they staying?" He asked, motioning to Jim and Phil.

"Yes."

"They're tourists, here to steal our traditions or mock them."

"Is that so?" The shaman looked over the bruises on the side of the biker's face and the injuries on Jim's face. "I have asked them, and they have answered well. They're of the earth, differently than you or me, but connected still." The shaman looked at them both. "Do not think I don't know what goes on in the world." Jim noticed that the shaman's voice, though still soft and even was chastising them. His voice didn't raise even an octave. He didn't sound angry but there was power in his words. The shaman went back into the house.

One of the younger boys had put on a ceremonial necklace and leggings. He'd found a long stick somewhere and he drew a circle in the hard sand about three or four feet in diameter, and then drew a cross in the middle dividing it into quarters. The Indians then scattered into the surrounding desert. Before Jim or Phil could figure out what they were doing, they started returning with pieces of wood, branches and scrub and stacked it for a fire. Jim noticed that they had stacked the wood at the eastern point of the circle, being careful not to break the circle's boundary. Jim and Phil joined the search. About half an hour later the pile was deemed big enough. Then everyone found places in the shade of what seemed a cool spot and waited—waiting for what, Jim still didn't know.

As the sun lowered itself in the western horizon, a vaporous moon appeared over the desert not yet fully revealing itself in the coming night sky. A signal must have happened that Jim hadn't noticed because, without any words spoken, the fire was lit. Everyone gathered in a semi-circle between the fire and the drawn circle. The three elders came out of the house along with the shaman, who was dressed the same except that now he wore a necklace of feathers and shell. At the bottom hung a rattlesnake's head. He walked towards the fire. One of the elders came up to Jim and Phil and motioned for them to come with him. He guided them to the front of the fire and motioned for them to sit.

There were already three others sitting at the fire, including the biker. The elders started drumming, slowly, the sound of a heartbeat. Soft rhythmic chanting began, creating a sound all its own, an insect sound like it was something that should have always been there. It built up until Jim could feel the resonance of the sound in his chest. One of the teenagers came around the front of the circle holding a clay jar out towards Phil, who was first in the line. He looked at the shaman questioningly, the shaman shook his head affirmatively, making a motion with his hand encouraging Phil to reach in. He pulled out a peyote button. Jim followed suit, and the shaman said, "chew slowly." They each raised the buttons to their mouths and started chewing the bitter plant. The boy walked down the row offering the peyote to the other supplicants. The boy then appeared with another jar, which he again held out to Phil. There seemed to be a liquid in it, he could feel it sloshing around as he took the jar, "what is this?"

The shaman shot him a sharp look. "Drink but do not swallow. Rinse your mouth and spit it out and ask no more questions." Phil did as he was told. Jim drank without question. It was Mezcal. The ritual was repeated six times.

The shaman started dancing, Jim watched him closely, one foot tentatively put forward, and pulled back, then short hops and staccato steps, his arms outstretched, in each hand a feather, the left hand tilted towards the ground, the right towards the sky, another step his arms rotated, the beat increased, so did the shaman, twists and turns, jumps, reeling around the circle, his body became fluid with the music, part of the music, his body threatening to fly out of control, but always just within control.

A door opened.

The shaman was now a swirl of color, stars were falling from his hair, silvery beams shot from his fingertips. Jim looked to the sky. It was dark, the moon full and bright, holding dominion over the desert. The music throbbed in his head. Motion started breaking up into the flickers of the fire's light and rose into the night sky until they became stars. Images flashed across his consciousness, animal sounds. A crow's wing, Indians lying dead on a highway, his mother's voice softly saying, "it was just a dream, Jimmy, it was just a dream," it turned to a song, it was familiar, he'd heard it before, it was the spirit of music. The music pushed against his chest, from the inside. It wasn't the drumming anymore. He looked around and saw more clearly than he had ever seen before. The scene was bent, curved, as if he was looking through some other lens. The music pulsed through him like a storm, and there was a sea of people, swaying like grass in the wind at his command. Then all he could see was a coppery, gold horizon, it moved slightly, coming into focus, it had some weird stippling, almost a tactile appearance, then it undulated, it was alive! It moved away from him, it was a rattlesnake and all the facets on the scales of the snake were scenes from his life, past, present and future. The farther it moved away from him the harder it was to discern those scenes until the snake had disappeared. The music pulsated through his body, it was scintillating, a scream came ripping through the atmosphere and he realized it was from him, but he wasn't afraid, it was a part of him, it was him. Out of the darkness he saw a silvery spiderweb then nothing, he felt the prickling of fear at the edge of his consciousness, then some silvery nails pushed down out of the darkness, and he knew he was in a coffin, he told himself not to be afraid if he let the fear seep in it would become a bad trip. He felt like he'd discovered power, or maybe a new science, or perhaps a very old one.

Jim woke to the rising sun prying open his eyes. He was cold, confused, unsure of where he was. He looked around and saw he was in front of the shaman's house. He tried to stand up, but he was weak. Everything came back to him—the night before, the trip, it had been more than a trip, more than random images thrown together by a subconscious struggling to find context out of the chaos of a drugged mind. It seemed more of a journey—it had coherence, meaning. In that moment he realized he was alive he was on the edge of life and death. Either was within his grasp. It was real, maybe all too real. He was living in the moment. The shaman was sitting on a rock poking the smoldering embers of the fire with a stick. Felix was sitting nearby; Phil was sitting next to the shaman, and they were talking quietly.

"And you were there, and you," Jim said.

"Welcome back to Kansas, Dorothy," Felix said.

"Where is everyone?"

"They're all gone," the shaman said.

"Already?"

"They're Indians, they're used to it." Jim made a move to get up.

"Don't try to get up," Phil advised, "you're probably a little weak."

Jim let out a little laugh, scoffing at the idea, he tried to stand, but his legs were awkward and unsteady, like a newborn deer trying to walk for the first time. He sat back down on the ground.

Felix laughed at the effort. "You should have seen Phil baby trying to stand."

"You need to eat," the shaman said. "I've prepared breakfast for you." He pointed to a large platter covered with a cloth and a jug that was between them. Jim pulled the cloth off. On the plate were dried meat and tortillas. The jug was filled with water. "You need something elemental to rebuild your strength, meat, bread, water. Eat and drink slowly and soon enough you'll be strong enough to fight again."

"What happened?"

"You tripped your asses off." Felix said, laughing.

"Oh, shit." Jim said.

"You traveled dawn's highway; you had your journey through joy and the dark night of the soul. Now the world is new, it was born anew with the dawn. You discovered power, you must be careful, and you must be prepared."

"For what?"

"For the moment when life breaks your heart."

"No chick can ever do that to me."

"No, it's not something so trivial, it's deeper and you must recognize it for what it is in the moment. And you must be ready, or you will succumb. Within a destiny lies fate."

"I heard a song."

"You must remember the song, if only for yourself. You forget at your own peril."

"What does it mean?" Jim asked.

"We find the lessons in life we want to."

"And there it is," Felix said, "the vague mystical statement of the fraud." The shaman smiled benignly.

"Was that what it was like for you Phil?" Jim asked.

"It doesn't matter," the shaman said. "If you tell each other what you saw, it wouldn't have the same meaning to the others as it did to you."

"I'm going to Sonora to meet a friend of Senor Reyes'" Phil said.

"Yeah!" Jim said, "let's go to Sonora then all the way down to Mexico

City, find some hookers, do the whole Kerouac *On the Road* trip!"

"No, Jim, you still don't get it. It's just not kicks and adventure. Didn't this mean anything more to you?"

"Man, I'm just looking to have a good time, for the experience, to inscribe them on my consciousness, so when I die, I'll have something to remember."

"Is every experience equal? One experience is as good as another?" Phil looked at Jim and Felix, "don't you see? This is a revelation, the moment when physics becomes metaphysics."

"But you're still looking for something with a set of rules," Jim said, "imposed by a tradition. You may want something new, but you want the safety of rules. I've spent too many years locked up. I've already served a life sentence, now all I'm interested in is freedom."

"What about all those aphorisms you're always spouting from Nietzsche and Rimbaud? Aren't those your rules?"

"I'm beyond that, man. You have to be more Dionysian in your thinking, you have to immerse yourself in madness, in the unconscious. Nietzsche and Rimbaud are just sign posts in the wilderness—they tell me I'm on the right trail."

"Jim, you seek chaos wherever you go."

"The universe is chaotic. It's the mind that imposes order."

"Philosophy without wisdom Jim, that's more of Felix's getting fucked up, and not Rimbaud's rational disorganization of the senses. That's the choice you're going to have make sooner or later getting fucked up—or real searching."

"Fuck you, Phil!" Felix said, he headed back to the car, "c'mon Morrison, let's go. He'll probably end up dead in the desert anyway."

"I have a philosophy. That's a lot more than a lot of people have, and I'm willing to live it until the end. Can you say the same?" In that moment Phil saw the difference between Jim and himself. He saw the fork in the road, the paths that he and Jim diverged from here, moving farther apart until they would only be able to see each other from afar.

"'Excess leads to the palace of wisdom,' huh Jim? What have you learned?" Phil turned and headed to the shaman's house.

In Jim's movie mind, he saw the final scene of this modern western, of the new sensuous wild west for a turned-on generation that wasn't afraid to see everything differently, in disconnected images with the mind choosing the order, creating its own context. The car raced across the desert floor, the asphalt fleeing behind them, in front of them the mountains in the far-off distance, the car racing after the setting sun, chasing the ever-receding horizon.

❋

"Is that the god's honest truth as to what happened?" Hanson asked.

"Hmmm," Jim said, cocking his head to the right, a smile on his face. "There's a truth in there."

"Listen you little prick!" Hanson said, jumping out of his chair. At that moment Ellison walked back into the interrogation room, leaving the door open.

"Mr. Morrison," he said, "you're free to go."

"Why?"

"The charges have been dropped. Phillip has returned home, mystery solved." Jim got up and was as far as the door. "Mr. Morrison," Ellison said behind him.

"Yeah?"

"Stay out of trouble son I don't want to see you back here again."

"Right, dad."

Jim walked out of the police station. He was downtown and had to walk all the way back to Sunset. He walked at his laconic but purposeful gait, taking in everything, remembering it. It was late afternoon. The few people on the street were straight—short hair, suits and not turned on. The tan and white buildings all seemed to recede into the landscape. As he moved away from the moment, it was the past. It didn't make any sense to look backward, to remember. It would be a sorry nostalgia. The future was forward, in front of him.

On Sunset, it was a neon infused night which was never quite dark and hummed with the electricity of creation. He could feel it; the energy rippled across his skin like a soft breeze. He was ready to change the world. He had changed his. The street was swarming with people, and he was a part of the Sunset scene. He would spread his wings huge against the night, the stars would fall from his hair. He was a force of nature. With a wave of his hand, the storm was at his command. As he neared The Whisky, he could feel the music thumping through the walls, and the doors. He walked in and was swallowed by the music.

 # JUDGEMENT NIGHT

(with Jovan Thomas)

*"What do you know better than
your own secrets?"*—Raymond Carver

urid, strobing images flickered in his mind, illuminated by lightning flashes crashing off each other, in and out of focus, in the swirl and fog of a fevered dream. Wet darkness, a young woman's face washed out in the rain, a bus placard that says: Nashville. Men's ruddy faces, cruel masks of people, distorted, laughing. A whiskey bottle, a disembodied voice that echoes the words "guilty! I condemn you!" A bus sitting on a darkened road, its lights stretching out into the night. It was steeped in sepia and chiaroscuro, the color of memory. A scratching sound at the edge of consciousness. It doesn't seem human, a chittering sound that sounds far away but growing louder. As it gets closer the sound becomes coherent until he recognizes it as a voice speaking to him.

"Wake up pops!" The man opened his eyes. His head was resting on a window, a drop of rain splotched on the window, then another, and another. He didn't know where he was. He looked around, blue painted metal walls and the oblong windows of a bus, the scenery fleeing past, as the bus drove into the night.

"Hey pops!" One of the insect voices was saying, "are you all right?"

The man looked around; a young cowboy was hanging over the back of his seat looking at him.

"Where am I?"

"Out in the middle of nowhere man."

Another cowboy poked his head above the other seat, "you ok, pops?" The cowboy asked, seeming concerned. "You look like you was havin' a bad dream."

"I'm fine." He said, not too convinced of what he said.

"Well, you look white as a sheet."

"Like you said, I was havin' a bad dream."

"Well, this is the place to have 'em." The second cowboy said.

"What'd you mean?"

"Doncha' know, pops?"

"Know what?" The man asked impatiently.

"It's just hereabouts they say this stretch of highway is haunted."

"Haunted? I don't believe in ghosts."

"Be careful they don't believe in you."

"Remember, not even the darkest secrets of men are safe."

"What's that supposed to mean?"

"I don' know," the cowboy said, "that's jus' how the story ends.

"I don't cotton to no stories."

"Take it easy, pops. It's just a tale mothers tell to scare their children."

"What's your name pops?"

The man looked around the bus as if its walls contained the answer. "I don't know," he said mystified. "I just woke up...here."

"Doncha' remember anything, pops? What about your pockets?" The man did a fast pat down of his shirt and pants pockets and found them empty.

"Man, you been on some kind of bender? You better remember before we get to the end of the line."

The man looked out the window but, saw only his face staring back, reflecting off the darkness outside. A thought came to him, "Forrest. I think Forrest may be my name."

"You mean like, you can't see the forest for the trees?" The cowboys fell back into their seats choking on their laughter. One of them picked a up a guitar sitting on the floor between them and started strumming on the out of tune instrument, their drunken singing closer to a caterwaul, "bury my body down by the highway side, so my old evil spirit can get a Greyhound bus and ride." Their laughter degenerated into guffaws as they collapsed further back into their seats.

A couple of rows up a young mother reached into her satchel for a baby's bottle. One rolled out of the cloth bag, clinking down the aisleway, glass on metal, coming to a stop against Forrest's boot. He looked down at it apprehensively, as if it were something to be afraid of. The young black woman leaned around her seat, a baby in her arms wrapped in blankets.

"You mind sir?" He looked up at her as if trying to remember what the words meant, "sir?"

"Huh? What?" The woman pointed to the bottle at his feet. "If you don't mind?" He picked up the bottle, a feeling of foreboding washed over him. He walked up the aisle to the woman and child.

"Thank you," she said holding out her hand for the bottle.

"Oh," he said, still distracted by his thoughts, "yes, of course." He handed her the bottle, then walked to a seat a row in front of the woman. Everything seemed familiar, as if he'd been there before, yet unfamiliar.

He turned back to the woman. "Excuse me." She looked up.

"Yes?"

"Do I know you?"

"No sir."

"Do you know me?" She looked at him, trying to place him in her memory. He looked wan, sick, sweating nervously.

"No sir, I don't think so."

"It's just that you look familiar to me, but I don't know you. It's like I've seen you..." his voice trailing off. He saw the woman's face in the dream, it was her. "Maybe it was just the dream," he said softly.

"Are you ok, sir?"

"I...I don't know," he said. "Did you see me get on the bus?"

"No, you were already on the bus when I got on. I was busy with my boy getting us settled in. Is something the matter?"

"I don't remember getting on the bus."

"What do you remember?"

"I've been thinking about that. I remember a dream then waking up here on the bus when it started raining. That's it. I can't remember anything before that. I don't even remember who I am."

"Did you check your pockets to see if you have a wallet?"

"No, I've already checked. I don't even have a bus ticket." He looked around the bus, "the faces of the people, your face, I think I saw them in my dream, but it's all smoke and haze, there's nothing there to hang onto."

"It was only a dream, sir."

"No, it's more than a dream, it feels like something I...something I don't understand, a future or maybe a past I don't want." He looked out the window apprehensively at the passing night. The woman looked scared.

"Maybe you just need more sleep an' you'll feel better."

The tension seemed to leave Forrest's face. "You're probably right," he said trying to change the conversation. "You have a beautiful baby."

A look of sadness passed over the women's face. "Thank you, sir," she whispered, meekly.

"Is something the matter?"

"No sir...yes sir," she tripped over her words, her thoughts. "The truth of it is I was raped a year ago and I couldn't get an abortion."

"I'm sorry," he said, "sorry to hear that."

"I know he's just a baby, an I should love him. I know he's innocent an all and he didn't have anything to do with how he got here, but sometimes I jus' look at him and see the father's face and I jus' want to get even with him, an it's all I can do not to push him away, or worse." A tear ran down her cheek.

"I, I'm sorry, I wish there was something, I, I...."

"Somethin' you could do?" She asked.

"Yes...." Forrest said, realizing there was nothing he could do. His voice trailed off. He turned around in the seat and faced forward.

Forrest fell into a discomfited sleep. Something was gnawing at his consciousness, trying to break through, trying to get in, to get him. At the same time, he was vaguely aware of everything that was going on around him—what people were saying, the motion of the bus, even the static of the radio as it struggled to play the driver's race music. It sounded vaguely like the song the cowboys had been struggling to sing. The thought that had been gnawing at his mind solidified into an urgent question. He opened his eyes and made his way to the front of the bus. The driver was an old negro in his 50's with gray hair, and a rounded stomach. He was wearing the gray pin striped uniform of the bus line. His clothes were oversized on him. They billowed and flowed around him like a robe. His jacket hung off the back of his seat. On the far side of the man's shirt hung an engraved name plate with the letters C-h-a-r. That was all he could see the rest was obscured by a fold in the shirt. The driver's foot pressed down the big flat accelerator pedal, pushing the bus further into the night. He noticed the man sidling up next to him.

"What's your name boy? Charles?"

"No sir. It's Charon. Take a seat, sir."

"I have to ask you something."

"Take a seat," the driver said, motioning to the closest empty seat. "Company rules, safety precautions, sir." Forrest sat down on the edge of the nearest seat. He leaned in towards the driver so he could hear him.

"When did I get on the bus?"

"What?" The driver asked, annoyed by being distracted from his job by the obviously ridiculous question.

"I asked, when did I get on the bus?"

"At the terminal," the driver replied, incredulously.

"You saw me?"

"You paid your money and got on jus' like everybody else."

"I paid you?"

"Yes, sir, two silver dollars, jus' like everybody else."

"I don't have a ticket."

"I didn't give you one, I know who paid."

"Where'd I get on?"

"Lethe."

"Where'n the hell is that?"

"Lethe, Tennessee." Just then the radio crackled with static and the sound of frayed wires just this side of shorting out, and a faraway voice came from the speaker. "Breaking news. Convicted rapist, *crackle*, Forrest, *crackle*, escaped earlier, *crackle*, and may be trying to leave the area. He's described as being six feet tall, white, *zzzzt*, thirty-five years old, sandy hair…" Then the radio cut out altogether. The driver banged on the dashboard.

"Damn radio." He looked over at Forrest. "That sounds like it could be you."

"What do you mean by that!" Forrest snapped, jumping towards the driver.

"It was a joke, sir! I din't mean nothin' by it."

"That description could be a lot of people."

"Yes, sir that could be a lot of people."

"Rapist!" Forrest whispered louder than he meant to. He looked over at the girl with the baby. "Where's this bus going?"

"Nashville."

"How long until we get there?"

"Usually, a couple of hours from here, but with all this rain the roads are all muddy, and it looks like another storm is rollin' in." Forrest looked out the window and saw storm clouds illuminated by lightning visible in the distance. He sat back down. He noticed the man who was sitting in the seat next to him. He looked to be in his late fifties or early sixties. He had white hair, rosy cheeks and the pacific look of a cleric on his face.

"Would you like a sandwich, my boy?"

"No thank you, I'm not hungry."

The old man looked out the window. "It's been raining something terrible; I'm surprised it's not a river out there. Although, I guess this road is ferrying us to where we're goin'. What's your name, son?"

"I can't seem to remember who I am or where I'm going, or why I'm going there. And to tell you the truth, like the driver said, that guy on the radio sounds a lot like me."

"The escaped prisoner?" The old man looked skeptical. "Look at your clothes, those aren't prison issue."

"The only part of a name I can remember is Forrest, and that convict's name is Bedford Forrest."

"Son, around these here parts Forrest isn't an uncommon name. Just because you remember the name Forrest doesn't mean anything. Your name could as well be Smith or even Jones."

"I guess you could be right," Forrest said. "You see the woman back there with the baby?"

"Yes?"

"I think I saw her in my dream."

"Are you sure?"

"No."

"I thought so. Could it be you had a dream with a woman, and you filled in a blank with the face of the first woman you saw?"

"Yes! You're right! I just wish I could remember."

"It's a dark and stormy night, it's enough to throw anybody off. You don't remember, you're struggling to put things together, you hear a report, your mind wants to make order out of the chaos, and suddenly two and two make five."

"The cowboy in the back told me this road is haunted."

"Old wives' tales, ghost stories. Around these parts folks like a good, dark, gothic story. It's a part of us, a part of our culture. But still a good many terrible things could happen out here."

"What do you mean?"

"Do you know the original meaning of the word 'uncivilized'?"

"No."

"It means to live outside of the city, and my boy, right now we're uncivilized."

"I have this feeling of foreboding like something is coming to get me. What if I am that guy?"

"What makes you think something like that?"

"This feeling of dread, like something evil is coming for me, that's part of me."

"My boy, I've just met you, and you do seem haunted. But before you let it go to your head, I don't mean by ghosts or anything like that. Something is haunting you—it may be an event, or even something you didn't do or did do. To find forgiveness in the world you have to find it in yourself. You have to make amends with whatever is haunting you."

"Are you a priest or something?"

"No," he said chuckling a little, "I'm just a retired teacher, traveling around the country to see the things I've always wanted to see, and now I'm heading home."

"You seem pretty wise."

"No, I've just talked with a lot of people on the bus and listened to their stories. You should see all the stranger souls I've met on this bus."

"How am I supposed to make amends for something when I can't even remember what it is?"

"It's hard to see what's inside a man's soul, what haunts him."

"Back to the ghosts."

"Maybe we're all ghosts," the teacher smiled, "ghosts of memory. We're held by our memories or other's memories of us, or even by events and places. Maybe ghosts are created because we remember. So, as you see, in a manner of speaking we're all ghosts."

"What do you mean?"

"You may not remember what it is, but you know in your heart what is haunting you. When you do remember, you can make amends if you want to, but you have to want to make peace with it and ask for forgiveness. It'll be the hardest thing you'll ever do, and you may not be able to do it on the first try. From what I've seen in life most people prefer the easy road. You're on a hard road, my boy," he said, smiling, "but you'll make the right choice."

"How do you know that?"

"Because you're worried about it."

The bus turned off the road into a small town. It drove through the streets of the closed-up and dark town until it pulled up in front of a small wooden building. Forrest woke with a start from the braking of the bus and the idling engine. Forrest looked out the window, the bus was stopped in front of a building that had large wooden windows from which a warm light shone out into the night. Inside, there were four or five wooden benches, on the back wall, some dime lockers, and off to the side a ticket agent's window with bars across the front. It was closed.

"What're we doing here?"

"One last passenger to pick-up, one last soul to get to where they're going," the driver said. Forrest saw that there was one person standing on the platform in the rain, a dark shrouded shadow. The driver opened the door and a woman got on. She paid her fare to the driver, turned and saw Forrest.

"Oh my," she said, recoiling a bit.

"You know me?" He asked.

"No, not really, but…."

"But what?!" He almost screamed.

"You look like the man in the newspaper that they locked up and threw away the key."

"Why, what'd he do?"

"Serial rapist, been terrorizn' Nashville and hereabouts for a coupla' years. But you can't be him, he's in prison."

"Prison," he said, dejectedly.

"An' he's gonna' be there for a long time, he got a coupla' life sentences, an' I hope he serves every last day of them, an' then some. A lot of the things he did happened right around here."

"Well, if he's the same guy, there was a report a while ago on the radio sayin' he escaped." The driver said.

"There's only one like him. I hope they catch him soon," the woman said.

"And you're sure I look like him?"

"Pretty much, there's some semblance."

"I'm getting off here," Forrest said, getting up and moving towards the door.

"What do you want to get off here for?" The driver asked. "This town is closed up tight until morning, and I don't think it's all that lively then either."

"If something is out there in the country, something wild and evil, something uncivilized," he said looking at the teacher, "I'll be safe here in the city." There was an awkward moment, where nobody knew what to do or say and nobody moved. The radio came to life with a crackle of static and the news report came on in mid-report,

"…who broke out of prison earlier today has been found dead in a field. The police think he was heading to the woods to a hideout." Forrest looked relieved. He noticed the rain had stopped.

"See you ain't him sir, you ain't dead," the driver said, "at least you don't look dead to me." Everybody within hearing distance laughed at this including Forrest, who finally seemed at ease, his fears put to rest. "What's it gonna be sir?" The driver asked. "You know the guy is dead, the weather's improvin', and I have a schedule to keep, you comin' along or you gonna' sit here in this empty bus station with not another soul in sight?" Forrest took a minute to consider, looked out the door at the dead city, and back to the bus, considering what it was—the only world he knew, the only place he was safe.

"I'm comin'. There's nothin' here for me and nothin' I want from here. Let's go."

Everybody settled into a seat, Forrest at last looked peaceful and at ease. The door hissed closed, and the driver put the bus in gear. It lurched forward through the dead town. Forrest watched the bus's headlights reflected off the darkened buildings and shiny streets as it wound its way back to the road. As the bus turned onto the highway, he noticed one side of the road was a forest and the other was open country. The road cut them in half like an asphalt river. The yellow headlights of the bus stretching out into the night until they were absorbed by the surrounding darkness ahead. The red break lights at the back of the bus got smaller as the bus moved down the road and farther into the night. Forrest nodded off into a peaceful sleep.

Everyone in the bus had fallen asleep except the driver. The inside lights had been turned off. The only light was the eerie green fluorescence of the dashboard lights and the bus's headlights reaching out into the darkness. Raindrops started hitting the windows and Forrest's eyes jerked open. He heard the rain splotching against the glass. Through the front window he could see lightning in the near distance. His eyes again betrayed desperation. He remembered something from the dream. Frightened, he jumped out of his seat, rushing towards the back of the bus where the cowboys were. He shook the nearest one. trying to wake him.

"Wake up!" Forrest yelled.

"Wha???"

"You said this road is supposed to be haunted?"

"Yeah, so what? I wanna' go back to sleep."

"What's the story?"

"What?"

"What's the story? What happened here? What ghosts are supposed to haunt round here?"

"Don'cha know?" The cowboy asked, "haven't you figured it out yet?" Forrest looked perplexed. "This is the ghost story. The ghost bus that rides these roads carrying souls to their redemption or their damnation." Forrest pushed himself away from the cowboy.

"I'm not dead," he yelled, "what am I doing here?" Suddenly there was a loud bang, and screeching tires. The bus swerved back and forth across the wet road as the driver struggled to keep the bus under control. Forrest was thrown to the floor by the unseen forces of nature which he'd never been educated on, but of which he was nevertheless subject to. The driver slammed on the brakes and the bus skidded off the road coming to an abrupt halt. The bus sat silently on the side of the road its headlights shining out into the rainy night.

"Here it is boy, the end of the road."

In a panic Forrest got up off the floor and headed up the aisle to the driver. "What was that noise?" He screamed. "Why have we stopped?!" The driver didn't answer. "I asked you a goddamned question! Why are we stopping?"

"Sounded like a tire blew. I'm gonna' go out and check it, be right back. Sit put."

"Sit put?! We can't just sit put! We have to go! They're coming! I can feel them! They're out there. Hiding. Waiting."

"I thought you was over this?"

"Everything I know, I can feel it in my bones. I know there's something out there waiting for me, something I don't want to meet up with."

"What's out there, boy?"

"I don't know, but I can feel it waiting for me, coming nearer." A memory tripped in Forrest's mind; a connection made. He turned to the woman with the baby. "But maybe it's already here. Stop this!" He yelled at her, "I can't do this anymore!"

"Stop what sir?" She asked, frightened. "I ain't doin' nothin'."

"I...I...I," he stammered, looking around as if expecting an attack from any side. He slumped into the nearest seat, drained. All emotion had left him, his will was gone, his energy sapped. "I'm tired," he said to the woman. "It feels like I've been here before, done this before, like I'm locked into some cycle. It's like dying every mornin' only to be reborn back to this moment, night after night, year after year. It feels like centuries. It's like some jail sentence, and I have a feeling you have something to do with it, and you can stop it!"

"You have to stop frighten' my passengers sir," the driver said. "There's nothin' out there except the night. I don't know what has you spooked. Maybe it's just you're in a country you're not familiar with, the storm, the escaped prisoner. I've driven this route every night for years, I know every turn, every bump. If you knew the road like I do, you'd know there's nothin' out there to be afraid of." The driver opened the door and took a step towards it.

"No! Please! Don't go out there!" Forrest jumped out of his seat, "they'll catch us, me. I'm tired, but if I stop, we stop, there'll be no saving us."

"I'm goin' out there." Forrest grabbed the driver's arm.

"You can't go out there!"

"Sir, if you don't take your hand from my arm, you gonna' find yourself picking yourself up from the floor right there."

"But I'm telling you!" The driver punched Forrest, who fell to the floor rubbing his face.

"Now, if you know what's good for you, you better stay down there, or get back on your damn seat, or I'm gonna' put you off the bus." The driver pulled a flashlight off the dashboard and got off the bus.

Through the front windshield the passengers could see the beam of light plying the night like a searchlight. It seemed to be bobbing around randomly, first in one direction, then another. Forrest got up off the floor and followed the driver out the door. The bus was sitting off to the side of the road in the wet grass. In the distance he could see the woods, but the driver was nowhere to be seen. He seemed to have disappeared. Forrest walked around to the rear of the bus, to see one of the tires had been shredded, with slashes running across it, like a clawed hand had reached out and grabbed it. He ran his hand over the torn apart rubber.

"Jesus, how did that happen?" He asked himself. There was a snap of a twig and he spun around to find the driver behind him.

"I thought I told you to stay in your seat?"

"I came out here to see if I can help. What happened?"

"Looks like the tire blew out."

"Blew out!?" Forrest said incredulously, "that's not a blowout! Look at it! It's been shredded!"

"It could be anything sir," the driver said, "a factory defect."

"Factory defect?! It's been shredded! How do you shred the tire of a moving bus?! It looks like some beast hand reached out and grabbed it."

"It doesn't matter sir, we're on the other side."

"The other side of what?"

"The river." A sharp, distinct sound came from the woods. Forrest looked around for who, what or where the sound had come from, but there was nothing. A look of realization came over his face. "Only something evil can reach out like that, and its coming for me, and we have to get out of here!" He became frantic he started tugging at the drivers arm who stayed solidly in place. Forrest pulled again and slipped, falling into the mud. When he got up the driver was gone. He'd disappeared almost in front of his eyes. And it was quiet. Forrest realized he didn't hear the bus's engine anymore. It hadn't stopped, it didn't sputter out, and it hadn't been turned off. It was just gone as if it had never been there. He ran to the door of the bus. Inside it was empty and dark, the seats were torn, and the windows broken or gone. It looked abandoned, as if it was a dead thing that had been rusting away in the weeds for decades. He looked into the night in horror. Everything he knew, everyone he knew, gone, his world was dying away.

He started running down the road, away from the woods, away from the bus. The road was wet and muddy, but he kept running. Running until his face was more sweat than rain, until he couldn't inhale or exhale anymore, until time and distance had separated him from the bus, until he forgot what he was running for, what he was running from, until he felt like a clean slate, new, and without a past, without a future, only now, only the moment. He slowed to a walk, finally catching his breath, finally feeling what was chasing him was behind.

Ahead of him, he saw a figure in the darkness, walking slowly. He could only make out a shape, a shadow that was a little darker than the surrounding night. As he got closer the shape solidified. It was a woman. He could see the outlines of a skirt and her small frame.

"Miss! Miss, what're you doing out here?" He called out. She stopped and turned around. He looked at her puzzled. She looked like the woman on the bus, yet she didn't. She looked younger her face untroubled, confident, happy. "What're you doing out here so late and alone?"

"Jus' walkin' home from work, sir."

"Weren't you just on the bus with me a while ago?"

"Bus, sir?" She said looking puzzled. "The last bus came through here hours ago."

"It's running late because of the rain and a flat tire." She looked at him as if he was crazy. "Let me walk you home, make sure you get there safely."

"I appreciate that, sir, but I'm just up the road a bit."

"There's something I have to make up for and I want to make sure you get home safely. I think it'll atone for what I've done."

"Suit yourself."

They walked along the road silently. She watched him warily out of the corner of her eye. He kept his eyes focused ahead on the road. It was barren, only the asphalt and the open spaces that surrounded it. As they walked along, he saw a light coming over the horizon, the crack of dawn as his mother used to call it. She used to say it was an in between time where anything could happen. It was neither light nor dark, as if a door was opening and they had walked through, between the worlds of darkness and light. It was the crossroads of eternity.

In the distance was a copse of trees and walking towards them on the road were two men. As they got closer, he could see they were swigging off a bottle of whiskey and passing it between them. They were dressed in black rain slickers, jeans and cowboy boots. Although their faces looked harder, and there were no jokes between them now, he recognized them right away—it was the cowboys from the bus.

"Bout time you showed up, boss," one of the men said.

"You're from the bus. Do I know you?"

"We're here." The woman said.

"Where!?" Forrest asked, the panic back in his voice.

"Where you've feared to be," she said, "that far shore you've been afraid to reach, the moment to atone for your sins or be bound to them. The decision is yours."

"Course, you know us, boss," the other cowboy said, "you said to meet you out here."

"And you brought us this tasty morsel you promised us." One of the cowboys grabbed the girl, twisted her arm behind her, while the other groped her.

"No! Please stop this!" She screamed, then looking right at Forrest, "Bedford, you've always been the one who can stop this!"

"Bedford......?" He mumbled, "so it is me. I am the escaped prisoner, the rapist."

"It's ok Bedford, you've spent your life crossing the river to death. It may seem like you're stepping over a chasm, but it's only a step over a stream."

"I'm afraid, I've only known this life." A wall in his mind crumbled as if from the pressure of a flood, memories rushed from his subconscious. He remembered his cruel life, the predator, nameless faces of women, faces that were battered, afraid, women's limbs that were bound, writhing, faces that had been gagged. He smiled cruelly at the memory of remembering who he is, what he is. He remembered the power he had over the moment, over the woman's life or death. He wasn't afraid anymore. The knowledge had changed him from the frightened man of the bus to the confident, fiendishly dangerous creature of the night. "Bedford Forrest," he spat out.

"What'd you say, Bedford?" One of the cowboys said.

"Nothin.' It took you two long enough to get here, where you been? Never mind," he said, grabbing the whiskey from them and taking a long swig from the bottle. Then he turned to the girl. "This whole time on the bus lookin' at me with those big innocent eyes. Were you hopin' I wouldn't remember you? Or did you think I'd forget you? Did you think you were goin' to get away from me?" She struggled desperately against the arms of the cowboys.

"You don't have to do this! You can break the cycle. You don't have to do this night after night."

"There's only tonight," he said.

"Yes, there's only tonight, there's always just tonight. But you wish there was something you could do. You said that on the bus. The person on the bus is your true self, the one that doesn't want to hurt anyone! YOU CAN STOP THIS! END THIS TONIGHT!" She screamed.

"I bet you liked that me on the bus, afraid of what the future held, afraid of what's around the next bend."

"That's your true self."

"Is it?" Bedford asked. "That guy was a little twerp, a goody-two shoes, and what did it get him? Beat. I killed him. Now I control destinies, you're here because I will it."

"No! You're wrong! It's a trap! All this is a prison! All you have to do to break the cycle, end this and you'll find the freedom and the peace you want."

"End this? I've been looking forward to it ever since I first saw you." Bedford closed in on her, a cruel lecherous look on his face, he pulled her away from the cowboys and dragged her off the road into the wet grass, he pushed her down and raped her. It was like Bedford, brutal, inhumane, monstrous.

When Bedford was done with her, he walked off into the grass, one of the cowboys called after him, "where you goin'?"

"It's going to be light soon, she's all yours." He wandered off into the glistening frozen blades of grass which sliced at his feet like razors. He walked until he was outside of hearing the girl's screams. He walked until he came to a circular clearing that was burned into the grass. It was about ten feet in diameter. In the middle was a mound of earth that couldn't be anything except a shallow grave. He walked around the perimeter looking at the mound when a voice boomed out of the night.

"Guilty! I find you guilty on all counts!" It was ubiquitous, everywhere and nowhere, it surrounded him. It was the voice of the teacher from the bus, but now it was harsh, judgmental, accusing. "I see no signs of remorse or efforts to redeem yourself! I hereby condemn you to your sin until such time as you can rectify your crime. You've lived outside of civilization we condemn you to the outside of society. You're condemned to the night."

Bedford walked to the center, to the head of the grave. He knelt down, reached out to the mound. Hesitating he pulled his hand back in fear. Did he really want to know? It was the final piece of knowledge that he'd been searching for all night. He reached out again and brushed away the dirt to reveal a face, his face. It was bone white and the features were etched by the dirt that had worked its way into the crevices of his skin, but it was recognizable. It was his face. He sprang backwards in shock landing on his back, sprawled out over the scorched earth, looking at the corpse in uncomprehending horror and fear. Behind him he heard the double click of a shotgun's hammer being cocked and locked. He turned around to see the girl standing there, her clothing was disheveled and wet, and she was holding a shotgun leveled at his chest.

"What're you doing here?!" Bedford asked.

"I am the instrument of justice, of what you put inside of me, of what I have to carry around for the rest of my life, maybe longer. You've locked me into repeating this nightmare with you, again and again."

"The child?"

"Now you remember him? Yes, this is the night you gave me the child but that's not what I have to carry around. It's the hate and fear you implanted in me, that you felt tonight, but that I have to walk around with for the rest of my life."

She jerked the rifle up.

"No! Don't shoot!" He yelled. She pulled the triggers, and a blast of white flared out of the gun's barrels, overwhelming his vision. Lurid, strobing images flickered in his mind...an insect voice said, "wake up, pops!"

THE SEAS HAVE NO STARS

"For the animal shall not be measured by man. In a world older and more complete than ours, they move finished and complete, gifted with extensions of the senses we have lost or never attained, living by voices we shall never hear."

—Henry Beston

The fishing boat was riding low in the water, returning to port with a full hold after months of wandering at sea, hunting for the next school of tuna. Danny was alone in the glass enclosed cabin of the ships bridge. The trawler was a workhorse of the sea. It wasn't large by any measure, not like an ocean liner or an aircraft carrier which are essentially skyscrapers that float ten stories above the water, so the passenger and crews may never see the sea or feel the roll of the ship. On a fishing boat the sea is right there, it's a personal relationship between you and a primal force of nature you can't ignore. You have to learn what the rules of the sea are and understand them in order to survive and make a living. That's why I named the ship Oceanus after the titan of Greek mythology, more powerful than even the gods. People were always amazed that the Oceanus was a sea-going vessel. It was old, the paint was peeling, the engines chugged along with a full hold, and it reeked of fish and offal even when empty. Danny was used to a life on the sea. Sometimes the water was so calm and still it was like skating on glass, but other times at a moment's notice, the seas could change, and the bow of the ship would plow into a wave and disappear. The wave would break on the cabin window and for a heartbeat, you wouldn't know if you were sunk or if you'd continue to bob on the ocean's surface. It was easy to see why the ancients could believe in Poseidon and other gods.

The season's hunt had taken them well away from usual fishing grounds that seemed more and more fished out every year. They had followed the dolphins and found prime fishing grounds, but they were where most people would call 'the middle of nowhere,' well out of the shipping lanes and far from where any pleasure craft would be. The light on the bridge was the only light in the darkness and seemed to shoot out of the cabin and was quickly absorbed by the night as if it had never existed. The sky was clear, stars were visible on their velvet background. Danny looked out into the night, to the horizon where the sky met the sea, although there was no way to tell the sky from the brackish waters of the sea. The only difference, Danny mused, was the seas had no stars. It was still a long way home and all he had to rely on was his instruments to get him and his crew home.

The water was the separating line of the worlds. He knew there was a whole different world down there. He understood life and death in the oceans. Since he was a kid his father would take him out on shorter fishing runs. He would look through the fish they hauled out of the sea and find rare and beautiful fish that weren't commercial, and he'd dreamed of being a diver and exploring the seas, seeing all the wondrous and alien creatures, discovering new species, exploring a reef, to be one of the few to observe an alien world. Now, as an adult he hunted the seas and pulled life up from the depths. He didn't want to take life but now he had a responsibility to his crew and their families to make a living. Occasionally, the high powered lights they used for night fishing would draw up strange creatures from the depths and he would find something odd or beautiful, but they were delicate and already dying the colors draining from them as they floundered on the deck, gasping, drowning in the air and without the pressures of the depths to support their bodies, their appendages were limp and flopping around without purpose. He had no context for what he saw and could only wonder at what these creatures' place in the environment was. When he could and it didn't seem too late, he returned the creature to its world and hoped it would survive his intrusion and live the lives they were intended to live.

He loved the sea but differently than his father had. His father was pragmatic, he saw the sea as a source of income, while Danny had loved the abundance and diversity of life in the sea. He had a more romantic, more poetic vision of the sea than his father. His father thought of him as a dreamer, and he had to admit, he was right, as did some of his crew. When his father was too incapacitated to fish any longer, Danny felt a responsibility to his father and to the crew who depended on him and the boat to make a living. Now, he no longer looked at the seas and the stars in awe and wonder. It had become a job, a way to make a living. His life had been pre-ordained, to be a fisherman. He argued to his father that his dream was still a life on the sea, but his father didn't consider diving work; his own separating line between the worlds and started taking him out when he was seventeen, which his father thought was late, but he started at the bottom, his father made sure he worked every position on a ship. Now he had lived most of his life on the sea, forty years since he was that teenager learning the ropes, literally, and now he was afraid that whatever moment he was waiting for had passed.

Most of the time he didn't have time to worry about things like this. The work kept his mind off of those things. The muscle weariness of his body made its way to his mind, and he easily passed out in his bunk. But it was times like this when the work was done, when the holds were full, and the nets were stowed away when there was nothing to do, when he had time to think. He went over the events of his life replaying them in his head. With the knowledge he had now, if he would, could he change things? He tried not to be bitter, but things were the way they were and couldn't be changed. He'd discovered some of his ideas now resembled his father's. His idealism had been dashed on the rocks of an unchangeable reality. Not so long ago he wouldn't have thought that way, He wondered if his father had any dreams. He never mentioned any. He soothed his mind with the knowledge that the important thing was that the hold was full, which meant a good payday for everyone involved. The boat rode a little lower in the water chugging along a little slower, and they were headed home. The crew would make a lot of money from their cut of the haul. Danny was happy.

Suddenly there was a blip on the radar, and it was a big one, but it didn't seem to be on the water, it seemed to be above the water. He got on his radio and called up to the watch, "you see anything out there?"

"No, captain, it's pitch black out here. Nothing happening except a couple of dolphins surfing on our bow wave."

"Keep your eyes open, we have a contact on the radar that we seem to be coming up on fast."

"What's going on, Danny?" His first mate Marty had come up to relieve him. He still looked sleepy. He'd known Marty since they were teenagers. He'd grown up with most of the crew, they were the sons of his father's crew locked in from an even earlier age than him. Most of them had already been crewing on this ship or others when his father brought him on. He was captain by virtue of the fact that his father had owned the boat and passed it on to him. God only knows how far back this legacy of primogeniture went back, probably centuries of fathers and sons on the seas. Most of the crew didn't seem to mind their place in the universe. They were part of the environment. Even though there were titles like captain and first mate, everybody fished. The chain of command only came in after the fishing was done, or when they were stressed and needed to be quick and concise to keep the ship from sinking, or something like that. Otherwise, everything was pretty equal.

"Captain," the watch came back on the radio, "off our port bow, I think I see something."

"What is it?"

"I don't know, I can't make out anything. There seems to be something hovering above the water! It's dead ahead, if we stay on this course, we'll get a good look at it." Danny pushed a button that rang a bell below deck. The sleeping crewman were used to jumping out of their sleep at the sound. Danny's voice came over the intercom, "All hands-on deck! All hands-on deck!" The crewman arrived on deck pulling on the last of their clothes. There was no reason to ask what they were summoned for; their questions were instantly answered as they saw it. They could only stand at the rail of the ship staring at the object. It was hovering about twenty-five feet above the water, they couldn't make out anything except the shape. It looked smooth and dark, darker than the surrounding night. It was like a hole in the sky hovering above the water, a void. All Danny could hear was his ship's diesel engines lumbering along. He cut the engines. The night went dead silent. There wasn't a sound from the object as they glided past.

"Tommy, turn on a spotlight and aim it at that thing!" A light snapped on. The beam looked solid in the night, it swung around and up at the object. Nothing was distinguishable. It was solid, no protuberances, no wings, nothing that seemed to stabilize it. The water under the object wasn't being disturbed at all. It was the same dark waves under it as the rest of the ocean. If this was some kind of craft, it didn't seem to have a propulsion system acting against the water. As the ship slowly passed the object, the crew all stood mesmerized by it. It didn't seem to notice they were there. It took a minute or two to move past the object. Everyone rushed to the stern to get more perspective on it. It didn't help shed any light on to what it may be, it seemed just as immutable and ineffable as it had before.

"What was that thing?" One of the men asked.

"Boys," Danny said, "I think we've seen a UFO."

"What're we going to do now?" Danny thought about it.

"Report it, I guess. Marty, get on the horn and radio it in."

When the ship was well clear of the object, Danny felt the ship starting to drift. He'd forgotten to turn the engines back on. Danny's watch was over and ordinarily he would have gone to sleep, but he was too amped up. He didn't know what the object was, and his mind was firing off ideas at the speed of thought, jumping from a thought to a scenario, to a possibility, to a daydream. He knew he wouldn't be able to sleep so he was just going to stay on the bridge until he got tired. The excitement he felt was shared by the whole ship. It was alive with energy. Nobody was sleeping, they were all talking about what they had seen, trying to figure out what it was. They were so excited by what they had seen that they weren't even listening to each other. They were just talking, trying to get it out of their system, trying to make sense of what they had seen. Except for Marty and Danny, it was a comfortable silence on the bridge as each tried to assimilate the experience in their own way. It couldn't even be categorized as a silence, as they probably knew what the other was thinking. About a half an hour past the object, the sonar started pinging like crazy.

"What's that?"

"A huge school of…looks like dolphins." Marty answered.

"Dolphins?"

"Yeah, the largest school I've ever seen,"

"Which way are they heading?" Although Danny already knew the answer.

"In the direction of the object."

Danny looked astern there was a light coming over the horizon. He would have sworn it was sunrise, but he was looking west, out to sea. "We're turning back."

"Why?"

"Something weird is going on."

"Weird?" Marty said, "what's weirder than a UFO?"

"I have no idea, but I want to see what it is."

"It's still dark."

"Look back in the direction we came from."

Marty looked back and saw the glow, "holeeeee…"

"It'll be dawn in a couple of hours," Danny said, as he turned the wheel hard and pushed the throttle to full.

It only took about twenty minutes to get back to the object, because Danny had pushed the engines. When they came within sight of it, they saw the light was coming from the object. As much as the object had been a hole an hour or so ago, it now seemed to push out light, illuminating the surrounding waters. It wasn't blinding, it was cool, no heat emanated from it, and of course, as before, there were no visible features on the object. Weirdly enough, even though he was by no means religious, all Danny could think of was Moses' burning bush. The watch radioed back, "Captain, the water up ahead is filled with dolphins!"

"Cut the engines!" Danny yelled, "steer away from them!" They could see the surrounding waters were filled with dolphins, wave after wave of dolphins breeching and diving. He had never seen so many dolphins in his life. It wasn't a pod or a school. Rather, it looked like, damn near every dolphin for God knows how many miles away, were all swimming towards and around the craft. There seemed to be a static charge in the air, a weird hum, like some kind of organic generator. He didn't know if it came from the object or if it was from the action of so many living creatures in close proximity. Or maybe it was his imagination or something he was projecting onto the circumstances? Directly underneath the object it was calm, dolphins bobbed on the surface looking up at the object.

"What is that?" Marty asked.

"I don't have the foggiest idea." Danny said.

"It looks like they're receiving the word of god."

"Could be Marty, could be."

"Do you really think so?"

"Just keeping all the possibilities open."

"You think they're communicating with the object?"

"Or it's communicating with them." Danny looked thoughtful for a moment, then seemed to reach a decision. "Ok, steer clear of the dolphins and drop the sea-anchors. Let's see if anything happens. With all the light that thing is providing we can see well enough, besides, it's almost dawn."

After an hour and nothing happening, and the object showing no observable recognition of their being there. Danny came back to the ships bridge. He had walked the ship from bow to stern to see if a different perspective revealed anything; it didn't.

"Anything going on up here?"

"Nothing from the object," Marty said, "but I've been monitoring the radio. There are reports coming in from all over the world. These objects are showing up, hovering out in the middle of the sea."

"And dolphins?"

"Yep, they're reporting that dolphins are massing around these objects or moving towards the nearest one."

"Wow! What's going on?"

"No one knows. The navy is sending the nearest ship, but in some cases, it may take a day or two for them to get there."

"Let's go over this with everybody. Call a crew meeting in the wardroom in five minutes."

The wardroom also doubled as the mess. In their off-watch time, the crew would hang out in the room, reading or watching movies. Whatever section you wanted to call it, it was the one place on the ship where most of the men could comfortably be stuffed into to talk.

"What could that thing be?" one of the men asked. They all looked at each other. They were all practical men of the sea, pragmatic. None of them went past high school, and some of the old prejudices and superstitions of the sea were carried down from father to son. It was their inheritance. For the most part they didn't believe much of what they couldn't see or touch, and they had seen almost everything there is to see on the ocean.

"A UFO?" one of them ventured tentatively, everyone laughed nervously.

"Well, that's the known, everything we've seen. What's the unknown?"

"What's with all the dolphins?" Tommy Jenkins the night watch asked.

"Has anybody ever seen anything like this before?" Marty asked. They all just looked around the room, no one said anything.

"Still doesn't answer the questions about the dolphins."

"Well, dolphins are as intelligent or maybe more intelligent than us." Danny said. "They communicate with each other, they're social animals, they have extended family groups. They hunt like early man surrounding their prey or driving them to an area where they can eat them. They use tools, they learn and pass knowledge on to other dolphins, they have different clicks for individuals—in effect, a name. They even have the same bad habit as humans, killing for fun."

"Let's hope that isn't a sign of intelligence too." One of the men said almost inaudibly.

"We see dolphins all the time," Marty said, "they're just..."

"What?"

"Animals."

"Look into their eyes and you'll know they're sentient beings."

"I've fished a few out of the ocean in my lifetime and all I've seen in their eyes has been dull and gray."

Danny hung his head in disappointment. "That's because you've only seen them on the deck and dying."

"If these are aliens looking for intelligent life, isn't that us?" One of the crew asked.

"Dolphins have been in the seas for thirty-nine million years using echolocation, and I would assume that implies an amount of intelligence as well. If the beings in the object have been visiting the earth for millions of years, dolphins were the most intelligent species around. People always ask how much older an alien intelligence would be. Dolphins have almost thirty million years on us! Maybe, to the aliens, we're the animals, apes with some fancy tools."

"If this object has been visiting for millions of years, why haven't we seen them before?"

"Because man has only been on the water for only a few thousand years, and for most of that time we've stayed close to shore. We're pretty far out in the ocean and off the main lanes. Another question is how often do they visit? How many times have they been here since man became an intelligent species?"

"How do you know all this?" One of the men asked.

"I wanted to be an oceanographer, and I'm curious and still keep up with things."

"How do we know this thing is alien?"

"What else could it be?"

"Who or what an alien is, is just a matter of perspective. What do you think the creatures we fish think of us as?" Danny looked around, again to some blank stares. "Let me ask you this, what's a standard description for a UFO.?"

"A cigar or saucer shaped object with bright lights."

"What do our ships look like to the dolphins or any of the life down there?"

"I don't know."

"The bottom of a ship is definitely cigar shaped," Marty said, "and we have our lights blazing at night."

"A UFO by any other name to the life below us. Then think of this, a diver in a wet-suit, mask, tanks, regulator, lights on the suit, we're the aliens."

"What's that have to do with the object outside?"

"Think of it this way, maybe the objects coming down into our atmosphere is like us going down into the sea."

"Allriiiiiiiiiiiiiiiiiiiiiight," Jenkins said, more of a disbelieving exhalation.

"It might mean we're misunderstanding what we're seeing or don't have enough information to comprehend what we're seeing. Maybe we're just seeing the bottom of the boat."

"Well, they're not coming for the fish." Marty said.

"If they're here to visit the dolphins, why doesn't the ship, craft, object, whatever the hell it is submerge?"

"Maybe they're not aquatic, maybe the object can't operate in a liquid, maybe they need air to communicate, maybe they know the dolphins need to come to the surface to breath, God! It can be any number of things, all of them, or none. The sun's coming up. Let's get back up there and see what we can see. Marty, have you tried broadcasting some kind of message to the object on the radio?"

"No."

"Give it a whack and see what happens. Tommy, use the light, signal over to that object and see if it responds."

"We don't have many channels available, and certainly no higher, exotic ones." Marty said.

"Try your best, see what happens."

"What do you want me to say?"

"I don't know, anything. Why don't you and Tommy work out a simple message, and both of you transmit it to the object."

As Danny came up on deck, in the light of dawn, he saw from the southeast a couple of F-16's heading his way. He watched as they came down in altitude and did a flyby of the object, then went around again, circling before heading back, off in the direction they came. Danny went up the ladder to the bridge.

"Well, there's the results of us reporting the object."

"What?" Marty said.

"Those jets, they just did a flyby."

"I didn't really hear them, I was preoccupied on the radio, I guess."

"Did you get anything?"

"All the usual channels had the usual traffic and the higher ones, just static." There was a pause. Marty knew they'd done most of what they could. "What do you want to do now?" Danny looked out at the object and the circling dolphins, and the enigma they represented.

"Whatever is happening is happening in the water under the object. If they are communicating with the dolphin's we need to see what we can hear down there."

"You want me to listen by hydrophone?"

"I was thinking of something a little more direct."

"Like what?"

"Putting a diver in, and if there's any communication from the object, record it."

"With all those dolphins flying around down there? They're pretty big, a diver could get hurt accidently."

"That's why I'm going down."

"Danny," Marty said quietly, thoughtfully. Danny recognized the tone, he wasn't Danny's first mate anymore. He was Danny's friend whom he'd known since kindergarten. "I know you've been waiting for something like this..."

"Something like this?"

"Yes, I know being a fisherman isn't what you wanted to do with your life, and it's not hard to see your frustration and anger that you take out on yourself. You work yourself until you pass out, and when we're in port, drinking to forget. But you're smart, that's why you're the captain. You're smart enough to realize this is dangerous for you I don't want you to be obsessed with this, only to end up disappointed, and let it break your spirit."

"I don't think it will."

"Danny, I remember when we were teenagers and talked about our dreams and ambitions."

Danny smiled warmly at the memories, "yeah, wanting to be an astronomer until I discovered all the math, diving with Jacques Cousteau, being his head diver, traveling the world, discovering new species, hanging out in Monaco, dating Princess Caroline." He thought for a moment, remembering himself as a kid. "The thing is all I wanted to be was a kid who looked at the stars."

"You've always been a dreamer, Danny."

"Yeah, now I just see every day as being closer to death and farther from what I want."

"And that's why I'm worried about you and this object. If it doesn't work out to be whatever you're building it up to be in your head, it could..." Marty's desperation rendered him wordless.

"Maybe the real reason I didn't go off and become a diver was fear. Maybe I was afraid I wouldn't make it, so I clung to the safety of what I did know."

"So, you're going to risk your life for this?"

"You know, every day out here is dangerous, and we risk our lives for some money. If I don't do this, it'll be giving in to that old fear."

Marty looked into Danny's eyes and saw his friend, the boy he'd known since childhood, and relented. "Fine. What're you going to record it with? We don't have equipment like that on board."

"I do, I have equipment in my cabin. I always bring it with me."

Danny sat on the edge of the diving platform at the rear of the ship. The water was a little choppy and opaque. He knew it was an alien world that he couldn't enter without life sustaining equipment to keep him alive. It would be as if he fell from the sky, an Icarus of the water, legs and arms thrashing about, the water surrounding him, cold and suffocating. Would the inhabitants of that world be able to make sense of him? Would they return him to his world if they could?

"You know," Danny said to Marty, "I've been thinking lately that the seas have no stars, but I remember I used to dive and just go to the bottom and look up at the fish, just hanging there, like they were hanging in mid-air. I'd forget the science of what held them aloft, and they shimmered like the stars in the sky." A microphone was built into the diving mask and Marty would be recording everything. Danny double-checked to make sure everything was secure, put the regulator in his mouth, gave Marty a thumps-up, and dropped into the water. He broke the plane to the alien world below and became an alien in that world.

The water was turgid but clear enough that the visibility was good. Danny felt a bit of pressure in his temples. He blew into the regulator equalizing the pressure. He swam to within visual range of the ring of dolphins, circling under the craft. He could see that it was much more furious and dynamic than what they could see from the surface. The dolphins were moving at nearly full speed around the object. It was frenzied but not chaotic, he wondered how long they could keep that up before burning themselves out? He looked down to see how far the circle of dolphins went. It looked like they went pretty deep, like a tornado of dolphins spiraling off into the depths. He wondered how they cycled up for air. He couldn't tell but there must have been some system, some logic to it. Going through the dolphins was the best way to the center. He felt a bit of trepidation in his body. It occurred to him maybe this was an invitation only party. Were the circling dolphins meant to keep other species out? He saw a hole in the circle, and he swam at full speed to get into it before it closed. When he broke through the ring, he was hit almost head on by a dolphin who only side-swiped him, but it buffeted him into another dolphin. He knew he would be bruised up when he got out of the water. Then the dolphins started accounting for him in the group and steered clear of him, and he knew he'd be okay as long as he didn't make any unexpected movements. He could hear the dolphins' whistles, clicks and echolocations. It was cacophonous, like being on a city street in the middle of rush hour, and all you can hear is the roar of the traffic and the sounds of people all mixed together, echoing through the canyons of buildings, but you couldn't make out individual conversations. He wondered how the dolphins could. As he swam through the dolphins, he noticed it wasn't a solid ring of dolphins, but circles within circles, moving in towards the object. He again thought of this as some kind of generator. He could feel the accumulated energy of all the dolphins in one place. It was like a living engine. It was a bit unnerving. He wasn't sure if this was something that was actually happening, a trick of perception, or his imagination running wild.

He slowly made his way through the rings until he emerged into the center. The water under the object was nearly calm. If the outer rings of the dolphins sounded like a city street, the center was almost pastoral. He looked up and he could see the object's shadow on the surface of the water. Every once in a while, a dolphin would breach the surface for air, otherwise the dolphins under the object were calmly swimming around. Periodically, there was a perceptible echolocation, whistle or click from the dolphins, otherwise it was quiet. Danny turned on the recorder. Then he heard it, something totally unexpected and weird sounding, like a pulse coming from above. No, it wasn't a pulse. It was a wave that he felt move through his body. He had a moment of panic, worrying it may have some physical effect, but then he realized the signal was probably geared to be safe for the biology of earth. As the wave moved through his body, he relaxed. He heard it too, and it sounded…alien. It sounded like a variation on the dolphin's language, but he could hear other elements in it. Did the dolphins get their language from the aliens? Or are the aliens adapting to the dolphin's language? He knew the sound was being refracted by the water. He was sure the aliens had accounted for that. Otherwise, the dolphins wouldn't understand the message. It stopped after a minute or two, then repeated. Danny stayed for one more cycle to be sure it was the same message repeating, and he had it all.

Immediately under the middle of the object he saw a column of water about seven to eight feet in length and three feet wide. It was placid, like glass. While all the water around it was moving, the column was stationary, a pillar in the water. He saw dolphins swimming into it and disappearing! Were they being transported to the object? Surely it couldn't be anything else? They wouldn't be destroying them; it didn't make any sense to come from wherever they came from to kill dolphins. Then Danny remembered what had brought him there, that his holds were filled with fish. He discounted the thought. That had to be the way in. He checked his air; it was getting low. He had to take the chance. He swam into the column of water and found himself in a void. He was still suspended in water. He didn't see any dolphins; he didn't see any horizon or limits to his vision. It seemed infinite, but he knew that was impossible. Had he been transported into the alien ship? Then he began hearing clicks and squeals. It was the dolphins' language they were trying to communicate with him in—the only language they knew? Maybe they didn't realize he was a different species from the dolphins? The clicks became louder, filling his mind, insistent on an answer. They were trying to communicate but he didn't understand, and even if he did, he wouldn't know how to respond. The clicks became louder and more insistent, he could feel the pressure in his skull. He tried to clear the pressure as he had before but couldn't. It felt like bone was about to shatter or fracture. He could hear the blood pulsing through his ears with every beat of his heart. It was like the roar of a locomotive or a jet engine. He doubled over in pain. He could still hear the clicks echoing in his head like a whisper trying to be heard over a scream. Danny knew he was dying. He would die in the void alone, no one knowing what had happened to him. Just as he thought he couldn't take it anymore. The sounds stopped. It was quiet. Had his eardrums shattered? Had a capillary burst in his head, and blood was flooding his brain? Or was his air gone and his brain was suffering from oxygen deprivation? An image of a being filled his mind. It must have been one of the aliens. He couldn't understand its form as he didn't have any context for what he was seeing. He couldn't tell if the alien was in water or not. The creature looked at him as if studying him. He heard a questioning click or two as the creature looked at him in a way that could only be described as quizzically. He heard a few more clicks from the being, they sounded soothing. Then he heard a voice awkwardly mimicking English the best it could, "return." Then Danny saw a column of the calmed water coming towards him. He knew it was his way out. He tried moving towards it, but he was immobilized. It kept moving until it enveloped him.

Danny came to in the fetal position on the trawler, his hands over his ears. He shivered, cold to the core. He couldn't breathe. Something was in his mouth, something hard, that tasted of rubber. He spit the regulator out of his mouth. Air rushed into his lungs, the cavity filled, and he moaned. He could feel his body involuntarily rolling around on the deck. He heard his crew, he felt the bodies around him, looking at him. Suddenly he was warm. The creature had returned him, and he knew he was safe, back in the world in which he belonged. He wasn't going to die today.

FATHER'S SON

Preface

The head of the charging bull elephant filled my vision. I'd angered it with my presence, I was too close to his harem. His head was down, his ears extended, making himself as large as he could, tusks pointed forward. There was good reason the Indians had used them in war, and Alexander and his battle-hardened army had quaked in fear when they first saw them. A charging elephant is a massive, thundering, unstoppable creature capable of trampling any human and horse underfoot, its thick skull, a battering ram, crashing into anything, up to and including a jeep. The ground thundered with each step of his charge. I could feel the vibrations through the earth with each foot fall pounding in my ears. Knowing the cause of those tremors was from a creature consciously aiming itself towards me added to the tension. Elephants don't know fear. They're the largest land animals. Lions may be, quote, the king of the beasts, end quote, but elephants truly are. Every other creature respects their strength and power, they hunt them only if they're sick or wounded. But I've been out in the African bush long enough to know that sooner or later every predator becomes prey.

I lifted my head from the rifle's scope to clear my vision. The elephant was still a hundred yards away. I put my head back down to the sight, 'no challenge,' I thought, it was like being right in front of the creature, point blank range, how could I miss? I waited until he was close enough for the bullet to shatter the heavy bone of his skull, bringing the creature crashing to its knees. The momentum of its mass would send him skidding though the brush like a locomotive jumping off its rails until it came sliding to a halt in front of me. My eyes blurred. The enraged elephant's head became my father's face, it was as if my father's spirit inhabited the elephant at the last moment. I pulled the trigger. I shot every time.

I

The jeep rattled, bounced and lurched over the veldt as I drove back to the base camp to escape the afternoon heat. My father was a legendary writer, a legend in his own time which had met with his conception of himself. He'd always lived his life as a larger-than-life character. Long before the world took notice of him there were James Eastman stories among the small orbit of friends that surrounded him. Long before there were any books written, and long before any newspapers or magazines reported on his every move, there was belief, belief in himself as a great writer.

I was expecting a new safari to arrive that evening. It was a safari in name only because the whole week was booked by a would-be biographer of my father. What could I tell him about my father that others hadn't already? Could any of my experiences lead to any insight about or understanding of my father's writing? Or even as a person? People sought out my safaris because of my father. To them he's a historical figure, etched in memory as marble, configured to what they want him to be. To me he was a living, breathing creature that filled my vision every bit as much as the elephant's had, and every bit as frightening.

As a young man he had all the gifts the gods could dispense, talent, good looks, and charisma. He seemed to pull everything he needed his way. When he became famous with his first novel *The Road to the Sun*, quickly followed by *Tender Fury*, the reviews and articles went from laudatory and respectful, to worshiping and idolatrous. Later, his 'Africa' series was judged to be some of the most seminal writing in American literature. He became regarded as a legend and an icon while still a relatively young man.

My father lived his life fully in public view. Newspapers and magazines wrote about his exploits, divorces, marriages, every aspect of his life. A lot of it reads like hagiography, and what had started as a joyous, youthful excessiveness, the celebration became a habit until he expected, then demanded things. As he grew older, he ossified, he became a fossil while being labelled the last writer of the 20th century.

There was a lot of death in my father's books. He once told me that he'd discovered death when he was eight years old. He'd been reading in bed late into the night and when he was finally trying to get to sleep, he was awakened by the thought that he was going to die and there wasn't anything he could do about it. Because he was eight years old, he was scared. He was going to run to his parents for comfort, but he realized they were going to die too and there wasn't anything they could do about it either. He finally lulled himself off to sleep by realizing that even though he was going to die, it was about eighty years in the future, so there wasn't any reason to be scared. In that realization he'd fused death and literature in his mind.

He next met death in his early twenties when he went off to war. He confronted it more closely, personally; he was wounded and nearly died. Death is easy when you're young, you still think you're immortal, especially if you survive. But still, you recognize that death can come at any moment. You may fear it, but you laugh at it, and live to the fullest. You drink more, you pursue many women, you seek experience. When he started to write, at first his stories about war were sympathetic and realistic because he wrote about what he'd experienced. As he aged and moved away from the rawness of the experience his stories became romanticized and dogmatic, and he espoused a great belief in war and death as a way to prove yourself. From that came my father's great literary aphorism: that all stories end in death. The older he got the more obdurate he became in that belief. I've often wondered how many generations have gone off to war stuffed with my father's stories, visions of glory in their eyes, but came back old men. The horrors they'd witnessed beyond the wildly romanticized imaginings of my father. When death finally came to him, did he turn and face its skeletal stare? Was he ready for it like he always claimed in his stories and novels? Or did it take him by surprise just like everyone else? Maybe my father's life was trying to understand death, to study it and to come to terms with it in his writing. He did tell me, "the world didn't exist before I was born and it will die away at my feet when I die."

Throughout his life my father was open and approachable to other people. People always came up to him as if they knew him, and they probably believed they did know him from his books. My father was considered an 'autobiographical' writer, and the details of his biography didn't contradict that idea. He'd based his novels on people and experiences from his own life, so when his next novel mirrored what they read in newspapers maybe you can forgive them for thinking they knew him. My father was a collector of stories and people, he was always surrounded by a circle of friends that revolved around him. He had a special kind of charisma, like a light shining out in the darkness, and when that light shined on you, it was warm and enveloping, people felt special, and they found themselves telling him things they never would have told anyone else. Maybe, they even thought they were auditioning to be characters in his next book. They'd regale him with their most outrageous stories, or embellish the stories of their lives, hoping they were 'characters' enough for the next novel. My father always said those who want to be written about weren't interesting enough, and those who were interesting enough didn't want to be written about.

And to his children? He'd made himself an object of fear, he was aloof, the child rearing was the wife's job. My father's work was always important, so when he was around, we were to be quiet and not bother him or suffer his wrath. When he was mad at you it was cold, he would cut you out of his life, that warm light was shined elsewhere until he thought you'd been punished enough. When I was outside of that light, I tried to recreate the conditions and situations that won that attention, even when that attention was negative. I became my father's son.

Which was the real James Eastman? The gregarious bon vivant or the terror of his children? One? Both? Neither? Was there another aspect of my father, another 'him' that he hid? I heard my father tell stories that I knew were lies, stories he put me at, that I knew didn't happen. As I grew up, I recognized it as old Irish blarney, his naysayers called it bullshit. He used to tell me he had lived the first twenty-three years of his life in his imagination. I used to think it was just one of his dramatic pronouncements to seem like the romantic brooding poet he imagined himself. My mother explained that my father, as a writer, that sometimes the world of his imagination met this world and it wasn't really a lie, that he was trying things out, working a story out in his head, and maybe in a world of my father's creation it really happened. Then she said, "what a marvelous life, all the lives he's lead."

As his son, I was supposed to know the intimate details of his life and have some insight into his writing. But I didn't have any insights into his life or his writing. I'd read all of my father's books in an effort to understand him. By the time I was in college, there were courses on my father and his writing, I took them all, and I learned when and where he was in the war, the dates of his marriages, his publication dates, the themes, symbolism, foreshadowing and all the other literary nuances and devices of my father's writing. None of that helped, I didn't understand my father any better than anyone else.

II

That evening I was sitting around the compound having a cocktail, watching the sun set and trying to catch a cool breeze off the veldt, waiting for my new charter to come in. Every once in a while hearing the occasional roar of a far-off lion. Minute after minute, mile after mile brought the would-be biographer closer, a concordance of events that made the inevitability of the encounter closer to reality. An encounter I wouldn't have control over. I imagined the passengers getting knocked around the cab of the jeep by the rugged terrain and their reaction to it. Were they rolling with every bump, pitch and lurch? Or cursing every bump, pitch and lurch? It became entertainment, a television program of my imagination as I played out the various scenarios in my mind. Finally, I saw the truck coming in from a long way off. At first it was just a dust trail, but as it got closer. I made myself another drink before he arrived and checked to make sure the servants had setup the dining room table with the fine tablecloth and China.

When the jeep pulled up in front of the tent, I was there to greet it. All the big game hunters were of a type: well-off, middle-aged men who could afford the trip to Africa, the fees for licenses, as well as my fee, increased accordingly because of my status as the son of James Eastman. As he got out of the jeep the client didn't disappoint, he was middle-aged and dressed and outfitted with the latest in hunting gear and fashion including wearing a green hunters vest, I walked up to him.

"Are you Talley?" I asked.

"Yes, John, John Talley."

"Welcome to the base camp."

Looking around, he said, "I was picturing more of a tent."

"You shouldn't let your expectations color the reality."

"Are you Jamie? Jamie Eastman?"

"Yes," I said extending my hand, you can call me James."

"Jaaaames," he said, with some skepticism, trepidation in his voice as he shook my hand, as if he wasn't sure I was who I said I was. All through my life I've had to suffer the diminution of my name from James to Jaime as if I was supposed to live in my father's shadow forever. Forever infantilized to be 'Jamie,' a character created by my father, forever trapped in my father's pages like amber, people can only see 'Jamie,' a construct of my father's fiction. I think it had somehow arrested some part of me.

"It's because of your father I'm here," he said excitedly, "it's because of your father I became a writer."

"And now you want to write a biography of him? A lot has already been written about him, books, magazines, newspapers."

"Most writers who have a best-seller, hell, most actors, singers, directors or artists have their moment in the sun, their fifteen minutes of fame with one song, movie, or painting. Your father, has held the public's attention for forty years."

"And?"

"You've never cooperated with a biographer."

"Don't you think there's a reason for that?"

"What was your relationship with your father like?"

"Contentious."

"I've read all of his books. Your father used you in a lot of stories, didn't he?"

"Used is the right word." Jamie lit a cigarette and the threw the lighter on a nearby table in disgust, "and you feel like you know me, because of what my father wrote?"

"Well, not quite, I guess, but can I ask you something?"

"Sure."

"What was your father like?"

"I thought I already answered that."

"No, you know what I mean."

"Probably nothing you want to hear. You want to hear what a great guy he was, that there was always some adventure hanging out with him, that he was a great guy to have a drink with, and perhaps you'd become friends with, and maybe you'd even be right, but that was only one aspect of him, he was more complicated than that. My father would purposefully do things or push people to an extreme to see how they'd react he'd watch them and make notes. He once said, he was like an anthropologist with a knife."

"I thought he used a lot of his life for the raw material of his stories."

"My father wrote fiction." I said sharply.

"Did I say something wrong?"

"No, dinner is about ready, let's sit down and we can talk."

"What about my things?"

"Don't worry, they'll be taken to your hut and unpacked while we eat."

We sat down at the dinner table covered with fine linen, China and crystal glasses.

"This is quite a set-up for the African savannah."

"A hunting trip is rugged, so this is one last taste of luxury and civilization before we go out into the bush." Just then, there was the keening roar of a lion, it sounded closer than before.

"Are the animals close by?"

"Close enough, predation almost outside your door. A few weeks ago, we found what was left of a lion's kill just outside of the camp."

"Just outside the camp?"

"Don't worry, they won't come into the camp, they avoid humans, they understand we're the dangerous animals."

"What about the one out there?"

"The local tribesmen had a ritual hunt; they only wounded the lion, but they'll kill it tomorrow. So, what're you after Mr. Talley? Any game or just my father?" He looked confused by the question. "Do you really want to hunt, or is your prey on this safari my father and me?"

"Yes, I want to experience a safari so I can write about it realistically."

"You may be more my father's son than I am. What animal are you after?"

"What animal? Elephant. Your father had a preference for elephants."

"I hope you're a patient man, we may be out quite a few days without seeing any animals much less elephants."

"Isn't that what I'm paying you for? Because you know the habits of these animals."

"I know their territories, I know their migratory routes, but any variable can throw them off, it's like kinetic balls, one hits the next, then another until the chain reaction builds and their actions become random, disorganized, unpredictable." I looked at him trying to see his reaction, "this isn't some tamed overnight campout with raccoons and a deer walking by. We're out in the wilderness, it's lions and hyenas right outside your door. No, there's no door, just the flap of your tent. It's life and death, and the sooner you realize you're not as close to the top of the food chain as you've imagined yourself, the better. There are a few rules on a safari. The foremost is don't shoot anything until I say it's ok. There are a lot of factors and conditions out here you aren't aware of, or there may be another predator nearby. There may be a nearby mate of what you're shooting who may charge. Not so long ago a hunter was gored by the mate of a water buffalo he had just shot."

"That's fine."

"Elephant, really big game, huh?"

"Your father wrote that the elephant was the biggest test of a person."

"He wrote that, but they're not the simple allegorical animals my father wrote about. They're quite sociable animals with a clear hierarchy, I've seen them mourn the deaths of another."

"Are they close by?"

"We'll be going to a lake, some of the animals go down there in the morning to forage. The larger animals come later to escape the heat of the day. The predators follow them, they're vulnerable, they know this, and they're wary, they want to live, as you and I do. Something unexpected like our presence can kick in a survival instinct and unpredictable behavior, and you can quickly become prey before you realize it. You understand?"

"Yes, of course."

"Good. Now we can talk about anything you want, the weather, my father, anything."

❋

After dinner we were sitting at the front of the tent where the evening fire was set up. We each had a cocktail. An evening breeze was cooling the savannah, as we watched the moon hold sway over the plain. An air of nostalgia permeated the scene. I could see Talley was imbibing the atmosphere, the romance of adventure, the sights, sounds and smells surrounding him, nostalgia for my father. He was seeing it all through the prism of my father's writing, a romantic vision of life and death, I could already tell that his mind was forming a memory of this evening, that would be told and retold as a story for the rest of his life.

"You don't know what it means to me to be out here with you," he said, "your father and his writing has really influenced my life, and now here I am out on safari with his son as my guide! I learned about what being a man meant through his stories."

"When my father was writing a book he wasn't an easy person to be around, reality and fiction often merged for him."

"He had to have been a keen observer of people."

"My father used people. He put them in extreme situations to see how they would react. He was interested in the behavior of people, he would test those around him, challenge them, all to evoke a reaction." I felt sorry for Talley, he was a fan of my father's and wanted to be close to his idol, by visiting the landscape my father described, with his son as his guide. But what he'd read about, I'd lived. "Look, I should have told you this over dinner. This isn't one of my father's adventures, it's not literary. It's hot blood pooling on the dirt, the light behind the eyes fading and finally flickering out, it is the smell of offal and decaying meat in the hot sun, the

55

swarm and bite of flies, it can be made to seem like a parable of life, death, and survival, but there's no easy resolution at the end, no easy moral, especially for the animal, only its death."

"Your father was a great believer in war and death as a way to prove yourself."

"How does killing a living thing prove anything?"

"If you panic in that moment or keep your head." I shifted uneasily in my chair.

"My father's writing influenced generations, young men marched off to war with visions of glory in their eyes because my father romanticized it. I have no illusions why people come on my safaris, I've had presidents' sons take my safari, government ministers, movie stars, scions of industry, the un-nameable wealthy. And it's not because I'm the best hunter, it's not because I'm the best tracker, or because I find the rarest game. It's because they want to hear about my father. Inevitably, the first question they always ask is, what was he like?" Talley looked somewhat abashed. "Hunting is like war - all you have to do is pull the trigger, that's all there is to it. There's nothing easier in life than pulling the trigger, you're a machine, a piston firing. It's an artificial moment created by being there. There's no reason to be there, it's not truly life or death, the animal isn't needed for sustenance, it wasn't a threat to you until you put yourself in that position. The only outcome is man kills. Something equally important could be learned by walking away."

"That doesn't sound like something a hunter would say."

"I'm not a hunter."

"What are you then?"

"A survivor."

"Of what?"

"My father. I'm not the hunter, the character my father portrayed in his Jamie stories." I didn't know how to put it any more clearly, I felt like I was smashing an icon in front of him. "My father loved this place, loved the hunt. Look, I've learned that out here in the bush, hunting is a passion play that you're only vaguely aware of what your true role in it is. Hunting was once for survival. We had to eat, we had to clothe ourselves or die. The hunt was sacred, the animals revered for their strength, their prowess and their sacrifice. There is a lot of ritual surrounding the hunt."

In the distance the lion bellowed his rage and pain into the night.

"Those tribesmen didn't mean to wound the lion, but they know they have to kill him, or they will have to pay the consequences." I took another long swallow of my drink. "In the hunt humans would wear the hides of animals, some would say it was only to get close to them, but anthropologists would tell you that it was just to get closer to the animal's spirit, to possess those traits they were in awe of. In a sense hunting was possession. Now man only wants to possess the physical, the skins, the tusks, or a head on a wall. Tell me mister Talley, what part of the elephant do you admire? What part do you want to possess?"

"I...don't know, I haven't thought about it like that."

"Perhaps something you should think about before you pull the trigger."

"I was thinking about your father's story, 'The Hunters,' that was about you, wasn't it?"

"Yeah, although, it's more a character named Jamie, but based on something that happened to me. It wasn't what actually happened, he made it fiction, something for his own purposes. If he was proud of anything, he was proud of the character named Jamie in the story, he was a hunter. Maybe that's how my father wanted it to be, but that wasn't me. I'm not a hunter. It was his version of 'Lord of the Flies' he thought he could do it better."

"It was based on that something that happened to you?"

"The first time I went hunting was when I was a teenager. I went out with some friends to a nearby prairie, hunting birds. I saw one sitting in the broken window of some abandoned shack that was out there. I aimed and shot it, and when the bird fell it was a sickening feeling to see the bird just drop. It looked unnatural. We went behind the shed to verify the kill, I guess. The bird was dead, and we left it there. It seemed there was some implied, unstated idea that there was some satisfaction in just the act of killing. I didn't reload my gun after that, and the rest of afternoon I walked around with the breech open and the gun pointed at the ground, I never even aimed it at anything else the rest of the afternoon. If any of my friends noticed they didn't say anything."

"That's not the story your father wrote."

"No, his story is about fathers and sons, one generation creating or destroying the next. What you want to remember is that in the story my father is both the father and the son."

"What about the holy ghost?"

"That was my father too, as the author of the story." I looked away to that faraway time. "There's another story, one my father didn't tell. When I was a kid, after a rainstorm I would always pick-up worms off the driveway and put them back in the grass. My father used to stand on the porch with a drink in his hand and laugh while I saved the worms. He said I was a 'worm savior.' That probably reveals my father's idea of me as a hunter more than anything else."

"Surely, he loved you?"

"To my father children were an after-thought, a by-product of sex. He considered himself the end result of evolution, not a link in a continuing chain. Raising children was the purview of the wife, and my mother did her best to fill the void. She made sure me, and my brothers learned how to play instruments, we took dance classes, we went to charm school, she tried to make us as well-rounded people as possible." I thought for a moment. "For a man of letters, love wasn't a word in his vocabulary. Happiness wasn't a goal of my father's generation and eventually he died of a broken heart."

"A man like your father? He was a living legend, people hung on his every word, he was hailed as a genius, he was welcome anywhere, he had marriages, children."

"That's the view from the outside. What people don't understand is that the image you propagate turns against you, you come to resent it because it's not you, it's not real, it's not the reality behind the fantasy. Wives left, children left, friends moved on. Behind the image was a sensitive person. Life didn't live up to how he envisioned it in his mind. That's why he wrote, that's what broke his heart." The alcohol was starting to get to me.

"Didn't your father once say, that of his children you were the most like him?"

"You would know better than me."

"Marriages, restlessness in the world, alcoholism. Those things that describe your father can also apply to you." Talley paused to let the thought set in, "and yet here you are in a profession that your father would approve."

"I understand this country better than he did, I understand the animals better than he did and our place in the natural world."

"Aren't you living up to his ideals, trying to win his approval on the terms outlined in his books, books that you tell me are fiction." I gulped down the last of my drink. It was like an admission, I was sure now, the alcohol was getting to me.

"Maybe you're right," I said, "Africa is the cradle of man. He walked out of Africa and made a place for himself in the world. Maybe I never came to terms with my place in the world, maybe when I walk out of here, I hope I can do the same."

"I saw a picture of you at his funeral and your eulogy, you didn't cry."

"I didn't cry because I'd lost my father a long time before that."

"How's that?"

"I lost my father when I was fifteen years old, and I didn't cry then either because I understood the rules. They weren't my rules, and I didn't like them. They were forced upon me, but I lived by them. My father wasn't a large part of my life. When he was working, my mother always told us how important my father's work was and he wasn't to be disturbed even when he wasn't working. We understood it and walked around on eggshells so as not to rouse his ire. When my parents had a party, we were like show objects, paraded at the start and then sent off to bed. We weren't part of that world either. When there were vacations, of course, we went along and there were good times. Those are the pictures that show up in the biographies. But my father didn't get interested in us until we were older, and we could be enlisted as accomplices."

"You ran away from home at sixteen?"

"I left home and joined the merchant marines."

"Why?"

"I wasn't getting along with my father, he used to write at night so I would leave and wander in the night until he went to sleep. It was a wild time, I was getting into trouble, I was arrested a couple of times, I had to get away and I guess I had something to prove…it was probably all the usual Freudian Oedipal complex issues, although, Oedipus was lost on my father." I drifted off in the thought, "I haven't been home since."

"That sounds like things your father might do, it looks like you're trying to prove something here."

"What are you trying to prove here?"

"Nothing. Interviewing you for my book and get some hunting in."

"No, you'd like me to say I'm trying to gain my father's approval to vindicate your idea that I was trying to live up to my father's values. Well, no, it was for myself. I had lived so long in the shadow of my father and believed in his legend, so I went off to create the myth of myself."

"That sounds like something your father would write or do."

"It doesn't matter what I do with my life, it's always up for examination. I'm a hunter so people think I'm trying to win my father's approval or trying to live up to his ideals. If I wrote a book, it would be compared against my father's. It doesn't matter what I do. Sooner or later some magazine, newspaper, tabloid or TV show is going to send around a reporter with a 'where is he now?' story, and no matter what I'm doing, I'll be judged as a failure or success based on my father's accomplishments, values and ideals, and I'll always come up short."

"You were there the night he died?"

"You mean the night he killed himself?"

"I read in a newspaper you had an argument with him, and it was pretty, uhhh..."

"What?"

"Boisterous."

"You believe the tabloids? You think I killed my father?"

"They couldn't find you for a day or two after they found him, there was an investigation."

"Is that why you came out here? Is that going to be the thesis of your biography that I killed my father?"

"Not the only reason."

"Something more than your book?"

Talley smiled, "I want an elephant."

"No, I was right. The trophy you want is James Eastman, my father's head on a mantle, or mine too to say you were this close. But you're only a voyeur in his life, a tourist seeing the sights, taking the tour and wanting a picture in front of a façade, you can leave any time, me, I lived it, and I can't escape it." I took a deep breath, and closed my eyes to visualize the scene, catch it in my mind's eye. "You want the whole terrible picture? The final scene of a man's life? All right, they did find me three nights later, but it's because I was trying to forget, to wash the memory from my mind. But I still remember that night vividly, as if I were still in the moment, caught in a dream I can't get out of. He looked so different from the last time I saw him. Most of his life he was big, strong, larger than life. Even when we were kids, we knew there was something different about him, he was always sure of himself. But that last night he looked bewildered. He was sick already. He'd been an athlete and knew his body. It was hard to see a man so strong weakening and wasting away. A lifetime of burning the candle at both ends left him broken, body and soul."

"He seemed like he was one of the original advocates of, live fast, die young and leave a good-looking corpse."

"Thirty or forty years of burning the candle at both ends, what does that leave behind? Embers. But there are a lot of memories of my father as a generous and adventure seeking guy, he left behind a lot of James Eastman stories, and I know that price was worth it to him because that's what he had worked and sacrificed for his whole life."

"What happened then?"

"We had an argument and he accused me of something terrible."

"What was that?"

"He accused me of driving my mother to an early grave. He was drunk and unreasonable. I decided to leave. I looked back and saw something I'd never seen before in him."

"What?"

"Fear, he was afraid. He died believing no one loved him, that no one had ever loved him - not his wives, his children, no one. Everyone had only used him. Of course, he was roaring drunk, there's a reason they call it roaring drunk, it was dying majesty."

As if on cue the plaintive keening wail of the lion echoed in the distance.

"What did you do then?"

"I reacted as I would to any creature that was afraid, wounded, I reassured him, I told him I'd see him later, I never thought I'd never see him again. I guess I should have stayed, but it scared me to the core and sent me off on a bender. A family habit, I guess. It's anybody's guess what happened after I left. Did he purposefully take a lot of pills and wash them down with whiskey? Or did he just take a lot of pills to help him sleep? He was already drunk before I got there and I'm sure he didn't stop after I left."

"Why didn't you go back the next day?"

"When the news reports started coming out about his death, it depressed me, so I just kept drinking."

"And after the police found you and the media?"

"Well, it wasn't what the tabloids suggested, that I was a murderer. I've thought a lot about it, and I'm willing to bet he was just as surprised to wake up and find himself dead as everyone else. It's the surprise we'll all wake up to eventually and discover it's real. Even though he was declining I don't think he actually believed he would die, I think he believed writing would make him immortal."

"It has."

"You know the ending of 'The Hunters'?"

"Of course, *The Lion Communique*."

"Exactly. He was very fluid in his thinking. Like I said, a complex, and contradictory person. Anyway, the police found me three days later."

"Do you miss your father?"

"'Miss my father,' isn't the way I'd describe it. Sometimes I remember him at his strongest and I think he could have lived forever, but his habits brought on his downfall. I guess his books will let him live. The weird thing is how easily we let him go." The alcohol was getting to me, time had suddenly rushed forward on me. It was later than I thought, and I was almost beyond reason. I threw the rest of my drink out into the nearby dust. "We leave at first light, all the animals head to the lake at dawn. And forget about that green vest we have another for you that will blend in better with the landscape."

III

The next morning, Talley and I were out in the blind before dawn, downwind of the game trail that most of the animals used to come to the lake. As the sun rose over the savannah, the landscape emerged from the shadows of night, and revealed the surrounding terrain. What had been thought to be a skulking predator turned out to be nothing more than a cluster of bushes or a rock. We were able to see the rolling grasslands covered with thick clusters of scrub brush before it broke to the lake. A mist still hovered above the water, the grass was wet with the morning dew, and the wind was lightly blowing a still cool breeze across the water. Birds were wading through the marshy area close to the shore hunting their morning meal. The smaller animals would come get a drink and then retreat to the jungle to sleep through the day, while the larger animals would come later seeking relief from the sun and the heat of the day. I knew eventually the elephants would come.

As the day progressed the breath of coolness in the air dissipated as the sun rose higher in the sky, the air became heated. You could taste it on the wind. Talley was becoming bored and impatient. By the time the sun hit its zenith the heat was becoming oppressive, and even though we weren't moving, we were sweating. Our shirts were wet and sticking to our skin. The odor of our sweat had attracted big black flies, their bites were a painful nuisance that made the time interminable. People fear being devoured by a big cat or some other large predator, but it's the insects out here that will eat you alive. Out here the conditions test the mettle of a person. Would they break? Give into the harsh extremes of the elements? Or find it within themselves to bear the brunt of the elements? In this respect my father was right about hunting testing the character of a person. Perhaps it was his most challenging test of people. The conditions are extreme, the reactions are extreme. At least my hangover was burning away in the heat of the day.

Finally, the larger animals started to arrive seeking relief from the day's heat, but still no elephants. Talley was becoming noticeably more and more impatient.

"There aren't any elephants here," he complained. "Isn't there somewhere else we can go that to find them?" I could see Talley's face was getting red, I wasn't sure if it was from the sun, anger or frustration.

"We could go somewhere else, but we wouldn't find any elephants.

This is the best place. We could hunt across their territory, and probably get a lot of game, if that's what you're after. But you'd be lucky to run across elephants. It would be sheer, blind, dumb luck."

"Why"

"The elephants are moving too, one event leading to another. A lion could be in the area and they move around them, or they've found a grazing area they linger at. Anything can set off a chain of events to knock them off their schedule. I've heard of hunters missing an elephant by a few hundred yards. We'll have to be going in soon, it gets too hot in the afternoon."

"Can we wait just a little longer?"

"As long as you don't think the sun is getting to you."

We smelled them first. It was a heavy musty smell, over-powering. Even in the open air it was stifling. Then we saw them as they broke through the tree line. They were moving slowly, steadily, secure in the knowledge that nothing could hurt them. A large male with lengthening tusks reaching towards the ground was in the lead. I watched Talley as he saw them for the first time. He was in awe of the sheer size of them. It's one thing to know they're big, to see them in zoos or circuses, but those environments are out of proportion - they're surrounded by man, put in cages, kept under tents, housed in artificial environments, they're tamed, subdued, their spirits are broken. But here, out in the wild, their natural environment, they're free, free to live, free of man. Their lives are wild, vital, alive. To see them in their natural state is to see the true nature of the animal rising up to their full majesty. Man is small in comparison. The bulk of them moved gracefully in step.

As I watched the male, I could see that something wasn't quite right. He was moving strangely. To an untrained eye he was lumbering along like an elephant, but that's not how they moved. They usually covered ground more quickly. It seemed like he was taking half steps. I wondered if maybe he was wounded, sick, or had become lame. Just then Talley brought up his rifle. I yelled, "DON'T SHOOT!" Just as he fired. The elephant reared his head up in our direction. I don't know if Talley had missed, if we were too far, or if the caliber of the gun wasn't great enough, but the elephant didn't appear to be wounded. He was mad, and he had seen us. He started charging towards us. It was amazing how such large creatures could cover so much ground so quickly, the thumping footsteps soon were thundering in my ears. He passed the edge of the marsh splashing water with each footfall, Talley fired again, but now he was panicked. The shot was reckless, nowhere near the elephant. Shooting from an unseen position at a prey that isn't aware of your presence is one thing. Shooting at an enraged animal that is aware of you and is consciously after you, each step closing the gap between you and him is the difference between target shooting and being in a war zone.

The elephant increased his pace. I would only have one chance for a good shot before he was upon us. I aimed my rifle carefully, sighting his massive head in the telescopic sight. I had done this many times; all I had to do was pull the trigger. The head of the charging bull elephant filled my vision, the elephant's head was down, his ears extended, making himself as large as he could, his tusks pointed forward. I could feel the vibrations of his steps through the ground, each foot fall thundering in my ears, louder. It sounded as if I was standing in the middle of one of my father's famous battles, but something was wrong, I couldn't shoot. I had the shot, but I couldn't shoot, something was wrong. All I could see was the enraged elephant's head in the scope, not my father's. I remembered the last time I saw my father, maybe I hadn't understood his pain or rage. Then I understood, the elephant was an elephant, not some totem of my father, but I knew I had to pull the trigger now or this would be the moment of our deaths.

Talley yelled, "shoot!" I pulled the trigger and watched the elephant as his animate body instantly transformed from a living creature to a lifeless hulk, still in motion from the velocity of his anger. The body fell to the ground as if in slow motion, now inanimate and useless. I looked back towards the herd to see what their reaction was. I immediately realized the elephant hadn't been sick or wounded. From the middle of the herd emerged what he'd been protecting, a calf. Why hadn't I seen it before? Did I have some tunnel vision that blinded me? Had the heat, the flies, or Talley's impatience bled over to me and influenced my professionalism and demeanor? Blinded my judgement?

The calf walked around to the front of the adult. It looked at its parent for a moment not comprehending what had happened. Then it started running its trunk over the body of its dead father, it pushed against the body of his father trying to rouse him. The body gave ever so slightly but returned to its original position. The calf started a wailing, forlorn, trumpeting. In that moment it understood death, and mourning. I was a hunter now, I had fulfilled my father's vision of me as a hunter, I had pulled the trigger, I was my father's son. I suddenly felt the rush of adrenaline pumping through my body; a blind animal panic surged through my veins.

"NO!" I screamed, "DID I TELL YOU TO TAKE THE SHOT?! Do you know what you've done?!"

"You took my elephant."

"No, you fool! I saved our lives, I had to kill the male, or we would have been crushed under its massive legs. You killed the male!"

"Yes, I wanted it."

"You wanted it!?" I yelled, grabbing his rifle throwing it out if his reach, "you've killed that calf's future! They're social animals they depend on the male to teach them the rules of their society. You've condemned him to a rogue's life roaming the landscape without purpose, no territory to claim as his own, without a mate, without progeny. He'll fight with his own, he'll be wounded, and if he isn't killed by another elephant, sooner or later he'll be driven to desperation by loneliness, by the lack of society, by the lack of food or a combination of factors. He'll invade a human habitation and maybe even kill a person or two. He'll have to be killed they all may have to be destroyed now. You've killed the next generation. The merciful thing would be to kill him now to spare him that tragedy of a life." I was standing over Talley the rifle was tucked tightly into the crook of my arm, my hand covering the trigger and the barrel was pointed squarely at his chest.

"What're you going to do? Shoot me?" He cried. I stopped, I noticed my stance, it wouldn't have taken much, a minute twitch of my finger and a hunting accident, or worse, cold-blooded murder, it was like waking from a fevered dream.

"No," I said, throwing the rifle down. "Get out of here, take the truck to the base camp, get your things and get out of here. I'm refunding your safari."

By the time I'd returned to camp it was late, Talley had cleared out and was probably in the city by now sitting in a hotel bar drinking, working out for his biography how this experience proves I was capable of killing my father. I sat with a drink in hand staring into the flames of the nightly fire. It was entrancing. I could only stare into it replaying the day's events in my head trying to figure out how I could have changed the course of events. I didn't see any, it was like replaying the last night of my father's life over and over in my head. What could I have done differently? Maybe I was still blinded. In my disgust with the whole thing I had left the rifles where I threw them. I would let them rust where they lay. My father's assertion that all stories end in death, I guess is true, in the death of the elephant. The elephant was the proxy for us all. It was my father, me trying to possess that spirit. For Talley and me, all our sins were cast upon the elephant and dissipated in his death. I had been killing a whole species for a long time, symbolically killing my father, and it turned out the species I was killing, was me. This was my last safari. I would find something else to do. There's been too much death here already.

Epilogue
The Lion Communique

"*All stories end in death, and in death there is continuing life, some say, but the jungle, the land itself had other ideas how this would end. Outside the light of the fire there are lifetimes led that are never witnessed by people. Places where the outcome of a life seems inevitable, like Karma, and you can't stop the trajectory of the forces set in motion both inside and outside of you; a lion in the bush, finally, the predator becomes the prey. Before me, the world didn't exist, after me it will melt away.*"

'The Hunters'—James Eastman.

THE CHRISTMAS TRUCE

The battlefield stretched from horizon to horizon across the iron drawn dawn. What were once golden fields of wheat that had waved in the afternoon breeze, that were once surrounded by verdant fields were now scarred and barren. Trenches cut across the earth, stitches straining to hold the earth together. The furrows bit deep into the ground, now planted with the seeds of men, and cultivated with their blood. Rows of barbed wire cut across in a jigsaw pattern, breaking the landscape into opposing sides, whose logic could only be deciphered by man. The mud frozen in waves their peaks cut like shards of glass sticking out of the ground. Tanks crawled across the landscape, clanking, creaking, lurching over the frozen sea of mud, belching clouds of diesel fueled smoke. No colour from before was left, only mud, iron and rust remained. Bodies lay where they had fallen, the putrid smell of death was overwhelmed by grotesque fogs of the most unnatural green and grey that hovered over the torn landscape. Night fell, the rifles went silent, no cannons blasting, no shells screaming their warning across the sky, no man in sight except for the stray sentry. The only sound was an indecipherable murmur of English, French and German, that hung over the battlefield, Christmas songs and prayers for the war to end.

The temperature dropped one degree, an invisible force swept across the battlefield like an Old Testament avenging angel, silently, mysteriously.

Throughout time it had been given many names. It was known to man, yet unknown to man. In other times it may have been called the Holy spirit, the Christmas spirit, or in a more scientific age, the Id, consciousness, an entity. Or maybe it was just the accumulated feeling of like-minded souls that manifested the ineffable, a fervent wish, or prayer, the original impetus of man. Sound was sucked from the surrounding air and replaced by a solemn silence. Snow fell out of the darkness like stars from the sky, blanketing the battlefield, covering the wounds of war, trying to heal the scars of the earth. The flakes, white, pure, slowly shaping the brutal tools of war into something they weren't, beautiful. The barbed wire caught the flakes and soon started to look like feathery gates. The clanking, lurching machines of war were transformed, the ice crystals building upon each other to reform them into structures that evoked ancient shrines, and if left to the elements and time would rust away back to the earth from which the metals had been ripped.

Soldiers crawled up out of their trenches, the living dead enlivened, returning from the earth to life. The impetus had expanded their perspectives, their horizons broadened, their minds were lifted above the fray, all thoughts of killing and grievances were forgotten. A sense of wonder overcame them. It was all so incongruous, the silence, the snow, it was almost religious. They wandered the battlefield reaching for the snowflakes, it looked as if they were dancing a waltz. They met soldiers from the other side in no-man's-land. The same gaunt men dressed in the same ill fitting, dirty, torn, and sodden uniforms hanging off the same skeletal frames, it was as if they were looking at a reflection of themselves. The only difference was the uniforms were of a different colour. Looking at their changed landscape, the soldiers were overcome with the realization, the battlefield had become their cathedral, it was Christmas.

The soldiers scurried back to their trenches and found whatever tinned goods that had been sent to them, gathering whatever little luxury they may have carried in a pocket to remind them of home, tied them with an improvised ribbon, and met back on the now snow-covered battlefield. The men from the other side came back bearing the same sort of gifts, exchanging salutations of "Happy Christmas mate!" and "Frohliche Weihnacten!" songs were heard, jokes were told, the clinking of cups was heard. The dead were gathered and mourned.

The impetus whether angel, entity, spirit, deity, or just a wish was frangible, subject to the vagaries, moods and whims of man who could crush it like it a moth's delicate, powdery wings. Amid the milling groups were a British and a German soldier struggling to maintain their peace.

"Hello Tommy!" The German exclaimed.

"Jerry! You speak English!"

"I worked in London before the war, a lot of us have." The German felt something rubbing on his leg, he looked down to see a brown and black tiger stripped cat arching its back against his leg. The soldier picked him up.

"Ah, little Squeek there you are."

"No, that's my Budgie!" The Englishman said, grabbing the cat away from the German, "he comes and sleeps with me every few nights."

"He's mine, I found him and feed him."

The impetus wavered in the men until a nearby officer leaned over to them and said, "come on lads, none of this now, it's Christmas." The men smiled.

"The cat must be crossing the lines at night and visiting us both."

"No one owns a cat anyway," the German said, "they're their own."

The Englishman gave the cat back to the German, and both men broke out into smiles and laughed at their foolish jealousy.

A Christmas tree was found in the trenches and set-up in the middle of no-man's-land. Soldiers from both sides decorated it with whatever bits and pieces they could find. They gathered around the tree, sang and celebrated, "the war is over!"

Word of the truce got back to the generals and the politicians in London, Paris and Berlin. Their far-off voices raged and bellowed, screaming the same things at each other, the questions the same in any language, "why is there a cease fire?! Who ordered it?! Will it last? What will become of our war? Get those men fighting again! Find us a man to do this!" The word filtered down from the politicians to the generals, to division commanders, down to regimental commanders, "Start our war back up!"

✳

The headquarters of the List Regiment was in a ruined monastery near Bethlehem farm, it had been shelled earlier in the war when it was the front, but now it was far enough behind the lines it was no longer a target. It was a ruin. The stone walls had protected enough of the structure for it to house a command center, a billet for the officers, the messengers, a radio room and the bones of a martyr deep under the stone floors.

When the orders came through Lieutenant Colonel Englehardt knew the man for the job, he had saved the colonel's life a few weeks earlier. He was an unctuous little fellow, a bit slovenly and wanting of military discipline, but he was loyal and content to serve.

Alone, in a corner of the ramshackle headquarters a lone messenger collapsed in a heap, his long coat billowed around his slight frame, asleep on a stool like an unused puppet.

"Gefreiter Hitler get in here!" Englehardt yelled.

The slight messenger with the bushy mustaches appeared.

"Have you heard of this so-called Christmas truce?"

"Yes sir."

"What do you think about it?"

"They're traitors to the Reich and betraying the fatherland and selling us all out."

"That's what I thought. Good. The men at the front all seem to have been hit with some sort of mass hysteria, or religious fervor, or maybe just ordinary cowardice. Although, from reports we're hearing the English and even the French are undergoing the same thing, I've never heard of anything like this, I don't even know if something on this scale is possible. It boggles the mind, but it must end. I have an assignment for you."

"Yes sir," the gefreiter said.

Englehardt signed the documents, folded them, put them in an envelope, and sealed it, "take these orders, to the commanding officer at the front, they order him to resume fighting at dawn. Do you understand?"

"Yes sir."

"And now I will tell you something not in the orders. You will stay at the front under the guise of waiting for the commander's response. If they don't resume fighting, I'm ordering you to sabotage this so-called truce, do whatever it takes. Do whatever you need to do, but get those men fighting again, or you will find yourself staying permanently at the front."

"Yes sir." Hitler snapped a sharp salute and clicked his heels, executed an about face and exited the command center.

Hitler grabbed a bike and ploughed through the mud the best he could wobbling through the streets as he struggled to stay in the ruts of trucks and carts. The streets of the town were a miasma of mud. Unpaved country roads ground up by the machines of war, troops being marched through them, the shelling and the rain. The front wasn't far, but it was a world apart, a different war from what Hitler knew. For the soldiers at the front the war was a day-to-day struggle to survive. He spent the first few weeks of the war at the front, and he'd do anything to stay out of that war. Although he seemed a good solider and had saved the colonel's life, his idea was to keep his head down, he didn't stand out among the ranks, he didn't seek promotion, those would only get him sent back to the fighting. He preferred the company of the officers of the regiment they understood him. He'd been foundering in Munich before the war, tossed about in the seas of life. It was a city of artists, but his hopes of a life as an artist were dashed, he could draw but had no vision. He was a man without a philosophy, he tumbled from light to dark without any sense of perspective. When the winds of war blew, they had pushed him here. The army, the officers had become his family, they gave order to the chaos that had been his life up to now. Here he felt a larger purpose, something greater than himself, whether it was just an idea or something else, hopefully it was driving him towards some destiny.

The battalion headquarters at the front was burrowed deep into a hillock. Hitler almost threw himself into the makeshift command center after trudging through what seemed to be miles of muddy trenches. He came to attention, and threw a salute, "orders from regimental," he said proffering the order packet with his free hand.

The lieutenant grabbed them, looking Hitler up and down in disapproval before reading them. "They want us to start fighting again at first light." The officers around him scoffed. "How can you kill someone who you've exchanged gifts with? Danced with? Shared meals with? Exchanged regrets with?"

"I have orders to stay until these orders are carried out." Hitler said.

"Then you may be here a very long time, gefreiter." The others laughed, "do as you must Hitler, but don't interfere with my men."

Hitler walked through the trenches looking for a place to rest. Every open hole or notch was filled or taken by soldiers. Even though he and the other messengers were familiar faces in the trenches, Hitler wasn't friends with any of these men even if they were of his regiment and had trained together. He felt disdain for the men, they were pawns of an empire they didn't understand. Finally, he came to an empty place next to a man, the space was occupied by a cat, the cat looked up at him, tilting its head in curiosity. Hitler kicked at the creature, "get out of here you little pest!" The cat jumped up, arching it's back, hissing at Hitler.

"SCAT!" he yelled.

"Hey! That's my cat!" The soldier in the next notch said, as the cat screamed and clawed its way over the top of the trench in a sputter of snow and dirt and ran across no-man's-land.

"Come back Squeek!" The men watched as the cat scampered off to the other side of the battlefield.

"What did you do that for?" The soldier asked.

"I'm tired, I want to sleep. What was that creature doing here anyway?"

"He's always been here. He was probably a cat on this farm before the war. A British soldier and I keep him, he goes back and forth across the lines at night. We almost fought over him the night of the truce when we discovered we had both been taking care of him, but we at once understood the pettiness of our jealousy. What are you doing here Hitler?" The soldier asked, sounding exasperated. "Why aren't you back at headquarters waiting for the scraps to fall from the officers table?"

"I'm following orders. Why aren't you fighting?"

"The war was supposed to be over by Christmas, now it is."

"You're a traitor, you all are! Not fighting for the Fatherland, our pride! You would let those foreigners humiliate us?"

"You weren't there, Hitler, you don't know. This truce is bigger than all of us, it's bigger than the officers, bigger than the politicians, it's bigger than the war, it may even be bigger than the world. It moved over us and moved us to peace, and it moved over the English too, and the French, we all feel it.

"You need to peel the film of religion or whatever it is from your eyes and see life for what it is, a constant horrible struggle."

"Go over and look at those men, they look like us, they're tired like us, they haven't eaten well like us, their uniforms are dirty, they hang off them just like ours, the only difference is the color of the uniform. Talk to them, they don't want to be fighting either, they want to be home with their families. If they were the enemy, then surely, so are we. We realized we're brothers, the war is over."

"Brothers kill brothers all the time."

"If you and those officer's you love so much want the war, you can come down here and fight it." The soldier picked up a helmet and threw it at Hitler, "Get out of here little mouse. Scurry off back to your hole and your safe warm bed, nibbling off officers' plates." The soldier watched as Hitler scampered off to another part of the trench. He found another empty hole and stuffed himself into it. It was cold, he pulled the oversized coat close to him, taut. He fell asleep wishing for the luxury of his cot.

The next morning Hitler awoke to the bite of frost. A cold sun already hung above the horizon. Most of the men were sleeping. Others were up and starting their daily ablutions, washing up, the latrine, making breakfast. There was no shooting, no manning the parapets or anyone on watch. Rifles were placed nearby leaning on each other forming teepee shapes, but no one paid them any attention or made any motion towards them. The dream of peace still anesthetized them like an opiate. Hitler made his way to the battalion headquarters.

"What are you doing here Hitler?" The lieutenant asked.

"You haven't resumed fighting. You were ordered…"

"What is your rank Hitler?"

"Gefreiter."

"Exactly! You don't even rate a corporal over in the English army! And you presume to question me about orders? Get out! The war is over."

"The war is not over until we march into London!" Hitler yelled over his shoulder as he stormed out of the battalion headquarters, shaking his fist in the air at them. He wouldn't let this humiliation by the lieutenant go by, he would obey his orders, he would show these men what a patriot is, what it was to fight. He would be the spark that reignited the war. He understood man, he knew their taste for hate, fear and violence, he'd experienced it most of his life, but sometimes the weak had to be led to it or shown the way.

Hitler sat in the hole he'd commandeered, ruminating, plotting. He was relegated to this mud hell, cast out from the relative safety and comfort of the regimental headquarters until he could find a way to start the war again. He thought of any number of ways of starting the fighting, his mind wasn't devoid of devious ideas, from the simplest, grab a gun and just start shooting at the British, they would shoot back, then the Germans would return fire, it had a simple elegance and seemed like it couldn't fail. Then there were the more complicated, but they seemed contrived, they had too many components and too many coincidences would have to occur that he wouldn't have any control over. And they all lacked the quality of not exposing himself, he didn't want to be seen as the perpetrator of the crime. He didn't want history to remember him as a villain, he didn't want his name to live in infamy. Besides, the state the men were in, they seemed docile now, but their antipathy towards him and being jarred by the resumption of violence, he didn't want them turning on him. There must be a way to get these cowards fighting again. He started walking the trench; he couldn't think of a plan to restart the war, to obey his orders, he struck out in anger, kicking at an empty notch in the wall, the anger abated, and his eyes cleared, he realized where he was, it was the hole that the cat had been in. He remembered the soldier had told him he almost got in a fight with a British soldier over the creature. An epiphany shot up his spine like a hot fire, and he knew the truce could be broken! A plan quickly formulated in his mind, but he would have to wait until the cat came back to this side to enact it.

He sat watching the hole from a good distance away, he didn't want to be noticed by the men or the cat. It wasn't that much after dark he noticed the cat back in the trenches, and it seemed the animal was looking for food. He waited awhile, until it had settled down. He approached the animal cautiously he didn't want to scare it. He held out in front of him a tin of beef. The cat was leery, it sniffed cautiously at the food, staying just out of reach, he remembered the man's previous abuse. Hitler didn't move, a moment or two later, hunger got the better of the cat and he moved to get the food just as the Hitler's other hand came around and grabbed him by the scruff of the neck, he grabbed the animal in both hands and twisted its neck. The animal went limp in his hands and was dead. He looked around, no one had seen, 'no one will know,' Hitler thought to himself.

As the soldiers from both sides looked over no-man's-land in the morning light they saw the cat's body, strung up on the barbed wire for all to see, it was almost a crucifixion. The news of the murder ran up and down the lines like electricity, until it reached the ears of the soldiers who claimed the cat. They rushed out to the body, as the soldiers on both sides watched over the tops of the trenches. Jerry picked up the limp body and cradled the cat in his arms, petting him a last time. The grief, and anger, and rage overcame him.

"You did this!" He yelled at the Englishman.

"No! It was you! You killed my Budgie!" They pulled out their guns, a moment of realization registered in each man's eyes and minds, their boundaries snapped back to where they had been before and the thoughts of killing and grievance came rushing in. The impetus was pushed back to the realm of the hopes and dreams of man, each pulled the trigger and shot the other, the bullets tore through the peace, both sides opened fire at each other, and soon the bullets were heard in surrounding valleys up and down the lines, the roar of the cannon were heard again echoing through the valleys. The war had started again.

 # ARRIVAL FOR DUTY

The wheels of Air Force One bounced and screeched on the runway, jostling the president awake from a dream, or to the dream; the dream of being President of the United States. In his hypnopompic haze he slid up the visor of the window and watched as the plane ran down the runway. He could see the jungle running along the perimeter of the airport some distance away, kept in check, pruned and trimmed, not an errant branch sticking out. He was landing in a country he never wanted to go to, a country he never thought he would have to see, Vietnam. In his youth, his generation was called to fight a war in this country, a war deemed unnecessary and immoral from the start, he hadn't thought so, he was above that, the military was for the suckers, the stupid and the poor who couldn't get out of it, and he hadn't served. His father had paid a doctor to manufacture a note saying he couldn't serve.

Now he was in Vietnam, on much different terms, his terms. As president of the most powerful nation on earth. He would be feted, he'd be catered to, he'd be shown a few sites of historic importance and act impressed. He would meet foreign leaders and dignitaries, who would want their pictures taken with him, who would want to shake his hand, and they would seek his opinion and would act as if every utterance was shrewd or sagacious. He would be respected. All that he expected in life, all that he was due in life. The door to the plane opened and he felt the humid air flood in. As he walked toward the open hatch, he put on his suit jacket. He knew it would be hot in the dark suit and tie that he always wore, but appearances are what mattered. It provided a veneer of success, and authority. If you appear successful, you are. His imported model wife met him at the door. He was rich before he became president. Everything he had was imported—wine, suits, wives. He hadn't wasted his life as a community organizer, or even strategically positioning himself politically as his predecessors had. He'd imposed himself into the process, every process, business, socially, culturally and finally, politically. It was a classic submission technique—punch someone in the nose and they'll reflexively cry. He'd punched a lot of people in the nose, figuratively of course, and if they cried, he used them. If they didn't, he tried to enlist them. If they refused, he punished them. He'd broken down every gate that had been closed to him.

The president and his wife stepped out onto the platform, he looked around. He knew the cameras would all be on him. He struck a pose, made his face a mask, frozen in the practiced pose that he thought made him look important, iconic even. He'd lived most of his life in the spotlight, a light he made sure shone in his direction. He had directed it and dictated what aspects of his life it revealed, and which aspects remained in the dark. He'd made sure he was always presented in the best possible light, as a successful businessman, a playboy, a billionaire; all of which he lived in fear of being exposed as a fraud.

He could see the terminal of the airport across the tarmac, a modern design, all acute surfaces and angles. It was freshly painted and decorated for the occasion. The marine guard awaited him at the bottom of the stairs. Beyond the guard, the Vietnamese delegation of diplomats and military officials waited to receive him. They were all dressed in their finest military regalia. He thought they all were little men in oversize western suits and military garb, caricatures of their western counterparts, aping civilized dress. He grabbed his wife's hand, not a tender intertwining of fingers but a brusque, controlling grip of her hand. A bit of pressure one way or the other and she would move in the direction he wanted. He bared his teeth. He knew from practice that at a distance it would appear a smile.

"Shall we?" He said. It was a command, not a gallant request or question, but an order. They started down the stairway. The air rippled with heat as they walked. Suddenly the air felt thicker. It pressed in around him, it felt as if he'd passed from one state to another, like moving from a temperate zone to a tropical zone. His eyes became unfocused. He slipped a little and let go of his wife's hand, grabbing the nearby railing for support. When his vision cleared his wife was gone. He looked around, he was disoriented, he was trying to find something familiar to reorient himself. She wasn't at the top of the stairs or the bottom of the stairway, she was gone. Had she left him in that moment and returned to the plane? Had that much time elapsed that she could have gone somewhere else? It had only felt like a moment had passed, could he be wrong? Could more time have elapsed? Gaining his composure, he continued down the stairs, he noticed the jungle looked closer, wilder, and unkempt, like he could reach out and touch it, or worse, like something could reach out and touch him. The receiving party had seemed to have changed too. The countries dignitaries and diplomats were gone too, they were replaced by young American officers from every branch of the military services. Had the dignitaries left for some reason when he stumbled?

When he reached the bottom, a naval officer in dress whites stepped out of the ranks, walked up to the president and saluted.

"Finally, you're here, sir," the officer said. "We've been awaiting your arrival."

"Very good," the president said. He thought he recognized the officer. He looked at the man trying to remember where he knew him from. He knew he didn't know the young man, but his features were familiar. Although, he seemed to have prematurely white hair for such a young man.

"Do I know you?" The president asked.

"No, you don't know me, at least not this me." The president looked perplexed. "Don't look to the past to remember me," the officer said, "try the future, my future, your present."

"What do you mean by that?"

"I wasn't a hero, I was captured." The words rang in the president's ears. They were his words. How had they come back at him like this? The man he had applied them to wasn't here. Who was this man? He looked around, the buildings looked different then they had from the plane, even from the top of the stairs, they were more primitive, more basic, more utilitarian than before. The paint was peeling, and it looked dirty, as if the dirt had been driven into every pore of the wood by the wind and then baked by the sun over years. The design seemed to be from the 40's or 50's not the modern building he'd seen before. Had he seen what he had expected to see? If so, was this real then? It was disconcerting and a bit vertiginous.

"When I came here, I was as I appear now, straight and tall," the officer said. As he spoke, his features morphed into an older self, his hair thinned out, his face puffed out of proportion because of his injuries' toll. He hunched slightly to the years having pressed down on him. "When I left, I was beaten and broken." He was now dressed in a dark suit much like the president's, he was as the president knew him. The president's eyes widened a bit, registering both recognition and shock. He knew the older man as a senator. As soon as he recognized the shock moving through him, he covered it up. He didn't want to show fear. It was a loss of control, weakness. The president replaced his shock with bravado. The senator smiled knowingly. The president looked down the line of men. He recognized them all, as if some context had been suddenly provided. They were all the younger selves of men he knew, of men who had served in the war. "Would you like me to take you to where they held me prisoner and beat me?"

"Where am I?" The president asked.

"Where you're supposed to be, where you belong sir. Hanoi."

"Hanoi?"

"Yes, but a Hanoi that has long awaited you. It's a Hanoi where you were supposed to come a lifetime ago. It's a Hanoi where you were supposed to die." A pall came over the president's face. "It's a Hanoi outside of time."

"This is sick, what're you trying to do?"

The senator continued to smile benignly at him. "Did we get your attention?"

"I'm the president! Take me to the receiving delegation! Where are my secret service agents?"

"We are the receiving delegation. The others are back in their own reality living it out."

"*Back in their own reality….?*" The president repeated, trying to make sense of the words. "Am I still dreaming? Did I hit my head, and this is some kind of hallucination?"

"You don't believe this is real? You based your life and reputation on illusion, surely, it's not hard for your mind to adjust." The senator's eyes sparkled with mirth.

"How can it be?"

"What would trigger an episode like this?"

"Maybe I'm unconscious or in a coma, or I had a stroke."

"How about guilt? When was the last time you felt guilty?"

"Never," the president said in a clipped tone, "that's for the weak."

"How about nostalgia? But then you've never been here, and I don't think you'd have some misplaced nostalgia for this time and place."

"No."

"Fear would be the last," the president's face again became the mask he preferred, childish, and implacable. "Yes, fear."

"Very sad, I'm not afraid of anything."

"Yes, fear of, being…"

"What?" The president demanded.

"Exposed."

"What are you implying?"

A bemused smile crossed the senator's lips again. "A frightened child."

"This isn't reality, nothing here is real."

"What's left then? Reality is only a reference point with common elements that we all agree on. Just think of this as a new reference point and your mind will accept the reality of the situation. It's a fiction that reveals truths."

"How're they living out the other reality without me?! I can't disappear! I'm the fucking president."

"You're not gone, you're still there in that reality, just a facsimile, a shadow of yourself. But you, your true self is here."

"My true self?"

"This is your essence, the core of what makes you, you."

"I'm a very powerful person, they say the most powerful person in the world, I control what happens, I decide the fate of men and events. I'm the hero of the story."

"That's an illusion you've created so you can believe you're in control. The illusion that allows you to sleep at night. But the truth is, when have you ever been the hero? Heroes risk something. When have you ever risked anything? Any time you've been presented with a heroic moment in life you've skulked away, only to reappear when the danger was past and take up the mantle of the hero. You don't control anything. You're manipulated by people and events, that ultimately control you."

"They don't!" The president snapped, defensively, too quickly confirming what was known by all. "You can't just hold me here.

"We aren't holding you. You're free to go when you want."

"Then let me go. You were a naval officer. I'm the president and you're only a senator! I'm your commander-in-chief, I order you!" The president said imperiously.

"In the world of man, not here, something more is required."

"What?" He demanded impatiently.

"We've been here a long-time standing guard for those who died, and for those who lived, but we can't stand at post forever. You're our relief."

"Stand guard!" He snorted incredulously, "the war is long over, and it wasn't my war."

"It's not over in our memories, in our dreams, in our bodies. It's not over in the dreams of generations after. War belongs to all of us, even to the protesters."

"I was for the war."

"What did you do besides voice support for it?" The senator stared into him. "What actions did you take to fight it? To end it? You gave it lip-service while you sat back. You didn't fight for a cause you believed in. You let others fight it, while you grew rich."

"I understand your sacrifice. I was shipped off to military school because my father ...." Suddenly his voice went silent. He was still talking, his lips and vocal cords were still moving, but no words, no sound was coming out. The president clutched at his throat, a look of panic on his face.

"Don't worry, there is nothing wrong with your voice. Only the truth can be spoken in eternity. You may lie to yourself, rationalize it how you like. But we know the truth. It resides in your unconscious mind. You went to a military school for rich kids—crisp uniforms, brass buttons and braid, filigree, medals as ceremonial and as symbolic as the uniform. War is blood and mud. You played toy soldier. You know the child's thrill of a parade. You carried a sword that was every bit as blunted as you are, no rounds in the rifles you drilled with. The dirtiest you ever got was working up a sweat, then a shower. Not days or weeks in the bush, dirt ingrained into every pore so that when you finally did get a shower, your skin still had a dark tinge. It was all safety and no surprise. The only danger was getting VD from a girl on a weekend furlough who saw the uniform and didn't know the difference.

"I want to go back now. You served the country; I've served the country too. We've all served as we've seen fit."

"What master do you serve? Mankind or the world of man? What you fail to understand is that there is a greater service to life—serving your fellow man. You've failed and avoided serving your fellow man on all counts."

"I've built buildings, provided housing…"

"All for attaining personal wealth and self-glorification."

"You dare to judge me!" The president bellowed, red-faced and puffed out.

"Yes, we do. There is no rank here, no wealth, no status, no privilege. We are the balance of nature. To put it in terms you can understand there's a price to be paid, a balancing of the books, a reckoning."

"And you think you can bring this about?"

"It is done, it is the nature of things." The jungle started to move. There was no breeze, and there wasn't any sound that animals would make; no cackle, no caw, no cry or growl that would have randomly filled the air. Not even the constant buzz of insects that he thought would be continuously permeating the atmosphere. The trees and vegetation were moving of their own accord. The movement seemed unnatural. He remembered his unease of seeing the closeness of the jungle before.

"What's out there?"

"Does it frighten you?"

The president averted his eyes then brought his head up and struck a belligerent pose as he said, "Animals! Can't we kill what's out there?"

"What do you suggest?"

"Bomb what's out there or send some troops to flush them out."

"Without knowing who or what is out there?"

"It doesn't matter. There's something out there that's dangerous."

"What if I told you could go out there and quell it yourself?"

"That's not my job! There are others to do things like that."

"The first refuge of the bully to hide behind the skirts of someone else, to blame someone else. How easily the use of force and violence falls from your lips when you can send someone else to do it, but who has never lived in fear of it nor felt its repercussions in his life. You know what's out there."

"How in the hell would I know what's out there! Tell me!"

"Lives. Human lives."

"The dead?"

"The dead, yes, but the living as well. All those who served, those who took your place, those who continue to serve, those who died, and those who will die by your actions, or inactions. They're all locked here, and only when their replacements arrive will they be released."

"I will replace only one?"

"No, all these souls will be released when you take your place."

"Then my life, my contribution is greater than theirs."

"No, you misunderstand, no one man's life is worth more than any others. Your sense of self-importance is of no importance. You've valued and placed your life above theirs. In fact, in disregard for their lives. They have served while you've ridiculed them and lived your life in spite of them."

"It was their choice to serve, I chose…"

"The book of days shows a century's long tradition of not serving while at the same time others have served, others have paid for your fortune."

"Is this what this is all about? Because I didn't go into the military during a war?"

"No, there are many ways to serve. Being a soldier is but one, another is a desire to serve but were made to suffer for their choices." The senator turned to the formation of men. Out of the ranks stepped a man the president could see was a civilian. He recognized him immediately. It was his brother who had died forty years previously. He was as he remembered him, tall, blond, still slim and handsome at forty, the age he was when he'd died. He was dressed in a dark suit and tie.

"Eddie…" the president said, holding out his arms to hug his brother who stopped short, out of his reach.

"A warm greeting for me?"

"Of course, we haven't seen each other in such a long time."

"You destroyed me."

"That's a very unfair accusation...." the president said.

"Why did you do it? Because I didn't meet father's expectation of what success is? I had enough money to do whatever I wanted, except I couldn't. What good was the money then? Or was it simply that you wanted the money?"

"What gave you that idea? It's a complete con job."

"Con job? The only con is you. We were locked into this thinking early the difference is that you loved those chains."

"What chains? I've had the freedom to do whatever I wanted to. I have the power I want."

"That's all I asked for, what about my dreams?"

"Dreams are unsubstantial. What can you buy with a dream? They're like words on a page, meaningless."

"You can buy a lifetime with dreams. You think words are meaningless?"

"Yes."

"Is that why you throw them out with such carelessness, random strings of words with no thought as to meaning?"

"They become devalued in people's minds, showing them the uselessness of words." The president folded his arms across his chest.

"Are they now?" Out of the ether the president's daughter appeared as a child, "your own words are your indictment."

"Daddy, why didn't you come to my birthday party? You said you would."

"I had business, honey. I love you."

"You promised daddyyyyyyyy." Her tinny voice echoing.

"Oh, honey, they were just words they don't mean anything. Words are empty, they're just words, words, words," it echoed in his mind. The image of his daughter diffused, out of focus, then back into focus. She was her older self.

"It doesn't mean I don't love you."

"Words are empty daddy," then she was gone to the mists of eternity as if she'd never existed.

"That was cruel, vicious."

"So, it seems your words do have consequences. It was no more cruel then you have been, as your actions have been."

"You should have embraced our values Eddie; they would have served you well."

"Like they have you?"

"Yes."

"Those ideas, those values you hold so dear, have corrupted you."

"I'm getting my beliefs, our beliefs out there and they're taking hold. They're very, very strong, powerful ideas people can believe in."

"See you can use words when you find them…valuable. You think you can con me with those words? You forget, I know you, still the scared little boy."

"It's what I, my supporters believe."

"What you believe?" He said incredulously, "what do you believe? What philosophy or commitment have you ever had except to yourself? You never met a penny that couldn't convince you of the truth of its lie."

We're bringing back the old values and ideas. Strong ideas that never die."

"Of course, they do. Antiquated ideas die. Ideas that are no longer useful, that are rooted in fear and ignorance die away just as the old gods they served do."

"They say those ideas never really die out. They may recede but they always come back in fashion."

"You're right. Racism, bigotry, hate, fear, and ignorance always do seem to come back into vogue. But ideas and values that need to grow in the dark, that can't take hold in the light, are dead things, dead ideas."

"What's it matter?" The president said coldly. "You're dead, you'll never be remembered except in association with me. I'm an American success story."

"Be careful of legacy. Your history is written. You're a pariah, you'll always be an American horror story. It's done."

As the president watched, his brother's face became amorphous and indistinct, the stature of his form seemed to diminish. When the face came back into focus, it had morphed into his father. The president felt as if a weight were being lifted off him.

"Dad, good you're here, you can get me out of this."

"Sorry, son." The president seemed confused.

"Father?"

"Yes, son."

"Aren't you here to get me out of this?"

"You've lived too long looking into a mirror reflecting only what you've wanted to see, the mirror is shattering. I left you an empire and you squandered it."

"I built our company up, it's larger and greater than it ever was. I have buildings the world over!

"No, you pimped out my name, grafted it onto what others built."

"I've branded our name, it's known worldwide."

"Branding is for cows! I did what you've always claimed to have done, built an empire from meager beginnings. I built! I created! I left behind something tangible. What have you done with my legacy? You've run it into the ground and when I gave you money to keep what I built running you promised me you would turn it around, and what did you do then? You tried to cheat me out of my own money when you thought I was incompetent."

"You owed me! You never loved me! I was nothing to you except a tax write-off!"

"And you traded in my empire for the adulation and adoration of the crowd, politics. And what did that get you? Investigations and indictments."

"I didn't do anything you hadn't done."

"What did you think was going to happen? Sure, I cheated and schemed and scammed the government, but I never rubbed their faces in it and I never let my ego get in the way of business."

"I got the respect I deserve in life. When I walk into a room generals snap to attention and salute, everyone defers to me, and they all address me as sir. Everything else are hoaxes, like all the other hoaxes that have been played on me."

"I still see the little boy backed into a corner by his lie, insisting it's the truth."

"You told me the rules didn't apply to us, that we were better, faster, stronger, smarter than everyone else."

"I tried to instill you with a superior mindset, but you have the mindset of the slumlord or a pimp."

"That doesn't sound like you father?"

His father smiled, "it's interesting the perspective being dead gives you. Your perspective...adjusts."

"What if you don't adjust?"

"They're the damned." A look of sadness came over the president's father's face. "It's time for me to go. It's time for you to learn, son. You have to face up to the punishment you're due. I did."

He was gone, returned to whatever ether he'd come from. The senator stepped up to where the president's father had been.

"It's time to take your place at post." The senator intoned.

"Wait, wait!" Desperation filled the president's voice, "can't we work something out here? A deal?"

"You wish to negotiate?"

"Yes, yes! I've built my life, and my reputation on negotiating."

"You have the capital to bargain with?"

"Of course, I do!" He huffed. The senator motioned with his arm and a marine captain appeared from the ranks in front of him. The captain was lean and hard, the skin of his arms tanned and taut, a thin covering over the striations of his muscles, this man had not served in an administrative capacity, he'd been in the jungle, seen fighting, seen death, seen life, seen heroism, and cowardice, all forms of being human that the extremes of war bring out in a person.

"You wish to negotiate?" He asked.

"Yes,"

"What do you have of value?"

"Money, as much as you want."

"It's valueless," the marine said. "What good do you think it does out here? You need to learn what has real value." The man pointed to the roiling jungle. "Out here, lives have value, souls have value."

"What do you want?"

"On the day you graduated college, forty men died in the war. Do you want to trade their lives for yours?" The president looked stunned, chilled by a realization. It was real, that he would finally have to stand before the mast of some type of justice. "What we offer you is to stand at post in relief of those you left behind or return to your reality and face the charges of man."

"The charges of man?" The president mumbled. "They are all lies and hoaxes! Words that have been used against me in their efforts to cheat me of what is mine!"

"It has been said the universe bends towards justice, that is more true than you think. Truth and justice are natural laws. Sometimes entropy twists them, but they bend back, sometimes with great effort and sacrifice, but bend back, they do."

Panic rose in the president's voice, "what about due process?! A chance to defend myself?"

"We've heard your case from your own lips. Who better to defend oneself?"

"I'm not a lawyer!" "I don't know the laws."

"Of mankind?" The officer asked. "We're all taught the laws of mankind. It's your choice and at your own peril whether you ignore them or not."

The president's mask broke, and his face betrayed the fear and desperation that had been held behind the façade, his face was mottled with roseated, veiny blotches and patches, a portrait of corruption. The true self revealed at last.

"Your case has been heard. It is time to choose. Charges have been drawn in the world of man. Now you must choose how to serve. Here, standing at post—or back to your reality to face the charges."

"This is unfair! The system is rigged!"

"How have you ever been treated unfairly? You're one of the fortunate sons of America. Millions of dollars from before you can remember, the best schools, the most beautiful women, a reputation of success, a world which has given you a voice in the politics of the world, all of which you've considered your right. But all those freedoms, privileges, and power you claim haven't been paid for with blood, sweat or invention."

"I haven't been given the credit or respect I'm due, *I've* been treated as if I'm the outsider."

"It is your guilt that claws against your consciousness. The knowledge of how you've lied and cheated that makes you feel inferior, and the fear you'll be discovered and exposed for what you are."

"The charges are fake!"

"You know better than that, as do we, the bill is due. The sacrifice you make is your choice, but a choice must be made."

"Isn't there any mercy in my case? For a lesson learned? Is there no redemption for me?"

"Mercy? What lesson have you learned? This isn't a TV show, there's no happy ending, no reclamation for the villain, because you have never sought it except as a ploy for time. Sooner or later time runs out, time has run out."

The jungle growled and seemed to threaten to burst open and unleash some madness.

"What is that! What's out there, it seems, close."

"Maybe the mob you set loose, the chaos of the universe, the madness of man that needs to be kept in check. It is here." The president's face became a mask of fear.

The jungle parted, out of the void appeared a gaunt skeleton of a soldier dressed in a dirty worn uniform. He walked across the tarmac, each step an effort, carefully placed, stumbling once or twice but caught himself before falling. His body was broken, but his soul wasn't, it kept him moving forward, one foot in front of the other. He walked past the men in the ranks and up to the captain and saluted.

"You're relieved, your replacement has arrived."

"Who is this man!?" The president demanded.

"This is the man who has been standing in your place all this time."

"Why does he look like this?"

"He was the last man called to duty. He's been waiting a very long time, an eternity. Don't you think it's time he had some peace?"

"What will happen if I go back?"

"To the world of man?" The captain smiled, "you know what will happen."

"How long would I have to stand at post?"

"Until your replacement arrives."

"When's that?"

"There's no relief in sight," the captain said. "We await your decision?"

THE CAPTURED DEED

omancheria 1874

The dark of the night pressed in around the warriors, save the light of the fire carving a shelter out of the liquid darkness that surrounded and threatened to drown them. Each was dressed in brightly colored shirts of red, yellow or blue buckskin. Medicine shirts the shaman Isatai had given them. They huddled around the fire looking glum. They couldn't even look at each other. All they could do was stare into the flames. It was early June, it must have been warm, but they all huddled in, close to the fire trying to gain its warmth. The white man had driven them to this, into the night.

"Why are you not dancing, celebrating?" Isatai asked. "What you have done today is a very brave thing."

"We did a terrible thing, the wasichu will kill us all," said one warrior.

"It will bring the soldiers," said another.

"They will outnumber us, and their bullets are faster than our arrows."

"The wasichu believe they can take this country, but they have grabbed a rattlesnake by the tail and soon it will unwind and strike at them and shake off their grasp."

"How will this happen?"

"Have you no faith?" Isatai asked. "Did not the medicine shirts I've given you protect you from the wasichu bullets today?"

"They were farmers, and gatherers, not warriors."

"The soldiers are many. Like the tatanka were, now are the soldiers."

"Did I not predict the drought? Did I not ascend to heaven to visit the Great Spirit and look down upon the wasichu's god? The Great Spirit gave me the power to defeat the wasichu, and yet you do not believe?" The warriors all sat, doubting his words. "I will show you. Look into the flames and you will see." Isatai started chanting, drums began pounding, the rhythm gathered and met the beat of their hearts, and that sound matched their thoughts. It was one sound they could hear. Then they felt a deep pounding of hooves vibrating through their bodies. As they stared into the fire, they saw the face of a great tatanka, its mane, aflame. It grew in their eyes, engulfing them in its spirit, the vision raced through their hearts like an engine. They believed. "What we have done today will bring the soldiers," Isatai said, "and the dead will come to protect us."

The wagon train wandered aimlessly like a ghost ship over the prairie which stretched out in front of it like the sea. The earth as uneven as the waves, the prairie as unknowable as the depths of the ocean. The wagon train rumbled over the hard brown ground. The horses followed the trail etched into the hard earth by countless other wagon trains almost imperceptible to man's eyes. Most couldn't see it until they were shown the signs. The horses pulled their loads of wagons and supplies inevitably forward, without destination. The Indian scout didn't see any of the settlers through his spy glass. He handed it to the General on the horse next to him. Sherman looked through the spyglass, surveying the horizon. He didn't see anything other than what was there, desert. More scrub than brush, 'how can men survive out here?' He thought as he surveyed the horizon.

"Nothing there," he said, handing the spyglass back to the scout.

Sherman's grizzled countenance looked like he was perpetually in pain. Perhaps he was. The memories of the war were kept in check at the back of his mind. His beard seemed more a moss that covered the crags of his face. He pulled at the top button of his blouse, unbuttoning it. Summer was coming and it was getting hot, and wearing the dark blue blouse only made it seem hotter. Puffs of dust billowed out of everything with just a touch, the leather of his saddle creaked as he unconsciously adjusted himself. He was more used to life in the saddle, and the trail, of campaigns, too many and too bloody. For what he'd seen in his years in the War Between the States, what he had done to win the war, some vilified him as a criminal while others hailed him as a hero. The war had carried him to the edge of madness and back. He imagined it had pushed some of his enemies over that barrier too. His mind had become hardened by the horrors of war, but the Union still existed and that's all that counted. Now he had another job to do, another war. Not a declared war in the way the War Between the States was, but a war, nonetheless. End the Indian problem, get them on reservations or kill them as renegades. He was here to finish the job and finish it he would.

The scout with him was wearing a blue blouse, stripped of all insignias. The Indian scouts liked wearing the blouse; it made them feel like they were soldiers. Some even wanted to be sworn in, so he swore them in. It didn't matter a bit; it was an illusion Sherman could live with, and the Indians thought they were soldiers. The Indian wore the blouse open to the waist, as a savage will. Underneath was a necklace and some trinkets. He had two feathers braided in his unkempt hair. Sherman looked at the scout contemptuously. He didn't trust them. After all, they betrayed their own people and were helping hunt the renegades down.

"Sir, it must not have happened long ago. The wagons are still grouped closely together, and the horses haven't pulled them all over tarnation." Sherman signaled his adjutant, Mackenzie, who gave the command, "fooor-ward!" The company moved towards the ghostly wagon train in unison behind Sherman, like a snake moving across the desert.

The soldiers approached the wagon train cautiously, expecting an ambush. The wagon train a mere lure to pull them in, and in the course of trying to figure out what had happened, out of nowhere the warriors would appear. These men had cut their teeth in the late war, just as Sherman and the officers of that war had cut theirs during the war with Mexico. Coming within eyesight of the wagon train it still looked abandoned. They could see arrows everywhere, in the canopies of the wagons, in the wooden planking, and in the flanks of some of the horses.

As the soldiers came alongside the wagons, they could see the buckboards were awash in blood.

"Gawd almighty, lookit all that blood. How could they survive that?"

"Quiet in the ranks!" Sherman barked. "Where are the dead? They usually leave them where they fall. Colonel Mackenzie, take a squad of men and back track, see if you can find where the savages attacked."

"Yes, Sir!" Mackenzie saluted smartly and motioned to a few men, and they galloped off in the direction the wagon train had come from. Sherman motioned to the scout.

"Look in those wagons, see what's left behind." The scout jumped off his horse and looked into the back of the nearest wagon. When he turned back to Sherman, he was somber.

"They're in there."

"Who?

"The people. They're dead." Sherman motioned to a nearby sergeant.

"Check all the wagons!" Soldiers galloped to the wagons looking in, a few jumped off their mounts, looking ashen and falling to the ground retching. The sergeant went to a lieutenant and whispered something to him. Sherman watched all this from atop his horse waiting for the lieutenant to make his report. The lieutenant approached Sherman, grim faced.

"They're all there, sir, they're all dead. They crammed all the bodies into the wagons, sir. They twisted their legs and bent over torsos to make them fit."

"Your men have never seen the dead?" Sherman asked.

"It's worse sir."

"Worse?"

"They mutilated them. They chopped off their privates and stuffed them into their mouths. Some are disemboweled with their intestines draped over them. I think one has the top of his head chopped off and his brains scooped out."

"I'll never understand the Indian mind," Sherman said. "When did this happen?"

"By the ripeness of the bodies, sir, some time yesterday."

Sherman's adjutant, Colonel Mackenzie, whom Sherman had

dispatched to back track the wagon train returned, pulling his horse up short of the general.

"Sir, it wasn't that far back the attack occurred. All we found were some arrows in the ground and pools of congealed blood."

"That's all-right Mackenzie, we found them. Look in the wagons." Then almost absently, to no one, Sherman muttered, "I wonder what made them do this?"

"They wanted us to find them," the scout said.

❋

Sherman rode at the head of the column as they headed back across the desert floor towards their encampment. The orange sun was hanging low in the sky. In the distant haze Sherman saw dust being kicked up like something big was behind it. He squinted but couldn't see through the haze any better.

"Give me that spyglass," he said holding out his hand, knowing without even having to think about it that the order would be obeyed. The scout handed Sherman the spyglass, he opened it and looked in the direction of the haze. All he could see was a wall of dust. He peered into the gloom. Suddenly it parted. He could see the brown bulk of buffalo behind the dust, bobbing up and down like a living locomotive. There shouldn't be a herd that big this far south he thought to himself. But he could almost hear the pounding thunder of hooves, and the thrumming vibration in his chest. He saw the mane of the lead animal. He looked again, not believing what he saw. It looked like it was aflame, but it couldn't be. It had to be a trick of the eye, the golden light of the sun refracting through the haze and lens of the spyglass giving everything a reddish tinge. Still, it looked like the herd was heading straight towards them. He thought the buffalo was looking him right in the eye, that it would run right through him. "We better find camp before that herd runs us down."

"Herd?" The scout asked. "Herd of what?"

"That buffalo herd." Sherman said pointing out to the plain.

"Sir, there isn't a herd of buffalo anywhere near here." When Sherman looked out at the plain again, he saw nothing. What he had seen or thought he'd seen seemed to have evaporated into the haze of the horizon. The wall of dust had disappeared leaving only the fading sun. Maybe it had been a trick of the light, a weird refraction of the glass, an unusual swirling of the dust or a combination of any of them.

Among a grove of pitched tents, Sherman's stood larger than the others. It doubled as his field command center and would be considered by his men luxurious with a cot, desk, and a couple of canvas field chairs. Sherman sat outside the tent in one of the chairs. The night on the plains was a dark blanket of liquid black that was only cut through by the campfire's light. He stretched out his legs towards the fire, a tin of coffee in one hand, cigar in the other. He mulled over what he'd seen on the desert earlier in the evening. It couldn't have been a herd of buffalo. He thought his eyes must've been playing tricks on him, a reflection of the setting sun in the lens of the spyglass, perhaps. Or worse yet, his mind was playing tricks on him again. Maybe the slaughter of the settlers had affected him more than he thought, and it had unsettled his mind.

Sherman ordered the scout to report to him.

"Are the Comanche who committed that atrocity upon those homesteaders near here?"

"I don't know."

"What I saw on the desert or what I thought I saw…"

"What you saw?"

"A herd of buffalo."

"The white man has killed the tatanka, there are no more herds near here." Sherman growled at the scout. "I know there are no herds near here. I made sure as many of the buffalo are gone as possible. Have you seen the photograph of the stacked skulls of buffalo, a pyramid of bone on the brown prairie ground? Done on my orders. Kill off the buffalo and you kill off the Indian's way of life and kill them off."

"It is said by the shamans of our people that at dusk the horizon is where the visible world meets the invisible."

"What's a shaman?"

"What you call a medicine man."

Sherman stared at the Indian, "I don't understand why you help us track down your own people."

"The renegades are not our people-they're of a different tribe."

"You're all Indians."

"We are not one nation. We are among many. Do you not get along with members of other nations? Did you not fight amongst your own people?"

"I have hunted down a fair amount of my own people some were even friends, but it was a war. We fight for what is right, we fight for freedom. I don't think your savage mind can comprehend the difference between war and betrayal."

"I am not as educated as you."

"I do know that warring states know a lot about each other, their habits, and their customs. Do you know what those renegades may be up to?"

"It's hard to know what they will do."

"Do you know if they're planning an attack?"

"I cannot tell the future."

"Do you know where those Indians are?"

"It's a full moon tonight." Sherman stared at him not understanding what the scout meant. "If they're planning an attack, they'll be dancing tonight."

"I want to reconnoiter them; can we get close to them?"

"Yes."

Sherman threw his cigar to the ground with a determined look of intensity on his face. "Let's go take a look."

Sherman and the Indian scout lay flat on a ledge overlooking the renegade encampment, hoping the darkness would conceal their position, that they would look like part of the rock. They could see the glow of the campfire. It didn't throw off much illumination to the surrounding area. It was nothing more than a yellow triangle in the sea of darkness. Embers from the fire occasionally popped and shot up into the night before dying out. Sherman and the scout silently watched the shadow figures as they moved in and out of the light.

"What are they doing?" Sherman asked.

"It looks like they're getting ready to do the ghost dance. It's suppos' to bring back the tatanka and…."

"I know what it's supposed to do." Sherman snapped tersely. "Bring back the buffalo and get rid of the white man."

"Shhh, there's more," the scout said pointing down to the camp. Sherman saw the figures had stopped moving around the fire and now sat in a circle drumming. They could see their arms moving up and down in rhythmic unison. Soon they heard the sound and chanting. To Sherman there seemed to be a solemnity to it. Then an Indian dressed in ceremonial robes slipped out of a Tipi and began dancing.

The scout watched the dance intently. Then a look of horror overcame the scout.

"We must go now, General."

"What for? It's just a dance?"

"You can't watch, it is sacred."

"Heathen superstition!" Then Sherman saw the look of terror in the Indian's eyes. He'd seen the look in the eyes of hundreds, maybe thousands of people who thought they were going to die. It was a look he'd seen in his own eyes once—fear. "All right then." The two slowly and carefully crawled back off their vantage point, over sun hardened sand and rock grinding under their bellies as they noiselessly slithered off the overlook.

When the two were safely away from the Indian camp the Indian asked. "You see the medicine shirts they were wearing?"

"Yes."

"They believe those shirts will protect them from your bullets." Sherman looked at him not believing. "General you don't know about the rest of the Ghost Dance?"

"Yeah, it's supposed to get rid of the white man."

"There's more."

"What more?"

"It's suppos' to bring back the dead."

"Bring back the dead?" Sherman considered that for a moment.

"It's to break your enemy's heart."

"The south didn't break me, and no damned Indians will either. Let them dance to whatever god they have. We'll stop them before they can conjure their damned heathen ghosts and spirits. We'll attack at dawn."

"You believe in the power of the Ghost Dance General?"

"Hell, no!" Sherman spat out, "but they do, and I'll kill the belief right out of them."

✳

The next morning Sherman roused the company early, crossing the floor of the desert to meet the group of Comanches to engage them before they had a chance to attack. As they approached, they could see the Indians riding out in front. Behind them was the brown haze he had seen the day before.

"You see there, Mackenzie? That dust behind those savages."

"It's just the dust from their horses galloping sir." Sherman stopped and pulled out his field glasses. He saw the heathens had painted on their horror war paint, but the haze wasn't from their horses. There weren't enough of them to kick up that much dust, and the haze was farther behind the Indians than it should've been even if it was from their horses. It was separate from them, but it was following them! He tried to peer into the haze. Maybe there was a herd of buffalo here, somehow. He could see movement inside the haze but there was no definition to it, only movement. Sherman made a decision. In a singularly fluid movement he unsheathed his sword, spurred his horse to a gallop and charged! Sherman closed the ground quickly. He rode past the Indians and into the haze. Inside there seemed to be a whole regiment of warriors dressed in their paint and war clothes, screaming their war cries. Sherman galloped straight at the braves, slashing with his sword knocking them off their horses.

As he fought, he noticed something was wrong with these Indians. They didn't look right. Their color was off; even the color of their horses was off. They were faded, drab. They smelled of rot and decay, the smell of the dead. Sherman shrugged it off. A battlefield always had the smell of death, and bodies rotting in the sun with drying gore kicked up in the dust by the horses' hooves. The horses breathed vaporous blasts of visible breath. He came close to one and felt its breath through his blouse. It froze his skin. There was something repellant about it, something of the grave.

The Indians weren't acting right either. When they were knocked off their horses, shot, or wounded with a slash of a sword, they fell and then got back up and continued the fight. Sherman didn't see any blood. Maybe it was the heat of battle, and later he would see the gore when he surveyed the sanguinary scene. There was one other thing that ran a shiver down Sherman's spine. He recognized the Indians. Indians he had killed in other battles…but that couldn't be so. Sherman looked up at the surrounding ridge. There on their horses, were the Indians of the dance, in full war regalia. He recognized the medicine man and his warriors calmly watching the battle, just watching.

Suddenly a realization of horror passed through his mind, and his body shook involuntarily, as the scout's words of the night before rang in his ears; "*it's suppos' to bring back the dead.*"

Sherman barked out to his bugler, "Sound retreat! Now!" The bugler did so. Sherman pulled on the reins to turn the horse. It reared, whinnied and almost threw him. The horse bolted and Sherman thundered off the field of battle.

Shaken, Sherman sat in his tent trembling when Mackenzie came in.

"General, you shouldn't let those heathens get to you. Why did you charge?"

"Didn't you see them, Mackenzie?"

"Yes sir, we saw the Indians. As we approached the contingent of warriors, just as we were about to engage them, you spurred your horse, and drew your sword. The Indians moved aside as you charged passed them, then you ordered the retreat and left the field."

"That's all that happened?!"

"That's all that happened."

"No," he said to himself, his mind flooding with questions and answers that he feared, the world pressing down on him. His face froze in shock as he unconsciously took a step backward away from Mackenzie. Sherman regained his composure enough to dress down the man. "I never did anything that cowardly! If you repeat an accusation like that again I'll bring you up on charges of insubordination."

"Yes sir!"

"Mackenzie, can I ask you something?" Mackenzie stood at attention, eyes straight ahead, "are those Indians acting right to you?"

"Sir?"

"Those Indians aren't behaving right. Why are they forming a skirmish line? Usually they ambush, coming out of nowhere, in groups that attack different parts of our line."

"Maybe they aren't as savage as we think, and they've realized it's a more civilized way to engage your enemy." Sherman considered that for a moment.

"In this terrain? No, ambush is a better tactic. They know this land, they know the hidden valleys, ravines, plenty of places to hide. They could attack us seemingly appearing out of nowhere and disappear again. No…"

Then as if hit with a sudden realization of his fears, he said, "no, they're doing it to draw us out…why?" Sherman's voice and thoughts trailed off. Then he snapped, "get that scout in here!"

A few minutes later the scout appeared at Sherman's tent. "Come in," Sherman said, as he paced the small space of the tent, his movements agitated as he nervously spoke.

"Do some Indians paint themselves to look dead?"

"I have never heard of such a thing."

"You told me the Ghost Dance can bring back the dead. How?"

"How am I to know? I am not a shaman."

"I've been seeing things. The herd of buffalo and today Indian warriors I could've sworn were dead, but the dead can't fight."

"The shaman has many powers we do not understand."

"Do you expect me to believe that superstitious claptrap that you told me!? That the medicine man is bringing back the dead?"

"I am not a spiritual man I do not know the spirit world. The shaman does. We have great respect for them." Sherman glared at him.

"I am not a spiritual man either. But this country is our destiny, the Indian needs to be on a reservation, or wiped away. They're supposed to be gone but they aren't. I'll make sure they're gone; I'll make sure they're all gone.

"Why do you hate the Indian so much?"

"We've come to this country to settle it and the Indians are in the way. The Indian needs to be on a reservation so the white man can farm the land and make it useful."

"I hear talk your men say your name is after a great Indian leader Tecumseh."

"Yes, Tecumseh was a great leader. My father admired him. He thought naming me after him would imbue those qualities in me."

"Are you a great leader killing all the people?" Sherman was speechless at the impertinence of the scout. "You wasichu don't see the dead, we see the dead of our past. You don't remember your blood is of the sea, your bone is of the earth. The land does not belong to you; you belong to the land. We're connected to the land, even the world you cannot see or refuse to see. Your people consider it madness. Maybe the shaman opened your eyes to see the invisible world."

Sherman and the detachment approached the Indian war party. The warriors were dressed in their medicine shirts of blue, red, and yellow and painted for war. Sherman didn't see the brown haze behind the Indian party and felt more at ease. They continued their cautious approach. Suddenly the haze seemed to manifest behind the Indians, highlighting their silhouettes against the cloud. Sherman looked up and down his line of men none of whom seemed to have taken notice of the haze, but he kept his composure. He didn't call for a charge. He kept calm even though his nerves were like an electric charge shooting through him.

Suddenly, the Indians, in unison, prodded their horses into a gallop. In his own seamless movement Sherman drew his sword from the scabbard, raised it above his head, and simultaneously he and his troops spurred their horses into a charge. As they closed, the Indians started firing their rifles. Bullets whizzed past. Sherman's men returned fire. The forces clashed, and Sherman and his men were in the midst of the Indian war party. There was fighting all around him, but no one came close to him. It was as if he were in a bubble. The fighting raged around him. He passed through the battle; the Indian warriors moved aside like the waters parting for the

Israelites. As he neared the rear, he saw the haze. He could see the roiling movement, and he was drawn to it. As he got closer, the movement seemed more concrete, and then became clear.

There was a second skirmish line, but they weren't Indians. They were soldiers in confederate gray. Their uniforms, in tatters, ripped from what looked like bayonet slashes. There were holes in the uniforms, the edges smoldered as if a hot round had just penetrated the fabric, their wounds oozed a blackened gore. The Confederates came towards him, arms outstretched like they were going to pull him off his mount. Suddenly, the horse reared, he almost fell off, the hands of the confederate soldiers landing on the flanks of his horse like waves breaking on a beach. The next thing he remembered, he was surrounded by four of his men, their blue blouses reassuring. With their help, he reined in his usually unflappable horse, and they led him out of the fray.

Mackenzie escorted Sherman back to his tent. The usually stoic Sherman looked scared down to his soul. Mackenzie maneuvered Sherman through the camp so as few men as possible saw him in this state.

"Thank you, Colonel, for coming to my assistance in the mass of the enemy."

"Enemy, sir?"

"I was surrounded."

"Surrounded? You passed through the Indians line and then we saw your horse rearing like something had spooked it. I sent in a guard to calm the horse. It didn't look like..." Mackenzie hesitated, not sure how Sherman would receive his report.

"Didn't look like what?" Sherman demanded.

"If you don't mind me saying, sir, it just looked like your horse was spooked. If you had fallen, you would have been susceptible to attack."

"You didn't see the men...dressed in..."

"What sir?"

"Confederate gray. Some of them looked like rounds had passed through their clothing, suppurating wounds." Sherman saw the uncomprehending look on his adjutant's face.

"Didn't you see them? They looked like they weren't alive, they were dead! We were fighting the dead!"

"The dead, sir?"

"You didn't see those apparitions?"

"We just saw the Indians, and none had anything on resembling confederate gray."

"Am I going mad? What's happening here Mackenzie?" Sherman's voice bordered on the hysterical.

"Other than trying to round up the renegades…"

"It was the curse of my mother's people. I've always feared it. I've fought it all my life, but now, it may be coming to pass."

"What is?"

"Mackenzie, our profession courts death. Madness is always just over the next rise, the next hillock…" Sherman's voice dropped off. "I'm out in that landscape wavering between madness and sanity. Be careful Mackenzie, that you don't cross over that rise and find yourself in the arid desert of madness. I fear it is this desert for me."

"I'll call the medic, sir."

The medic gave Sherman some laudanum to settle his nerves and help him sleep, but his fevered dreams broke through the drug. He saw a city at a distance, illuminated by the glow of the fire. Flames danced in the night above the city. He could feel the heat from his vantage point. Refugees streamed out of the city like blood from a wound, their clothes singed and burned. Ash fell like a dark snow in the wake of their step. The flames of Atlanta burned in their eyes with their hatred of him. Not far behind them trailed Indians, their eyes charred black with still burning embers visible through cracks and fissures.

Sherman woke bolt upright in his cot, drenched in sweat. He looked around to get his bearings to remember where he was and reassure himself the dream had only been a dream. He swung his legs over the side of the cot, his head in his hands trying to clear the memories, the captured dead of his memories straight out of his mind. The dead of Atlanta still haunted him. He knew they were all dead and they'd stay dead, but they wouldn't stay dead in his mind. Maybe he really was going insane. Sherman looked up noticing Mackenzie had been sitting vigil over him.

"How long have you been here, Mackenzie?"

"All night sir. The doctor thought it a good idea for somebody to stay with you in case you needed something."

"I know what's going to happen tomorrow if we go into battle."

"At the Point, they always said a good strategist always knows what's going to happen."

"No—if we—if I, go into battle tomorrow, the dead of Atlanta will be there to avenge their deaths on me."

"You can't believe that. The war is over, and the dead…"

"Are dead? To the south I was the most hateful person ever to walk the earth. If the devil himself appeared, they would have embraced him over me."

"Sir, if you're afraid…"

"Mackenzie, I'm beyond fear. It borders on the edges of madness, and that is the truth. The war drove me to the edge of madness. Did you know that?"

"Yes, sir, I've heard that."

"Now, that Indian medicine man leading the renegades somehow used the Ghost Dance to bring back the dead to fight us, me, my dead."

"Sir, we have to go out and confront those renegades to either capture them and return them to the reservation or dispatch them. It would be an honor if you'd let me lead the command against them."

"No, Colonel, I know my duty and my orders, wherever they may lead me." Reveille broke the morning air. "Wake the men, Mackenzie. Our destiny or our fate awaits us."

❋

As Sherman took the field of battle, the dusky smell of smoldering, burnt wood and flame filled the air. His horse snorted. Could he smell it too? Sherman could have sworn he saw the glow of fire on the horizon. He saw the haze straight away, larger than it had ever been before, and he could see motion in it from a distance, like a great mass was concealed within, roiling, writhing. In the lead, before the haze, was a small contingent of Indians. One man in a blue medicine shirt stood out from the rest, Sherman took him to be the medicine man. Sherman pulled his sword from the scabbard.

"Take that Indian in the blue medicine shirt alive if possible, and the rest will follow." With that Sherman spurred his horse into a canter. The troop pulled their guns and followed suit. As they approached the haze, Sherman could see into it. He could make out individuals within the mass. The dead of Atlanta of every breed—women in hoop skirts, soldiers, negroes their clothes covered with soot, some smoldering. Sherman could see their full necrotic state, the burns that covered their flesh, the skulls indented by falling timbers, the peeled skin that hung from the bone.

A corridor opened in front of Sherman and his men. They entered the throng. The passage closed behind them, blocking their exit. They were deep in the throng of the Indians, confederates he'd killed, all dead. He knew that they would stay dead, but they wouldn't stay dead in his mind. He was surrounded. They were pushing him forward towards the dead of Atlanta. The dead started grabbing and pulling at his soldiers as they passed. Yet they were insensate of those hands and their intentions. Only Sherman could feel their pull and he was afraid of what would happen if they succeeded in pulling him from his mount. They'd rend him, tear him apart as a bit of cloth. The hands grabbed at him, all he could see were the hands, white, black, red. He felt them on his boots, pulling. More came and he felt the hands on his legs, pulling, each getting a better grip on him. He could feel their cold sepulchral hands upon him. Then the hands were pulling at his blouse, his arms, his chest. The dead were merciless. Sherman slashed at them with his sword, but the blade passed through as if only cutting through vapor. The hands were on his shoulders, restricting his arms, then over his head and face, he felt one last pull and fell to the ground with the ghostly hands and faces pressing in on him. Then, unconsciousness.

Sherman came to on his cot in his tent, the medic was holding smelling salts under his nostrils. "What happened?" Sherman asked. As he tried to rise the medic gently pushed him back into the cot.

"You suffered a seizure of some sort, sir." The flap of the tent opened, and Mackenzie brought the medicine man in, in chains. He was smaller than Sherman had thought he was, with long black hair, a bone necklace at his throat, and still wearing the blue medicine shirt. He looked calm.

"We captured all the renegades, sir."

"Very good, Mackenzie. What's your report?" Sherman asked weakly.

"We surrounded the savages and they surrendered without firing a shot. This one is the medicine man who's been stirring them all up, promising them he could rid them of white men. He is called Isatai."

"You really believe you could remove us from this country?"

"I am not like other men."

"My scouts have informed me you that believe your shirts can render you impervious to our bullets."

"None of my people have fallen to your bullets."

"How about bringing back the dead?"

"I have done no such thing. You brought them."

"How did I bring them?"

"I have captured the dead from your soul, those whose deaths have been impressed upon your soul and which you have refused to face. I made it so you could face them."

"But still, you're in chains. You and your people will be taken to the reservation. If you ever leave it again, you will be killed."

"You can put us on your reservation, prison, or even kill us. Your children may try to steal our religion. Our spirits will always be free. One day we will again roam this country as free as our spirits. There will be more battles of my kind, and you will lose until the invisible world is made visible to you. You do not understand the nature of the battle before you. You have no belief."

"No. Your day has passed. The Indian will be locked away on reservations or you will perish."

"It is you that is wrong, for the captured dead of your souls will haunt you forever."

GHOSTS

"Have you ever heard the story of Resurrection Mary?" I asked, breaking the silence.

"No, I don't think so."

"She was a teenager in the 30's or 40's, she was a pretty girl with blond hair. She and her boyfriend were driving to a dance at the O'Henry Ballroom, they got into a fight, she got out of the car and was going to walk the rest of the way. Her boyfriend left her there on the side of the road and drove off to the dance by himself. The next day a couple of drivers reported seeing her hitchhiking, but she was hit by a car, the driver didn't see her, or he was drunk, it doesn't really matter, she was killed. Ever since then guy's driving on this road have reported seeing a girl hitchhiking at night, they pick her up, and the driver asks where she's going, she says a dance at the O'Henry Ballroom."

"Never heard of it." The driver always says.

"It's just up the road a bit." The guy starts driving, the girl is nervous, it's around this time he usually notices she seems to be dressed a little old fashioned, she has a clutch purse, her hair is up, and she's dressed in a chiffon dress with a petticoat, he notices her skin is white, really white, pearly white.

"Is it a costume party?" The driver asks.

"No." she says, quietly.

"Why're you nervous?"

"I'm late for the dance. My friends are waiting." She answers. He reaches over to touch her hand, it's cold and clammy, enough that he pulls his hand back in surprise. Suddenly, she yells, "stop! Let me out here." The driver hits the brakes, they're in the middle of nowhere and there's nothing around except Resurrection cemetery on the side of the road. He turns back to the girl, but she's gone, and all's that's left is a wet spot on the seat where she was.

"Why are you telling me this?"

"It's just a story I've been thinking about."

"Why?"

"I mean, why is she coming back? What is she looking for? What's haunting her?" After that neither one of us said anything for a very long time.

I'm on my way to a friend's funeral, I'm coming back to my hometown, sitting in the back of a black SUV with my girlfriend Mia, she had seemed exotic and mysterious when I met her, but she was probably from Ohio or Iowa, or maybe even Orange. Now, she seemed a construct of L.A. She was just the latest girlfriend. We were at the point where there was one last barrier to step over, something we both felt between us, but weren't talking about and if we couldn't get past it, it was the end. The question that hung over everything was could I take that last step? I was afraid I would lose her.

I hadn't seen Sean in a year, since his father's funeral, When Brad called to tell me that Sean's father had died, at first, I thought he was talking about Sean. When I realized he wasn't, I was relieved, but it turned out to be a somewhat prescient mistake. Almost exactly a year later the call came that Sean had died. At his father's funeral I was shocked to see Sean's face had become a mask of itself, the years of alcohol and cocaine had caught up with him. Before that I hadn't seen him in almost a decade. He died in an old people's home, of a very common death for the superannuated, he fell and hit his head. The thing was, he was only thirty-eight. Cocaine had riddled the matter of his brain.

Sean and I had spent our early twenties hanging out together living out some rite of passage of angst-ridden young men of many lost generations, drinking, womanizing with the twist of cocaine adding to our adventures.

Nothing about this was new, wine, women and song had become sex, drugs and rock n' roll, but we acted like we had discovered it. Eventually, I wrote a roman-a-clef, it was a picaresque of the soul, a tour of the inner journey, a fictionalized version of our exploits. All the names changed to protect me. I was aiming to be the Thomas Wolfe of the 90's, and I became the new dark, brooding poet of American literature, it was probably one of the things that attracted Mia to me. There is a certain amount of dread in this return, when my book was published there was a hue and cry from the local citizenry about allowing such garbage to be published. The lifestyle I had described couldn't happen in the Midwest, maybe New York or California, but not the Midwest. It was a misrepresentation of life, a misrepresentation of people some thought. Others thought they recognized their 'characters' but since the characters were amalgams and the two main characters were different aspects of myself, there was some greater existential truth in there, not factual truths. It was misunderstood but I guess there was enough sex, drugs and rock and roll to make it a bestselling book, and for Hollywood to be interested. I'd hoped the controversy would spark interest and if I was real lucky, threats of my book being banned. I thought I was on the right track.

As the car wound its way through the streets the town glided by like a projection against the window. Time was merging and melting like a kaleidoscope, I saw the ghosts of myself and my friends passing by on the streets. The streets and buildings looked the same, but there was something different about them, as if they were built from memory, an imperfect memory, like a piece was missing, something was a bit off. It was as if I wasn't a part of the environment anymore, I was an observer of life unable to touch or affect it. I felt like a ghost passing through other's lives. It was a strange feeling as if just the act of being here again was resurrecting those ghosts. Thomas Wolfe wrote that you can't go home again, maybe you can, but not without catching up with the ghosts of your past. I wondered if others could see them? I wondered if Mia could see them? Would she be able to see them if I told her about them? It was like just being here was a revelatory act in itself. I tried to point out some of the sights to her to alleviate the dread I was feeling.

"I lived in this town for twenty-five years I can tell you stories about just about every building. See that one there, across the street, that used to be the Big Banjo pizza place, Bluegrass bands used to play there all the time. There's the movie theater I used to work at, the back door never locked, it was always ajar, we used to go in and sit behind the movie screen, getting high and watching the movies. The images were backwards, but we were stoned so it worked out." I chuckled a little to myself at the thought. "There's the record store that used to double as a head shop. One time me and Sean climbed onto the roof and drank a bottle of some liqueur one of us had gotten hold of."

"Is that all you guys did in this town, get fucked up?" Mia asked.

"No! It wasn't like that at all, it was fun and exciting buzzing around the town seeing things as they are. You try to add too many dark contours to my life, it's not as debauched as you make it sound. I'm not a dark, brooding poet."

"You are a dark brooding poet." I smiled, but turned away so she wouldn't see.

Sean was dead. So, what was the difference between us? Why was he dead and I was alive? It wasn't supposed to be Sean that died I was always the angst-ridden, darkly brooding writer that wore the sex, drugs, and rock n' roll lifestyle on his sleeve. It turned out, my real addiction was literature, writing was simply the best high I ever had. After the book's success I kept the party going and lived out my rock and roll dreams long after my friends were getting married and settling down. Now, I'm a big Hollywood screenwriter, I went out to L.A. to write the screenplay for my book. When I sold the film rights to the book I had it written into the contract that I would write the screenplay. I thought I was being canny. I knew that both Faulkner and Fitzgerald had written for Hollywood and didn't like it, but I thought I knew all the pitfalls and I could control it, that it would heighten my visibility and options in Hollywood, and I'd have something to fall back on in-between books. At least that's how it plays out in my head and here in the town where I grew up. The reality is, I write for a TV show where at the beginning of every episode is a murder, and by the end, the main character sees the ghosts of those they've laid to rest. I've laid to rest a lot of fictional ghosts. When I got the job writing the TV series it was supposed to be a job, I didn't have to bring home with me and I could write at night, that's how I had written the first book. Then a trap sprung, it felt like one of those sell your soul for a meal deals. I had money, a house, bills, a girlfriend…Now, I rarely found the time to do my real work, scriptwriting had become a day-job. I should have just worked on a book and got fired like many famous writers before me.

"Sean was probably the one person in this life who knew the secret I don't want revealed to the world that would expose me for what I am."

"What's the secret?"

"I can't tell you; you would see right through me."

"You think I'd use it against you?"

"Knowledge is power."

The insides of funeral homes always gave me the feeling of having a thin layer of dust over everything, or maybe it was a thin film of the accumulated sadness and grief. The dull waxed linoleum floors and hazy beams of light flooding through any open window only added to the gloom. I said hello to people I hadn't seen in years, we were all gravely serious, quick handclasps and awkward greetings, there wasn't much to say except the wishing of condolences and brief catching ups. When there was nothing left to say to anyone, we all settled into our seats, waiting. Finally, the service began, Sean's brother got up and started his eulogy.

"Thank you all for coming. It's been a long time since we've seen each other, we've been there for births, baptisms, first communion's, graduations, weddings, anniversaries, and now it seems all's that's left are funerals." I looked to my side, a girl, a woman now, I hadn't seen since high school was sitting a couple of chairs away from me. I watched her for a moment, it was like watching a silent movie, her face started breaking down like she had started crying on cue, it seemed a rehearsed moment, crying only because it was expected. I realized we don't cry as much for the dead person, as much as for the realization of our own deaths.

After the funeral we all gathered at a local restaurant, the men in dark suits, the women all in a version of a black dress, everybody with a drink in hand. Everyone knew Sean and I were close and kept coming up to me to offer their condolences. When Mia and I had a moment off in a corner her mood from the car hadn't changed. She had been aloof the whole trip and I didn't know why. It felt like she had only come with me as an obligation of the relationship. If she felt this thing between us, why didn't she say anything?

"Who was that woman?"

"What woman?"

"The woman you couldn't take your eyes off during the funeral."

"She was a girl I; we went to high school with together, Sean knew her a lot better than I did." It was true but I knew it wouldn't pay to tell Mia my brief history with the woman.

When too many people had wished me their condolences, all my ghosts were catching up with me…or maybe it was just the whiskey wasn't sitting well in my stomach, the drink was getting watery in my hand, "c'mon, let's go," I said, "I'm starting to feel like the widow here." We left before the repast.

In our hotel room, Mia and I changed clothes and tried to relax around each other, that last barrier was still between us, unsaid and unacknowledged, something that needed to be said, something that I should have said already, but at any given moment it never seemed to be the right moment. We turned on the TV hoping for the distracting blankness of television, we flipped around stations, nothing was on. Finally, we were left with only each other. She looked at me as if she was trying to figure out a small puzzle. It seemed as if for the first time on this trip she wanted something of me.

"You know all these ghost stories." She said.

"Yeah."

"Tell me one that is real."

"Real?"

"Something that is about you, that you care about."

"Real? Ok, let me tell you about Marley, it's a real-life ghost story."

"Marley?"

"No, this isn't some retelling of a Christmas Carol and 'old Marley was dead as a doornail' thing. Marley was a cat; he was the first cat I'd had since I was a kid. He found us. My sister had been hearing sounds in the basement for about a week, we all discounted it. Apparently, there was a broken window in our basement that he came through and one evening the basement door to the upstairs was open, my mother was making dinner, and the smells of simmering food must have overcome his fear, and he walked up into the kitchen, suddenly, we had a cat! He was a beautiful gray tiger cat. We found his owner and he let us keep him, I forget why he didn't want him anymore, but he was our cat then, and he became my cat. He slept on my bed, sat on my lap as I read, one time he didn't like that I was reading *The Sea Wolf* and not paying enough attention to him, he reached up with his paw and grabbed the edge of the page and bit it. That book now sits on the library shelf with two perfect holes in one corner of a page, he was my friend. We'd had him a little while when I noticed his fur rippling when it shouldn't have been, it's hard to explain, and at first, I didn't think anything of it, I thought it was just my imagination, but it just didn't look right. We finally took him to a vet, he told us Marley had leukemia we gave him what medicine we could, but it was too late, soon he was getting sick, I built him a cave under my desk, with a cushion, food and water. A few weeks after that I came home and found that he couldn't walk anymore, he had urinated and hadn't been able to get up to use his litterbox. I looked into his eyes, and he was so scared, he didn't understand what was happening to him any more than I did. I petted him and told him everything was all right, that he was a good boy. But I knew we had to put him to sleep, he was suffering too much, and it would be selfish to let him live like that. I took him to the doctor, and he injected Marley, and I petted him as I saw the light of life fade from his eyes. I went out that night unable to think of anything else except of my little tiger. The next morning, I woke up and by the side of my bed was Marley! He was there, solid, substantial, and healthy! I sat up in the bed and he was still there. As I woke up my conscious mind started kicking in and I told myself it was "only wish fulfillment" as the thought passed through my mind, he dissolved in front of my eyes, but I knew he'd come back to tell me that he was ok." My voice had broken a couple of times in the telling of the story and I hung my head as a tear ran down my cheek. "That's the only true ghost story I know."

"Tell me one thing John, do you care whether I stay or go?" I balked, I couldn't answer, she saw the fear in my eyes, "it seems like you were closer to your friend than to me. Tell me, why do writers have such problems with relationships?"

"Maybe we don't have more than anyone else, we just make it public."

"What are you trying to do? Fix them? Figure then out? Get them right?"

"We spend a lot of time alone with our thoughts, talking to ourselves, sometimes in other voices, you get used to being alone, being self-contained."

"Reliving that pain isn't good for you."

"I knew I was a writer when, after a girl broke up with me, I was wallowing in the pain, but it sharpened me and I realized I was using the pain to write, and I realized I enjoyed it, and I nurtured it as long as the words came."

"There's something so sad in that, you just don't see it."

I was already in bed when Mia came in, she got in the bed, her back to me, she said a perfunctory "goodnight," and was asleep. I reached out to touch her, to tell her…what? I told myself I would know when I got that far, my hand hovered over her shoulder, but something was wrong, she 'felt' different. I turned toward the opposite wall, I watched the patterns of blue and black play on the wall creating abstract paintings, until I wondered how long I had been laying awake. It reminded me of other nights. The night my grandmother died, and I stayed up all night watching the changing shadows play across the faces of gargoyles on the building across the street, and one other night…I fell asleep without any of the answers to my questions.

The wind was howling, rain splattered thickly against the windowpane, the screen door of my apartment flung open screaming against its rusted hinges. There was a pounding at the door, I looked out the window, huddling in the doorway being buffeted about by the storm was Sean. His face was ashen and looked necrotic like something out of a horror movie. He was dressed in a ripped and torn leather bikers' jacket, he pulled it closer to his body, against the storm.

"C'mon! Let me in!" He yelled; I was afraid.

"No! You're dead!" He pounded on the door again, I woke up, it had been a dream. I sat up in bed, I put my legs over the side and sat with my head in my hands for a minute or two reassuring myself that it was only a dream. Later, when I told this dream to friends, they said, "Sean, would never have hurt you." I agreed, I understood this instinctively, but the fear crawled around the primitive part of my brain like some reptile. I got up and walked around the partition separating the bedroom from the living room, and there was Sean. Not as he had been dressed in the dream but as he had looked in his twenties, before his face had become a mask of himself. He looked erudite, dressed in jeans, a button-down shirt and a sweater.

"What're you doing here?"

"I died, I'm a ghost."

"You're a ghost? You're not a ghost."

"Well, then, maybe it's you. What're you doing back here?"

"I'm here for your funeral."

"I guess it must be me then."

"What's it like being dead?"

"Seeing the big picture instead of the details, a little lonely, but maybe that's my own death and not someone else's."

"What're you doing here?"

"I don't know, you're the one holding me here."

"What do you mean?"

"You haven't let go of my memory you brought me here."

"I brought you here? How? Why?"

"Its energy stuck to a person or place and it's more your energy than mine."

"How can it be me? You…"

"Yes, I had some things I wanted to do, write a Civil War book, be with Brandi, we all have things but it's just stuff that we all think we can cheat death with. It's a little game we all play with ourselves while 'cheated' death laughs at us and waits. Your game is writing."

"I tried to bring you along. We could've been Hollywood moguls; we could've been big!"

"How do you figure?"

"Remember, I said we should buy the rights to that African adventure story, and I would write the screenplay and you would buy the rights? A couple of years later that writer had a best-seller, then another, and it became a series, the books went straight to film even before being published, we could've been on the ground floor! We could've ridden into L.A. like Bruckheimer and Simpson!"

"It wasn't where my head was at."

"I had it all planned out, write some books become a literary legend, die at twenty-seven, thirty-three at the latest."

"Dying is easy when you're young, it's abstract, you think you're going to live forever anyway."

"I wrote the fucking thing!"

"What're you mad at me for? I'm the one that's dead."

"Because you're the one that's dead! You're the one who had all the advantages, the money, the education, and you're the dead one."

"It was an accident."

"You died going through withdrawal. We couldn't blast you out of Otto's."

"You didn't duck addiction either, you had a need, a want, a desire that drove you one way, my need, my want, my desires pushed me another way."

"To an early grave."

"I guess I didn't plan that so well, but it was an accident, it's mostly accidental if you die young."

"Or you court it."

"It wasn't anything I, we hadn't done before, it's just one throw of the die, a turn of the wheel, and it comes up snake-eyes. You were there for a lot of it, it could've been you here, you did your fair share of coke."

"I know, that's what scares me. I know there were times I was closer to death then I realized or wanted to admit."

"And maybe you were a little stronger, or maybe you stopped before the number came up, or maybe your heart didn't break."

"You mean because of Brandi?"

"No."

"Some other woman? I always thought that when you came back from school…"

"No, nothing as paltry as that. It's a deeper cut, down to the soul, spiritually, when you've expended everything, when you look inside and it's not even a void, it's just… just, you're devoid of anything, emotion, caring, you come to realize you don't care what happens to you, you get arrested, a woman comes or goes, you die, it's just all the same."

"We sat in a lot of bars talking, and the alcohol, I told you a lot of things I haven't told anyone else, including girlfriends. You never told me anything like that before."

He nodded, "I kept it to myself, it was part of the problem, maybe if I had said something," a look of sadness passed over his face, "but how can you tell someone something that is an emotion, not even really a feeling, more like a gnawing, somewhere between the conscious and the unconscious. It runs deeper than the alcohol or the coke, they were meant to help me forget, to separate me from the pain, somewhere where there's no love, no hate, we didn't have religion, meditation, or even a philosophy, we had the drugs."

"No love."

"Does that still bother you?" I jerked my head up, "don't worry I never told anybody."

"No, I made my peace with it a long time ago."

"If you had you wouldn't have brought me back."

I woke up in the morning, the sun was streaming through the curtains. I was certain everything had been a dream or a dream within a dream, but I woke up on the couch in the living room.

On the drive back to the airport Mia and I were as quiet as on the drive from the airport.

"Here's a final story," I said. "After Al Capone was released from Alcatraz prison, his mind decaying and being eaten away by syphilis. He was taken back to his Florida mansion to live out the rest of his days. In its heyday it had been a magnificent estate. Cast in old world splendor, it was built with marble, had colonnades in the front, frescos and fabrics that were reminiscent of Italian villas. In the back he had a pool shaped like the Mediterranean Sea, all paid for by the blood of his enemies and rivals for power. Overlooking the pool was a portico. Every morning after breakfast he was rolled out in a wheelchair to sit and get some sun and watch over what was left of his fallen empire and 'fish' in his own Mediterranean. As he sat on the portico trapped in a body and mind that were quickly deteriorating, he would talk to the ghosts of all the people he had killed or had had killed, trying to make his peace with them. It was reported that he had long conversations with the ghost of Bugs Moran, the man he tried to have killed in The Saint Valentine's Day Massacre. The thing is Bugs Moran died eleven years AFTER Capone did. Capone was battling the ghosts he brought along with him."

"What does that mean?" Mia asked.

"Let me tell you about that secret, that I said Sean was the only person who knew the one secret about me I didn't want anyone else to know."

"You don't have to, it's not that important anymore."

"We were at a party, we were in our early twenties, and I had been talking to a girl all night, and she turned me down. I got really drunk and went off by myself. I don't remember much after that; it was mostly flashes of consciousness and disconnected images. I'd pushed myself to the edge of coherence. I had crawled off to some corner of the house, I think I was in a sunroom or something, all I remember is a lot of windows, the shadows of window frames like bars of a cell across the floor, the skeletal fingers of tree branches scratching at the walls, the tumult of blue and black creating abstract paintings in the night. It was a theatre of cruelty of my mind. When the party was over Sean found me, I was in really bad shape and out of it, I think I was delirious or the closest to delirious I've ever been. I was babbling 'nobody loves me, nobody loves me' over and over again. Sean got me to a couch, threw a blanket on me and I passed out. I woke up the next morning, the sky was starting to lighten, I was safely on the other side of dawn, I had made it through the dark night of my soul. I was cold, I pulled the blanket around me, tightly. I realized I was a raw nerve waiting to go off. It felt like my mind was scoured, no one had ever seen me so nakedly exposed, something that was so intimate. It was like I had gone through some catharsis; it was a new morning; literally." I looked at her to see if I could tell what her reaction was, she seemed blank, I didn't know how this would work out. I wondered if I should go on. But I was too far in, I had to finish what I started. "Do you know what it's like to see yourself in that light? To see that side of yourself? To have stripped yourself bare, to your raw essence, to zero? To come face to face with your worst fear? Do you have any idea what it's like to know that about yourself? And then, to know someone else knows that about you? Neither of us mentioned it ever again."

"And this has to do with us?"

"I was afraid that if I told you...I would lose you. Now, I know that if I don't, it's over."

"What're you saying?"

"What I'm trying to say is, it's that new morning again, I don't think those are things we need to carry around anymore."

A couple of weeks after I returned to L.A. I had a final dream or vision, or whatever you'd like to call it. I was in a white void there was nothing, no horizon, no up, no down, no sky, no earth, nothing. But it didn't feel empty, I wasn't afraid, it felt like it was a vestibule, a place to wait. There was no sense of urgency, it was a place where you knew someone would be along in a minute to help, and it didn't matter how long that minute was. Then Sean's father was there.

"Where's Sean?" I asked.

"He's here."

"Is he ok?"

"He's ok, John, he's with me."

"Oh." Then the dream was over. I was awake, Mia was asleep next to me, and I knew everything was ok.

GODWIRED

What we classify as U.F.O. sightings have been reported the world over for at least the last 2000 years. It wasn't until recently that it was noticed there was a pattern to the sightings, under further analysis it could only be concluded it was a search pattern.

J. Walker,
Department: **Redacted**,
Agency: **Redacted**

Jake sat in the communications center waiting for the sun to rise. After the briefing on the pattern the generals had all been skeptical about his theory, the only one that had shown the least bit of interest or belief was Admiral Charles, and at first, he was skeptical too. He asked, "what are they searching for?" I had to answer honestly, "I don't sir it's not in the numbers." He'd ordered the setup of a communications team, and commandeered a communications center then made sure all the proper intelligence was routed directly to these computers, which started broadcasting the search pattern the aliens were following with Jake's solution, the logical end point of their search.

THIRTY MINUTES UNTIL SUNRISE OVER TARGET, a chyron ran across his computer screen.

Jake wasn't military, at least not anymore. The intelligence agency he worked for was so far underground it didn't even have the usual government acronym, the alphabetic designation that for the more popular agencies rolled off of people's tongues with revered and romantic connotations, and people innately knew from birth what their missions were. Acronyms like NASA, FBI, CIA, EPA, FDA, but his agency didn't exist, it was a white hole on a document, a blackened line on government budgets, memos and directories, and if you called the Pentagon and asked for him or his department you were curtly told no one by that name works there and no such department existed. After you hung up the call was traced, and an investigation was started. The communications team assigned to him were asleep on the cots that had been brought into the room in the event of a response to the broadcast.

Jake had been watching for hours as the sun rose around the globe, and soon the sun would rise over the target city, from the data he'd collated, the end point of the search pattern. It would either prove or disprove his theory. He knew if the U.F.O.'s and aliens were real the ships wouldn't appear over the capitals of the world, or out in the middle of nowhere, nor en-masse scattered across the globe. The arrival wouldn't be foretold by prophesy, angelic visitations or mysterious lights. Jake had found the pattern out of the noise of the numbers.

TEN MINUTES UNTIL SUNRISE OVER TARGET

He started out with the raw data of all reported U.F.O. sightings, he eliminated all mistaken identifications, frauds, and natural phenomena. There were only a few sightings left that were authentic U.F.O.'s., but it was just a mass of data that looked more than anything like background noise. One afternoon, he was out in his garden and saw a praying mantis. He looked at it and it turned its head and looked right at him. He thought it was the most alien creature he'd ever seen, and started to wonder how it perceived him? How did it perceive the world? How many variations of the world did it see through the different facets of its eyes? He asked himself, is our perception of the world any truer than the mantis'? He started imaging how an alien might perceive the world using these insights and I just started applying different perceptual models to the sightings and when he was running the thousandth or so model the pattern 'popped' out of the numbers.

ONE MINUTE UNTIL SUNRISE OVER TARGET

As the sun rose over Jerusalem the computers in the communication center bounced to life filling their screens with incoming data.

"Well, that didn't take long." Jake said to himself, "wake up everybody," Jake said over the comm system, "we have company." There was a moment's hesitation of those drowsing on the cots, half-awake listening and waiting while the other half of their minds were off in a dream. As Jake's words seeped through their consciousness everyone jumped to their posts, fumbling over themselves to get their equipment functioning and collecting the data they were assigned to.

"O'Donnell get me some pictures of this thing; I don't care if you have to pull it off a video feed or even some kid streaming it to his Facebook friends. Clark, give me some information, what's it doing?"

"Just hovering, but it's broadcasting! And it's blowing our ears off! It's overriding and blasting past every other signal."

"What's it broadcasting?"

"The pattern…and there's some other information."

"What is it?"

"Looks like, coordinates and a time."

On the large video screen above Jake's head a coherent picture manifested in a flicker of excited electrons and protons, and there it was, a U.F.O. glimmering in the morning light, solid, tangible, hovering over the city. Jake picked up a phone unable to take his eyes off the image, he hit a button on the console, "admiral, we have a visitor," and he hung up the phone. It was only a minute before Admiral Charles rushed into the room, his eyes automatically drawn to the video image.

"Jesus, Jake! Your idea worked! You've called down the gods from the sky! What do we know about this thing so far?"

"At sunrise local time it appeared over the city and started broadcasting the pattern back at us with the addition of coordinates and a time."

"What do you mean it 'appeared' over the city? Didn't any of our satellites catch it coming in?"

"No, sir, there was no incoming track."

"Ok, what coordinates is it broadcasting?"

"Checking now," Clark said, then looked up from her computer screen, a look of disbelief on her face. "Sir, the coordinates are immediately below the craft."

"That's weird," the admiral said, "what's there?"

"The church of the Holy Sepulchre."

"Wow!" The Admiral said out loud, "Clark, we need to clamp down on this immediately, mark it as classified and move it to a code word protected server. This can't get out, at least not immediately, we need to get more information."

"What is it sir?" Jake asked.

"The church of the Holy Sepulchre?" Jake shrugged, "it's the area reputed to be where Jesus was crucified and buried."

A look of disbelief came over Jake's face, "that has to be a coincidence sir. You can't throw a stone anywhere in Jerusalem without it hitting something of religious significance."

"It's always been assumed that contact with an alien race would challenge our conceptions about God."

"Yes, but that was more of our psychological reaction to contact, a fear that our idea of God would become obsolete, not something so ...."

"What?"

"Overt, sir."

"God has always been part of the space program from "Godspeed John Glenn, to reading Genesis in orbit around the moon."

"Do you believe something of a religious nature is going to happen there, sir?"

"Jerusalem is the center of three religions, and has been for over two thousand years, and it's where your search pattern brought us to. There are those out there who won't believe it a coincidence, they'll misinterpret their intentions as divine, miraculous, they believe religion explains more than science."

"Are you one sir?"

"No. Don't you believe there's something out there greater than yourself Jake?"

"I believe the aliens would qualify as that sir. And I believe we're Godwired to a certain extent."

"Godwired?"

"We're hardwired to believe in God because it's easier to believe there's something out there looking over us, protecting us rather than being crushed by the knowledge that we're alone and there's nothing else out there, to keep ourselves from going mad as a species."

The admiral thought for a moment, "or if I can play Devil's advocate for a moment longer, maybe it's the memory of our creator implanted in us, so we won't forget?"

"Can you imagine being a primitive human standing under the canopy of the stars, the awesomeness of the universe threatening to overcome you, and the horrible silence to our questions, so we created stories to warm ourselves by torchlight in cold European caves, from the cave wall to television we've tried to answer those questions."

"You don't think religion has answered those questions?"

"Those answers are five-thousand years old, probably older. As far as I know sir, we're the only species that feels a need for a deity."

"Admiral," Clark said, "we have a top-secret communication for you from Mossad."

"Let me see it." He read the communique, then said to Jake, "Looks like those questions are about to be answered. The Israelis are setting-up a command center adjacent to the coordinates to observe and interact with the extraterrestrials if such an opportunity presents itself. We've had a team in place for this since the late seventies."

"A team?"

"In case of an encounter... of this nature, it was decided that there should be some protocols set-up and conclusions were drawn, protocols written, and directives issued. But no one could decide what disciplines would be best suited for the encounter. No one believed them and the protocols weren't maintained."

"What were the disciplines decided?"

"The first member has always been the person who made the breakthrough on the U.F.O.'s because it was assumed that person would be a scientist and that person and would have some insight into a way to communicate with the aliens. The other two are a little more dogmatic."

"What are they?"

"The second member is a member of the clergy because of the religious implications and the third, a member of the military to help keep a lid on everything. You better get going Jake, you don't have much time."

"Me?! I'm not so sure about that sir, I'm good at finding patterns that doesn't necessarily reveal their thinking process."

"Do you think you could communicate with them?"

"I don't know, perception is one thing, communication another. How might they communicate? A recent study has established that music from all cultures has universal themes, other species from earth are known to communicate in song, whales for instance, maybe music is truly a universal language."

"Are you saying they communicate by music?"

"No, it's just a hypothetical among thousands, maybe millions of variables of evolution."

"That's it Jake, your mind is open to the possibilities, whatever is going to happen out there, your mind is facile enough to act and react without being hampered by the constraints of either military discipline or religious dogma."

"If I may sir?" Clark said.

"Yes."

"They've been responding to our broadcasting the pattern, and whether it's a matter of perception or communication it seems they've found a way to understand our communications. Wouldn't they have found a way to communicate with us too? After all, they're the advanced race."

"Jake, we barely have time to get you there before the time coordinates elapse. The clock is running."

"Yes sir."

"What is supposed to happen when the local time matches the time coordinates?"

"We're hypothesizing ...contact."

"Contact?"

"Why else would they broadcast the pattern back to us with a time code? They could've just used the information of the search patterns end point and collected whatever they're looking for and left, leaving us with just another mystery. They Israelis are assembling a team to encounter the aliens and I want you there Jake."

II

Eleven hours later Jake was in Israel. As his car approached the command center, he saw the U.F.O. for the first time, it was huge, covering almost half a city block. Much of his life had been filtered by video feeds, pictures, data feeds, and intelligence reports, he'd never been a field agent, he was an analyst always confined to the walls of cubicles and offices. The reality of it was almost beyond his ability to comprehend. To Jake the juxtaposition of images looked incompatible, impossible, an advanced craft hovering over the ancient structure.

As much as he didn't want to admit it to the admiral there were the sociological and maybe even religious implications of a vehicle of probable alien origin hovering over the church, just the knowledge of its existence would lead to many a step forward for mankind.

The Israeli military had set-up a command center in a tent a couple of blocks away from the hovering craft. There was a lot of activity swirling around Jake, there were twenty to thirty people there and ten percent were always in motion, but never the same ten percent. There were communications, there was a reconnaissance team being briefed, the military had set-up a perimeter to keep the press and onlookers away. And there was a digital countdown clock that was in motion too. A lieutenant in the Israeli army came up to him.

"Mister Walker?" She inquired.

"Yes."

"Lieutenant Dahan, Israeli intelligence. Have you been briefed since you arrived?"

"No, I literally just walked in."

"We've reconnoitered the craft, done flyover's, flybys, sent drones in to get a closer look, we've even bounced radar off of it, and we've come up with what we think is a fairly good idea of the size of the ship and what the volume inside it may be."

"And?"

"We've estimated it could hold easily hold a couple hundred people, maybe more. You and me and one other are the team going up into the craft. The broadcast has ceased, we have about an hour before we catch up to the time coordinates the craft broadcast."

"Who is the third?"

"We're also waiting for Doctor Weinhart."

"Doctor?"

"Now, now," a voice from behind said, they turned to see a man who looked too young to carry the title of Doctor, but had the calm, peaceful countenance of a cleric.

"Doctor Weinhart," the lieutenant said, "this is Jake Walker, American intelligence." They shook hands, "Doctor Weinhart is an expert on the Torah as well as a scholar on all things ancient, and mister Walker was the one who solved the problem of the alien search pattern."

"Rabbi David Weinhart," he said extending a hand, "I have dual degrees in theology, so I am a rabbi and an archaeologist, so technically I'm also a doctor."

"Of which?"

"Both, theology and archaeology, for Israel it's the best of both worlds."

"I see."

"Jake, that would not be short for Jacob, would it?"

"Yes, it is, my parents named me Jacob."

"Is it not ironic then that you're one to make contact with the aliens?"

"How so?"

"In your Old Testament it was Jacob who climbed the ladder to heaven to talk with God."

"More like Jonah waiting to go up into the belly of the beast." Jake said, "I'm sorry, I'm afraid I'm not very religious. I'm not Jewish, I'm American. I've been Jake since the moment I was born it only says Jacob on my birth certificate because that is the formalization of Jake. I was raised Catholic, and that ended. "

"When?"

"When I learned to love the logic of numbers, they add up, they make sense. Numbers don't lie, the solution to a problem leads to a truth, it brought this craft here."

"You don't believe in God?"

"Depends on what day you ask me."

"What about today?"

"Maybe, you've been looking for God in the numbers all along Jacob? Don't you find it alien to love a number?" Rabbi Weinhart asked.

"Alien is what we're here for."

"This craft may be proof of something entirely different."

"Why is everyone of the opinion that something of a religious nature is going to happen here?"

"In Israel," Lieutenant Dahan said, "everything religious is political and everything political is religious. No one is sure what is *supposed* to happen here your guess is as good as any."

"It seems to me that U.F.O.s have been projections of what we want them to be, angels, demons, or Gods. If we've been nervous about nuclear weapons, they're here to stop us or to reassure us, what they've never been is a thing unto themselves." The countdown clock reached zero.

III

An aperture opened in the bottom of the craft, a pod emerged, and then it was hovering noiselessly just above the ground, had they blinked? Had the pod descended so fast that in one moment it could be in the air and the next hovering at ground level? Or had they witnessed some other process? Teleportation? Was it "beamed" down? Jake understood this wasn't magic just a technology he didn't understand, or perhaps couldn't yet comprehend. An aperture opened in the side of the pod, they all looked at each other.

"Well?" Jake asked.

"It's another step up the ladder Jacob." Rabbi Weinhart said.

Inside, the pod was spacious or at least seemed to be. It was all glossy white, there was a lot of light but no visible source of it. There was no horizon, no way to gauge the depth, size, or height of the room, no seam at a corner, no curvature of a rounded wall, or even an observable wall. An opening about eight feet long and three feet wide appeared. They couldn't tell if it was a window that had opened to an adjacent room of if it was an opening in space. Inside the window were four beings that were vaguely humanoid, though they seemed to change moment to moment, as if they were in some inchoate state.

"To answer your questions," the words and sounds appeared in their minds, an ambient voice that seemed to come from everywhere and nowhere, it wasn't sound reverberating off walls but echoing in their minds, they weren't sure which of the aliens was communicating with them. "We cannot join you because the gravity of your world and the composition of gases that sustain you would not sustain our life, we are beings of deep space, we live between the stars, we're no longer limited by terrestrial concerns. Each of you perceives us differently, the form you see in the window, think of it not as a window, but a mirror of your subconscious, our images conform to your expectations. The images you perceive as 'us' are there for your convenience, our form is quite different than yours."

"You understand our language?"

The answer came back so fast it almost bordered on precognition, "yes, we understand your languages. To us it is like one language, it's quite simple, although there are other creatures that inhabit your world who have much more complex forms of communication. You don't need to vocalize your questions we discern them from the chaos of your competing thoughts."

"Where are we?" Lieutenant Dahan asked.

"You're still in the pod."

"The pod is in the ship? I didn't feel any acceleration."

"If what we witnessed of the speed of the pod is accurate, I would have to say, yes, we're in the alien ship." Jake said.

"Why are you here?" Rabbi Weinhart asked.

"We're in search of knowledge." The humans looked perplexed.

"You're looking for answers?" Lieutenant Dahan asked, "I thought aliens were supposed to be the advanced technology, to bring us all the answers, to bring us knowledge, the cure for cancer, cheap power sources, new propulsion systems, the secret to immortality, peace."

"Those are the questions we have, they sought us out, they have their own questions." Rabbi Weinhart said.

"It makes sense," Jake said, "it's always been assumed they would come with answers for us but why would they travel vast distances of interstellar space to give us answers? How would they even know what the questions would be? On our voyages of discovery were we ever the bringers of knowledge? We were always seeking something whether it was a route to India or gold."

"And those explorers were never the bringers of peace." Weinhart said.

Everyone was silent. Were these aliens the equivalent of Columbus and all that he brought to the new world? Or were they the peaceful explorers of the stars we've always imagined ourselves to be? The arrival of extraterrestrial life has long been prophesized in science fiction books and movies, radio broadcasts, TV shows and speculation by visionaries, dreamers, the fearful, and even stoned philosophers. All had different theories most seemed to side with the benevolent alien hypotheses.

"We have many questions as well, where do you come from? Is there more life in the universe?" Jake asked.

"Life is common, life that advances to the technological is not so common, it isn't necessary to most life. Species that step out of the natural order are the ones that suffer the most. What brings us to your planet is a most serious matter. It is a matter of the soul."

"The soul?" Weinhart said, "you know of the soul?"

"It is an absolute in the universe. We're in search of the universal one."

"The universal one?" They all looked at one another, perplexed.

"What is that?"

"The universal one is a primal being, it is energy that incorporates into the beings it is helping. There is a lot we don't understand about it, there's a membrane between its nature and the rest of the universe."

"What makes you think this 'universal one' is here?" Jake asked.

"We detected it; it was a burst of radiation."

"Radiation? What kind of radiation?"

"It is far more than radiation though, it is a rift in the fabric of everything, it rippled through time and space. We have searched for it throughout the galaxy."

"What is the nature of this, uh, rift?"

"There's a lot about its nature we don't understand, it doesn't occur on every world, only those worlds that are in jeopardy."

"Where did you detect this radiation?"

"From another part of the universe from a measure of distance you think of as two-thousand light years away."

"What kind of radiation could have been released two-thousand years ago?"

"Your discovery of the pattern and its end point lead us to where it originated from, we are above that area now."

"Jerusalem?" The three looked at each other, again.

"Are you saying this type of radiation was released two-thousand years ago?" Jake asked.

"In your conception of time."

"Oh, my God," Jake said, "Jerusalem, two-thousand years ago, or more accurately, two-thousand and twenty-eight years ago?"

"Correct."

"The resurrection, of Jesus?" Dahan asked.

"This can't be?!" Jake said incredulously, "The first contact we make with extraterrestrials and they're searching for...for?"

"It could be a universal wish Jacob, they said the soul is universal," Weinhart said. "We know of this energy, we know it as Jesus, he lived in this land a long time ago. Some believe him to be the son of God. Is this search part of your religion?"

"What is religion?" One of the alien voices asked.

"It is how we worship God?"

"What is God?"

"The one who created the universe."

"The universe has always existed and will always exist."

"Is this energy or a being?"

"As we said, we don't understand its nature, whether energy or being, or as you believe, a deity. It exists in a state where physics meets metaphysics. We are scientists, we wish to study it and understand it."

"We wish to understand it, the universal one too," Weinhart said, "we have books to explain the universal one or that seek to explain it, they may be of help to you."

"This can't be real! They're searching for Jesus?"

"More than that Jake, they're searching for the Christ, the spiritual being, the metaphysical, resurrected entity."

"The resurrection could have been anything, the apostles knew a good story when they heard it, maybe they broke into the crypt and hid the body so it matched prophecy, mass hysteria from the grief of seeing their friend crucified, maybe it's a science these aliens don't understand, or it's just a coincidence and there was some natural release of radiation two-thousand years ago in Jerusalem."

"Jacob, even I have to admit that something happened here two-thousand years ago. Three days after the crucifixion the apostles start freaking out, running around saying Jesus was resurrected. Tell me," Weinhart said addressing the aliens, "why does the universal one visit these planets?"

"The universal one visits species in need."

"What kind of needs?"

"Worlds where the inhabitants have stepped out of the natural order, worlds that embrace technology and lose themselves."

"The universal one was killed here, one of our religions says that he was raised from the dead three days after he was killed, we call that the resurrection. Does that happen on every planet he visits?"

"The worlds he visits are in distress, they fear, and break the corporeal body, crushing the shell, the energy is released. It is indistinguishable from the beings that surround it until it disincorporates. We thought since the energy signature was so strong that he may still be here." The Rabbi in Weinhart felt sorry for the aliens they were chasing something they may never be able to catch.

The aliens seemed disconnected for a moment, their thoughts elsewhere as if communing with some other entity.

"We have detected the radiation in another part of the universe do you wish to come with us?"

The three looked at each other knowing what acceptance of the invitation would mean. Jake looked at Weinhart.

"What about you? Do you want to go? It's confirmation of what you've always believed. Maybe they will find the universal one this time."

"No Jacob, I don't need to, I have certainty, I know it's out there." Weinhart said gently, "this is the ultimate exploration, another step up the ladder, they're like you Jake, searchers, looking for God in the numbers, they want to believe, they're looking for a way, as you are."

"I guess, it's the last step up the ladder."

"Not the last Jacob but the next one."

Weinhart and Dahan watched as the pod melded back into the U.F.O. which accelerated and was gone as if it had never been there, nothing disturbed, as if it had never existed. Could it have been a dream? A mass delusion, a desire for the aliens to provide the answers everyone is looking for? The proof was in their number, they were minus one member. Jake was right, the truth lies in the numbers.

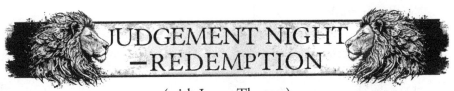

JUDGEMENT NIGHT
—REDEMPTION

(with Jovan Thomas)

"What do you know better than your own secrets?"
—Raymond Carver

L urid, strobing images flickered in his mind, illuminated by lightning flashes crashing off each other, in and out of focus, in the swirl and fog of a fevered dream. Wet darkness, a young woman's face washed out in the rain, a bus placard that says: Nashville. Men's ruddy faces, cruel masks of people, distorted, laughing. A whiskey bottle, a disembodied voice that echoes the words "guilty! I condemn you!" A bus sitting on a darkened road, its lights stretching out into the night. It was steeped in sepia and chiaroscuro, the color of memory. A scratching sound at the edge of consciousness. It doesn't seem human, a chittering sound that sounds far away but growing louder. As it gets closer the sound becomes coherent until he recognizes it as a voice speaking to him.

"Wake up pops!" The man opened his eyes. His head was resting on a window, a drop of rain splotched on the window, then another, and another. He didn't know where he was. He looked around, blue painted metal walls and the oblong windows of a bus, the scenery fleeing past, as the bus drove into the night.

"Hey pops!" One of the insect voices was saying, "are you alright?" The man looked around; a young cowboy was hanging over the back of his seat looking at him.

"Where am I?"

"Out in the middle of nowhere man."

Another cowboy poked his head above the other seat, "you ok, pops?" The cowboy asked, seeming concerned. "You look like you was havin' a bad dream."

"I'm fine." He said, not too convinced of what he said.

"Well, you look white as a sheet."

"Like you said, I was havin' a bad dream."

"Well, this is the place to have 'em." The second cowboy said.

"What'd you mean?"

"Doncha' know, pops?"

"Know what?" The man asked impatiently.

"It's just hereabouts they say this stretch of highway is haunted."

"Haunted? I don't believe in ghosts."

"Be careful they don't believe in you."

"Remember, not even the darkest secrets of men are safe."

"What's that supposed to mean?"

"I don' know," the cowboy said, "that's jus' how the story ends."

"I don't cotton to no stories."

"Take it easy, pops. It's just a tale mothers tell to scare their children."

"What's your name pops?"

The man looked around the bus as if its walls contained the answer. "I don't know," he said mystified. "I just woke up…here."

"Doncha' remember anything, pops? What about your pockets?" The man did a fast pat down of his shirt and pants pockets and found them empty.

"Man, you been on some kind of bender? You better remember before we get to the end of the line."

The man looked out the window but, saw only his face staring back, reflecting off the darkness outside. A thought came to him, "Forrest. I think Forrest may be my name."

"You mean like, you can't see the forest for the trees?" The cowboys fell back into their seats choking on their laughter. One of them picked a up a guitar sitting on the floor between them and started strumming on the out of tune instrument, their drunken singing closer to a caterwaul, "bury my body down by the highway side, so my old evil spirit can get a Greyhound bus and ride." Their laughter degenerated into guffaws as they collapsed further back into their seats.

A couple of rows up a young mother reached into her satchel for a baby's bottle. One rolled out of the cloth bag, clinking down the aisleway, glass on metal, coming to a stop against Forrest's boot. He looked down at it apprehensively, as if it were something to be afraid of. The young black woman leaned around her seat, a baby in her arms wrapped in blankets.

"You mind sir?" He looked up at her as if trying to remember what the words meant, "sir?"

"Huh? What?" The woman pointed to the bottle at his feet. "If you don't mind?"

He picked up the bottle, a feeling of foreboding washed over him. He walked up the aisle to the woman and child.

"Thank you," she said holding out her hand for the bottle.

"Oh," he said, still distracted by his thoughts, "yes, of course." He handed her the bottle, then walked to a seat a row in front of the woman. Everything seemed familiar, as if he'd been there before, yet unfamiliar.

He turned back to the woman. "Excuse me." She looked up.

"Yes?"

"Do I know you?"

"No sir."

"Do you know me?" She looked at him, trying to place him in her memory. He looked wan, sick, sweating nervously.

"No sir, I don't think so."

"It's just that you look familiar to me, but I don't know you. It's like I've seen you..." his voice trailing off. He saw the woman's face in the dream, it was her. "Maybe it was just the dream," he said softly.

"Are you ok, sir?"

"I...I don't know," he said. "Did you see me get on the bus?"

"No, you were already on the bus when I got on. I was busy with my boy getting us settled in. Is something the matter?"

"I don't remember getting on the bus."

"What do you remember?"

"I've been thinking about that. I remember a dream then waking up here on the bus when it started raining. That's it. I can't remember anything before that. I don't even remember who I am."

"Did you check your pockets to see if you have a wallet?"

"No, I've already checked. I don't even have a bus ticket." He looked around the bus, "the faces of the people, your face, I think I saw them in my dream, but it's all smoke and haze, there's nothing there to hang onto."

"It was only a dream, sir."

"No, it's more than a dream, it feels like something I...something I don't understand, a future or maybe a past I don't want." He looked out the window apprehensively at the passing night. The woman looked scared.

"Maybe you just need more sleep an' you'll feel better."

The tension seemed to leave Forrest's face. "You're probably right," he said trying to change the conversation. "You have a beautiful baby."

A look of sadness passed over the women's face. "Thank you, sir," she whispered, meekly.

"Is something the matter?"

"No sir...yes sir," she tripped over her words, her thoughts. "The truth of it is I was raped a year ago and I couldn't get an abortion."

"I'm sorry," he said, "sorry to hear that."

"I know he's just a baby, an I should love him. I know he's innocent an all and he didn't have anything to do with how he got here, but sometimes I jus' look at him and see the father's face and I jus' want to get even with him, an it's all I can do not to push him away, or worse." A tear ran down her cheek.

"I, I'm sorry, I wish there was something, I, I...."

"Somethin' you could do?" She asked.

"Yes...." Forrest said, realizing there was nothing he could do. His voice trailed off. He turned around in the seat and faced forward.

Forrest fell into a discomfited sleep. Something was gnawing at his consciousness, trying to break through, trying to get in, to get him. At the same time, he was vaguely aware of everything that was going on around him—what people were saying, the motion of the bus, even the static of the radio as it struggled to play the driver's race music. It sounded vaguely like the song the cowboys had been struggling to sing earlier. The song seemed familiar like he'd heard it before, in a long-ago half-forgotten dream, close enough to touch but still out of reach. Why did he keep hearing it? It was like it, or someone was trying to tell him something. The thought that had been gnawing at his mind solidified into an urgent question. He opened his eyes and made his way to the front of the bus. The driver was an old negro in his 50's with gray hair, and a rounded stomach. He was wearing the gray pin striped uniform of the bus line. His clothes were oversized on him. They billowed and flowed around him like a robe. His jacket hung off the back of his seat. On the far side of the man's shirt hung an engraved name plate with the letters C-h-a-r. That was all he could see the rest was obscured by a fold in the shirt. The driver's foot pressed down the big flat accelerator pedal, pushing the bus further into the night. He noticed the man sidling up next to him.

"What's your name boy? Charles?"

"No sir. It's Charon. Take a seat, sir."

"I have to ask you something."

"Take a seat," the driver said, motioning to the closest empty seat. "Company rules, safety precautions, sir." Forrest sat down on the edge of the nearest seat. He leaned in towards the driver so he could hear him.

"When did I get on the bus?"

"What?" The driver asked, annoyed by being distracted from his job by the obviously ridiculous question.

"I asked, when did I get on the bus?"

"At the terminal," the driver replied, incredulously.

"You saw me?"

"You paid your money and got on jus' like everybody else."

"I paid you?"

"Yes, sir, two silver dollars, jus' like everybody else."

"I don't have a ticket."

"I didn't give you one, I know who paid."

"Where'd I get on?"

"Dutchman."

"Where'n the hell is that?"

"Dutchman? Dutchman, Tennessee?" Forrest sat down, confused, something didn't seem right. Just then the radio crackled with static and the sound of frayed wires just this side of shorting out, and a faraway voice came from the speaker. "Breaking news. Convicted rapist, *crackle*, Forrest, *crackle*, escaped earlier, *crackle*, and may be trying to leave the area. He's described as being six feet tall, white, *zzzzt*, thirty-five years old, sandy hair…" Then the radio cut out altogether. The driver banged on the dashboard.

"Damn radio." He looked over at Forrest. "That sounds like it could be you."

"What do you mean by that!" Forrest snapped, jumping towards the driver.

"It was a joke, sir! I din't mean nothin' by it."

"That description could be a lot of people."

"Yes, sir that could be a lot of people."

"Rapist!" Forrest whispered louder than he meant to. He looked over at the girl with the baby. "Where's this bus going?"

"Nashville."

"How long until we get there?"

"Usually, a couple of hours from here, but with all this rain the roads are all muddy, and it looks like another storm is rollin' in." Forrest looked out the window and saw storm clouds illuminated by lightning visible in the distance. He sat back down. He noticed the man who was sitting in the seat next to him. He looked to be in his late fifties or early sixties. He had white hair, rosy cheeks and the pacific look of a cleric on his face.

"Would you like a sandwich, my boy?"

"No thank you, I'm not hungry."

The old man looked out the window. "It's been raining something terrible; I'm surprised it's not a river out there. Although, I guess this road is ferrying us to where we're goin'. What's your name, son?"

"I can't seem to remember who I am or where I'm going, or why I'm going there. And to tell you the truth, like the driver said, that guy on the radio sounds a lot like me."

"The escaped prisoner?" The old man looked skeptical. "Look at your clothes, those aren't prison issue."

"The only part of a name I can remember is Forrest, and that convict's name is Bedford Forrest."

"Son, around these here parts Forrest isn't an uncommon name. Just because you remember the name Forrest doesn't mean anything. Your name could as well be Smith or even Jones."

"I guess you could be right," Forrest said. "You see the woman back there with the baby?"

"Yes?"

"I think I saw her in my dream."

"Are you sure?"

"No."

"I thought so. Could it be you had a dream with a woman, and you filled in a blank with the face of the first woman you saw?"

"Yes! You're right! I just wish I could remember."

"It's a dark and stormy night, it's enough to throw anybody off. You don't remember, you're struggling to put things together, you hear a report, your mind wants to make order out of the chaos, and suddenly two and two make five."

"The cowboy in the back told me this road is haunted."

"Old wives' tales, ghost stories. Around these parts folks like a good, dark, gothic story. It's a part of us, a part of our culture. But still a good many terrible things could happen out here."

"What do you mean?"

"Do you know the original meaning of the word 'uncivilized'?"

"No."

"It means to live outside of the city, and my boy, right now we're uncivilized."

"I have this feeling of foreboding like something is coming to get me. What if I am that guy?"

"What makes you think something like that?"

"This feeling of dread, like something evil is coming for me, that's part of me."

"My boy, I've just met you, and you do seem haunted. But before you let it go to your head, I don't mean by ghosts or anything like that. Something is haunting you—it may be an event, or even something you didn't do or did do. To find forgiveness in the world you have to find it in yourself. You have to make amends with whatever is haunting you."

"Are you a priest or something?"

"No," he said chuckling a little, "I'm just a retired judge, traveling around the country to see the things I've always wanted to see and now I'm heading home."

"Not a teacher?"

"No, you could say I've taught people lessons in my judgements."

"You seem pretty wise."

"No, I've just talked with a lot of people on the bus and listened to their stories. You should see all the stranger souls I've met on this bus."

"How am I supposed to make amends for something when I can't even remember what it is?"

"It's hard to see what's inside a man's soul, what haunts him."

"Back to the ghosts."

"Maybe we're all ghosts," the teacher smiled, "ghosts of memory. We're held by our memories or other's memories of us, or even by events and places. Maybe ghosts are created because we remember. So, as you see, in a manner of speaking we're all ghosts."

"What do you mean?"

"You may not remember what it is, but you know in your heart what is haunting you. When you do remember, you can make amends if you want to, but you have to want to make peace with it and ask for forgiveness. It'll be the hardest thing you'll ever do, and you may not be able to do it on the first try. From what I've seen in life most people prefer the easy road. You're on a hard road, my boy," he said, smiling, "but you'll make the right choice."

"How do you know that?"

"Because you're worried about it."

✳

The bus turned off the road into a small town. It drove through the streets of the closed-up and dark town until it pulled up in front of a small wooden building. Forrest woke with a start from the braking of the bus and the idling engine. Forrest looked out the window, the bus was stopped in front of a building that had large wooden windows from which a warm light shone out into the night. Inside, there were four or five wooden benches, on the back wall, some dime lockers, and off to the side a ticket agent's window with bars across the front. It was closed.

"What're we doing here?"

"One last passenger to pick-up, one last soul to get to where they're going," the driver said. Forrest saw that there was one person standing on the platform in the rain, a dark shrouded shadow. The driver opened the door and a woman got on. She paid her fare to the driver, turned and saw Forrest.

"Oh my," she said, recoiling a bit.

"You know me?" He asked.

"No, not really, but…."

"But what?!" He almost screamed.

"You look like the man in the newspaper that they locked up and threw away the key."

"Why, what'd he do?"

"Serial rapist, been terrorizn' Nashville and hereabouts for a coupla' years. But you can't be him, he's in prison."

"Prison," he said, dejectedly.

"An' he's gonna' be there for a long time, he got a coupla' life sentences, an' I hope he serves every last day of them, an' then some. A lot of the things he did happened right around here."

"Well, if he's the same guy, there was a report a while ago on the radio sayin' he escaped." The driver said.

"There's only one like him. I hope they catch him soon," the woman said.

"And you're sure I look like him?"

"Pretty much, there's some semblance."

"I'm getting off here," Forrest said, getting up and moving towards the door.

"What do you want to get off here for?" The driver asked. "This town is closed up tight until morning, and I don't think it's all that lively then either."

"If something is out there in the country, something wild and evil, something uncivilized," he said looking at the teacher, "I'll be safe here in the city." There was an awkward moment, where nobody knew what to do or say and nobody moved. The radio came to life with a crackle of static and the news report came on in mid-report,

"...who broke out of prison earlier today has been found dead in a field. The police think he was heading to the woods to a hideout." Forrest looked relieved. He noticed the rain had stopped.

"See you ain't him sir, you ain't dead," the driver said, "at least you don't look dead to me." Everybody within hearing distance laughed at this including Forrest, who finally seemed at ease, his fears put to rest. "What's it gonna be sir?" The driver asked. "You know the guy is dead, the weather's improvin', and I have a schedule to keep, you comin' along or you gonna' sit here in this empty bus station with not another soul in sight?" Forrest took a minute to consider, looked out the door at the dead city, and back to the bus, considering what it was—the only world he knew, the only place he was safe.

"I'm comin'. There's nothin' here for me and nothin' I want from here. Let's go."

Everybody settled into a seat, Forrest at last looked peaceful and at ease. The door hissed closed, and the driver put the bus in gear. It lurched forward through the dead town. Forrest watched the bus's headlights reflected off the darkened buildings and shiny streets as it wound its way back to the road. As the bus turned onto the highway, he noticed one side of the road was a forest and the other was open country. The road cut them in half like an asphalt river. The yellow headlights of the bus stretching out into the night until they were absorbed by the surrounding darkness ahead. The red break lights at the back of the bus got smaller as the bus moved down the road and farther into the night. Forrest nodded off into a peaceful sleep.

Everyone in the bus had fallen asleep except the driver. The inside lights had been turned off. The only light was the eerie green fluorescence of the dashboard lights and the bus's headlights reaching out into the darkness. Raindrops started hitting the windows and Forrest's eyes jerked open. He heard the rain splotching against the glass. Through the front window he could see lightning in the near distance. His eyes again betrayed a desperation. He remembered something from the dream. Frightened, he jumped out of his seat, rushing towards the back of the bus where the cowboys were. He shook the nearest one. trying to wake him.

"Wake up!" Forrest yelled.

"Wha???"

"You said this road is supposed to be haunted?"

"Yeah, so what? I wanna' go back to sleep."

"What's the story?"

"What?"

"What's the story? What happened here? What ghosts are supposed to haunt round here?"

"Don'cha know?" The cowboy asked, "haven't you figured it out yet?" Forrest looked perplexed. "This is the ghost story. The ghost bus that rides these roads carrying souls to their redemption or their damnation. Here it is boy, the end of the road." Forrest pushed himself away from the cowboy.

"I'm not dead," he yelled, "what are we doing here?" Forrest looked out the window, at the slow-moving scenery, it was familiar, déjà vu, but it was more. He knew what was going to happen, he noticed he wasn't breathing. It hasn't happened, or hasn't happened yet, his eyes widened as revelation swarmed through his mind, "STOP!" He screamed. "Stop the bus!" The driver smashed his foot down on the brake, they caught, the tires screeched, and the bus swerved back and forth across the wet road as he struggled keep the bus under control. Forrest was thrown to the floor by the unseen forces of nature which he'd never been educated on, but of which he was nevertheless subject to. The bus skidded off the road coming to an abrupt halt, sitting on the side of the road its headlights shining out into the rainy night. The driver was out of his seat and headed back towards Forrest.

"I thought you was over this?!" He yelled at Forrest; a glint of light shone on the name plate on his breast. "You have to stop frighten' my passengers sir, there's nothin' out there except the night, I don't know what has you spooked maybe it's just you're in a country you're not familiar with, the storm, the escaped prisoner. I've driven this route every night for years, I know every turn, every bump. If you knew the road like I do you'd know there's nothin' out there to be afraid of."

"I know what's suppos'd to happen! If we went any farther, we'd have gotten a flat tire! Everything I know, I can feel it in my bones, I know there's something out there waiting for me, something I don't want to meet up with."

"What's out there boy?"

"I don't know but I can feel it waiting for me, coming nearer," he stopped to think, "or maybe it's already here," he turned to the girl with the baby, "stop this," he said, softly, "I can't do this anymore. I'm tired. It feels like I've been here before, done this before, like I'm locked into some cycle, it's like dying every night only to be reborn back to this moment, night after night, year after year, it feels like centuries, it's like some jail sentence, and I have a feeling you have something to do with it, and you can stop it!"

"Stop what sir?" She asked, frightened. "I ain't doin' nothin'."

"But things have changed this time! I know it!"

"You said you know what's going to happen?"

"You punched me before and…and I always got on in Lethe before!" He looked at them, no one said anything, they were dumbfounded, "can this change? I know this is different! Tell me! If events can change, can I change them?! Tell me! I can…change."

"If you like."

"I can prove it! Come outside with me and take a look at the tire!"

"Le's take a look," Charon said. They stepped off the bus, it had stopped raining, everything was wet. The bus was sitting off to the side of the road in damp grass, in the distance he could see the woods. They walked around to the rear of the bus and looked at the tires. Then they saw it, one of tires was shredded, the rubber was peeling off, and a blister of rubber was bubbling up in-between, ready to blow. It looked like a clawed hand had reached out and grabbed it. Forrest ran his hand over the shredded tire.

"See didn't I tell you!" He said, "another half mile, who knows, maybe a coupla' feet and the tire was going to blow!"

"It doesn't matter sir, we're on the other side."

"The other side of what?"

Charon smiled, "we've crossed to the other side of the river."

A sound came from the woods, it was distinct. Forrest looked around for who, what or where the sound had come from, but there was nothing.

A look of realization came over his face, "only something evil can reach out like that, and its coming for me!" He didn't want to confront it, whatever it was, but he knew if he didn't, he'd never be free of it. The sound of the bus's engine stopped, it didn't sputter, it wasn't turned off, it was just gone, as if it had never been there. He turned around, the driver was nowhere to be seen; he'd disappeared. Forrest walked around to the front of the bus, it was a rusted hulk, he looked inside, it was dark and cold, the seats were torn, and the windows broken. It was a dead thing, it looked as if it had been rusting away in the weeds for decades. He looked out into the night in horror. Everything he knew, his world was dying away, but something was missing, a final piece of the jigsaw just outside of his grasp. He started running down the road, away from the woods, away from the bus. The road was wet and muddy, but he kept running, running until his face was more sweat than rain, until he couldn't inhale or exhale anymore, until time and distance had separated him from the bus, until he forgot what he was running for, what he was running from, until he felt like a clean slate, new, and without a past, without a future, only now, only the moment. He slowed to a walk, finally catching his breath, finally feeling that what was chasing him was behind.

Ahead of him he saw a figure in the darkness walking slowly. He could only make out a shape, a shadow that was a little darker than the surrounding night. As he got closer the shape solidified, it was a woman he could see the outlines of a skirt and her small frame.

"Miss! Miss, what're you doing out here?" He called out, she stopped and turned around, he looked at her puzzled, she looked like the woman on the bus, yet she didn't, she looked younger, her face untroubled, confident, happy, 'is that all it takes to change someone's face?' he wondered, "what're you doing out here so late and alone?"

"Jus' walkin' home from work sir."

"Weren't you just on the bus with me a while ago?"

"Bus sir?" She said looking puzzled, "the last bus came through here hours ago."

"It's running late because of the rain and a flat tire." She looked at him as if he was crazy. "Let me walk you home, make sure you get there safely."

"I preciate that sir, but I'm just up the road a bit."

"There's something I have to make up for and I want to make sure you get home safely; I think it'll atone for what I've done."

"Suit yourself."

They walked along the road silently; she watched him warily out of the corner of her eye. He kept his eyes focused ahead on the road, it was barren, only the asphalt and the open spaces that surrounded it. As they walked along, he saw a light coming over the horizon. The crack of dawn as his mother used to call it, she used to say it was an in between time where anything could happen, it was still neither light nor dark, it was as if a door was opening and they had walked through, between the worlds of darkness and light, it was the crossroads of eternity.

In the distance was a copse of trees, walking towards them on the road were two men. As they got closer Forrest could see they were swigging off a bottle of whiskey and passing it between them, they were dressed in black rain slickers, jeans and cowboy boots. Although their faces looked harder, and there were no jokes between them now, he recognized them right away, it was the cowboys from the bus.

"Bout time you showed up boss," one of the men said.

"You're from the bus, do I know you?"

"We're here." The woman said.

"Where!?" Forrest asked, the panic back in his voice.

"Where you've feared to be," she said, "the far shore you've been afraid to reach, the moment to atone for your sins or be bound to them. The decision is yours."

"Course, you know us boss," the other cowboy said, "you said to meet you out here."

"And you brought us the tasty morsel you promised us." One of the cowboys grabbed the girl, twisted her arm behind her, while the other groped her.

"No! Please stop this!" She screamed, then looking right at Forrest, "Bedford, you've always been the one who can stop this!"

"Bedford......?" He mumbled, "so it is me. I am the escaped prisoner, the rapist," with the realization a final wall in his mind crumbled as if from the pressure of a flood, memories rushed from his subconscious, he remembered his cruel life, the predator, nameless faces of women, faces that were battered, afraid, women's limbs that were bound, writhing, faces that had been gagged. He smiled cruelly at the memory of remembering who he is, of what he is. The knowledge changed him from the frightened man on the bus to the confident fiendishly dangerous creature of the night. He knew the monster that was himself, he remembered all that had happened before, he remembered the ugliness, he knew he had a choice, be the person he'd always been and suffer the consequences he'd always had, prison, fear, hatred, loathing, or choose the unknown and let it all go. He didn't know what would happen, but he just might break the chains that kept him locked in this nightmare, night after night. "I'm afraid," Bedford said, I've only known this life."

"It's ok, Bedford, you've spent your life crossing the river towards death, it may seem like you're stepping over a chasm, but it's only a step over a stream."

"Bedford Forrest," he spat out.

"What'd you say Bedford?" One of the cowboys said.

"Nothin', leave her alone."

"What're you talking about Bedford?"

"Let her go!" Then he turned to the girl, "I've lived through this night for too long, I've experienced the fear and terror I put in you, you'll never have to live through this again."

"Nothin's stoppin' us." One of the cowboys said, pulling the girl towards him.

"Your power and strength flows through me, if you try to hurt her, I will stop you, without me your evil doesn't exist."

"Yeah?!" They tightened their grip on the girl and moved to drag her off into the grass, but they were nothing without Bedford, without his darkness they dissolved and dissipated into nothingness, the girl was free of their grip.

"It's going to be light soon."

Forrest wandered off into the glistening dewy grass. He wandered through the grass until he came to a circular clearing that was burned into the grass, it was about ten feet in diameter, in the middle was a mound of earth that couldn't be anything except a shallow grave. He walked around the perimeter looking at the mound when a voice boomed out of the night, it was ubiquitous, everywhere and nowhere, it surrounded him.

"Guilty! I condemn you…!" Bedford recognized the voice, it was the old teacher from the bus, "you've fulfilled your sentence you're no longer bound to the netherworld outside the realm of civilization and society, you're released. You're free to walk in the light of day." The girl was standing next to him.

"What's your name?"

"Clarabelle."

"I remember what happened Clarabelle, every time."

"It's something you're going to have to live with."

"I remember what happened when I got here. I thought it would be different this time." Bedford walked to the head of the grave, he knelt down and reached out, he hesitated, pulling back his hand in fear, did he really want to know? It was the final piece of knowledge that he'd been searching for all night.

"This is your grave."

"I thought this was my redemption, you mean I still die?"

"We all die Bedford, the grave was if you failed the test you'd die to awake on the bus and start the cycle over seeking redemption, you've broken the cycle."

"Why is the grave still here?"

"There's always a grave in our futures, but it's empty," she said. He looked skeptical, "go ahead, look." He reached out again and brushed away the dirt it revealed nothing, he pushed away the rest of the mound, nothing, it was empty, "satisfied?"

"What's next Clarabelle?"

"We're waiting for the sun." Clarabelle turned towards the east, the sky was starting to lighten, bars of light layered upon each other, from the black of night, to cobalt, then azure, down through the spectrum to white light as the sun began to rise over the horizon. She reached out to hold his hand. "It's over Bedford, you've freed the both of us." The morning's light crept into the circle and engulfed him, he took a last look at Clarabelle she had become luminous, every atom of her being iridescent, the light became stronger and stronger until he lost her in the light. She was free, free from the burden that he had unfairly put upon her. Finally, the light overcame him.

"Wake up," a voice gently said, "wake up." Bedford awoke in a bed the sun shining in his eyes, he turned his head, across from the bed was a mirror, he was an old man, aged, older than he thought he'd ever be, older than he had any right to be, but he remembered everything that had happened, the pictures in his head were ugly and brutal. The events felt recent in his memory, as if they'd happened only a few days ago. The past wasn't past for him even though he knew they had happened a long time ago now. He knew he'd wasted a lot of time lost in anger, fear and the self-hatred that made him lash out at the innocent. He had to live with that knowledge. Had he made amends? Could you make amends of that magnitude? Could the scales of Justice truly be weighted to redemption for his crimes? He didn't know. He didn't know how much time had passed or how much time he had left or what he was going to do, but he was at peace. He'd saved Clarabelle, her soul was free, the weight of the burden had been lifted from his soul. He no longer had to live in fear of what was going to happen or of the past haunting him. Nor was he afraid of what the future would bring, for the first time in a long time. At the foot of the bed stood the teacher.

"You're the teacher and the judge?"

"Yes," he said mildly.

"What happened, I was just young?"

"You used up the time trying make it right, to redeem yourself."

"I've been redeemed?"

"Yes."

"How many lives have I led?"

"Just one. But you used it up."

"Oh."

"Don't worry, most don't get it right."

"What happens to them?"

"What happened to you, a choice to be made."

Bedford smiled contentedly. He laid back down, pulling the covers up around him, a cocoon, warm and safe, he knew he'd rest. He wasn't afraid of what he might dream, or what life he might arise to.

THE THIRD DAY

I

Vlad was lying in the rubble of a bombed-out building amid chunks of concrete and twisted steel. The surrounding buildings looked like tattered paper, their facades ripped off and interiors exposed, furniture still inside, they looked strangely enough like doll houses. Blocks of concrete with steel sticking out of them twisted into abstract sculptures of war. Bricks and powdered concrete poured into the streets like rivers frozen in destruction. Everything was covered in dust, all shades of gray, black and white. War bleeds the colour out of life.

Vlad wasn't trying to blend into the rubble so much as to become part of the rubble. His rifle jutted out in front of him hopefully looking like nothing more than a piece of pipe. His face was caked in dust, his lips were parched and cracked. "Pfft," he spat out some concrete dust as soundlessly as he could. He lowered his head back to the sights of his rifle. If someone spotted him up here, they'd send a patrol to flush him out. He had a vision of an armed militia bursting through the door to the roof, machine guns blazing as he scrambled across the rubble like a wounded spider trying to get away, until his body gave out to the assault of the bullets and fell dead. The crimson of his blood pooling on the gray-white powdered plaster before soaking in, and absorbed away until it became nothing more than a dark blotch, part of the lifeless colour of war. Even worse, he could imagine someone on the street below simply aiming and firing a rocket launcher, toppling what was left of the ravaged building. These scenarios played over and over in his mind.

The sky was starting to lighten to a robin's eggshell blue. The streets were still, empty at this time of day. He could hear the twittering of the first birds of morning. The sound of the birds was the last remnant of when life had been normal. Sarajevo is a beautiful city of ancient traditions, culture and history. It's built on the same plan as many other European cities, a Platz at the city's center, medieval buildings, balconies lined with plants, and maybe a house that some historical personage had resided in. Along with that history came rivalries that were long submerged and simmered for generations, and when the lid was thrown off, war came.

Vlad saw a mangy looking dog sauntering down the street, stopping occasionally to forage in the rubble. Suddenly, the peaceful morning was shattered by the first gunfire of the day. The dog's head snapped up looking in the direction of the gunfire, his ears perked up at the sound of the next volley of gunfire. The dog scampered off.

"Even a dog has sense enough to avoid war," Vlad thought to himself. No more of the birds would be heard that day, leaving not silence, but an eerie emptiness.

This was the third morning of his lying-in-wait, the third morning without sleep, the third morning without eating, the third morning without his family, and the third morning of going over the events that had brought him here to kill his best friend. Maybe he'd been stalking Janus all his life, or maybe providence had put him here to study Janus, to know his habits, traits, idiosyncrasies, to be the balance to his counterbalance. Those events played over and over in his mind. His life had become an act of remembering.

He was thirteen when he and the other members of the national shooting team first heard of Janus. It was a time of great hope in their lives, they were training for the Yugoslavian national shooting team. Vlad had been recruited because he was thought to have been one of the best shots in his province, but so had the other members of the team. Still, it was a great honor to be chosen. Vlad was elected captain of the team because he was the best shot on the team, maybe in all of Yugoslavia, it was said. Like war, Janus was rumored before they ever met him. Janus *was* supposed to be the best shot in all of Yugoslavia, and that he never missed. They never believed the rumors, until he arrived.

One day shortly after those rumors of Janus had rushed past their ears, they were at the state-run training facility, it was formerly a military boot camp; that had been closed after the war and converted into Yugoslavia's Olympic training center. It was out in the middle of the country. The camp was about five kilometers from the nearest town, cut off from their families and the outside world. There was a television in the day room and, if there were any solitary moments, it was only a few minutes before someone else came in. Nothing was done alone. Everyone moved in crowds. This was meant to focus our attention on shooting and dissuade them from any interest or contact with the outside world.

One afternoon we were practicing on the firing line. There were human shaped targets at the end of a rope and pulley system that was used to deploy and retrieve the targets from the far end. We were all dressed in the team uniform, navy blue sweatpants with a white polo type shirt with the national emblem over the heart. We were all shooting when one of the coaches walked down the line.

"Krystof!" He barked at one of my teammates, "aim at what you're shooting at, don't just point the rifle and hope for the best!" We were, of course, the best shots in Yugoslavia, so we knew enough that this was just a coaching tactic to motivate us. To us, the coaches were all faceless, of the same mold—barrel-chested bullies, aggressive and belligerent. It was some ancient martial idea that it would make men out of us. They acted as if they were drill sergeants, and we were their recruits. They thought they would tear us down and rebuild us in their image. They parsed out their praise for only what they couldn't refute—excellence. It was our talent that set us apart from the rest of the world and made us rebels. We mocked and mimicked the coaches when they weren't around.

"Tomko! You're not holding your breath as you squeeze the trigger. It's not your dick, don't jerk it!" Each of us was subjected to these critiques as he walked down the line, Vlad could hear him getting closer, "Ranko! Concentrate on what you're doing! You can't bully the bullet into the bullseye!" The coach got to the end of the firing line where Vlad was, just as he had finished shooting and had retrieved the target. He grabbed it from Vlad as he took it off the line and looked it over. Vlad could see the light shining through the holes. It was almost perfect, with only one errant hole outside of the bullseye.

"Vlad! Your shooting is exemplary!" The coach said in his overblown tones. "The head coach is right, someday you'll lead this team to Olympic gold medals. Boys come and look!" The team gathered round, and all admired my shooting. I was feeling rather proud of myself at that moment. Most of the boys were from the country or at least the suburbs which then were still wide open and had a country feel and culture to them. They had a lot of experience hunting. Vlad was the exception. Coming from the city, he had always shot targets, it had always been considered the other boys who had the advantage in shooting. "Except what is this, Vlad?" He asked, poking a finger through the hole outside the bull's-eye. "This is what happens when you think before you shoot. Don't stop to think. Sight, shoot and squeeze the trigger in one fluid motion! How do you expect to lead this team to victory, or even remain captain with this kind of shooting?" Vlad heard one of the other boys behind him mutter "dick," the coach's head snapped around at the sound, like a hawk after a mouse, but he missed his prey. Their faces betrayed nothing except the innocent condescension that many a teacher knew. That was the afternoon the head coach brought Janus out to the practice field.

"Boys! Boys! Settle down," the coach said, "I want you to meet the newest member of our team, Janus. Janus is a remarkable marksman and I'm sure he will be a leader in our goal to win at the '76 Olympics. Vlad, as team captain you will make sure Janus is welcomed and acclimated to our team."

"Yes sir," Vlad said. The coaches stepped back and there was an awkward moment, as they all looked Janus over. He was already dressed in his "signature look," as he called it, a black leather jacket and a white button-down shirt with far too wide of a collar, the fashion at the time. It did give him an iconic look and accentuated his natural good looks and charisma. He appeared to be a dashing, romantic figure, like a western rock star, or at least people's idea of one. Later, when they were coming and going from matches, people would recognize him on the street. When he got off the bus, women would come up to him to ask for his autograph. He'd perfected the look of the sensitive artist with a faraway look in his eye. Sometimes when they were walking along, Vlad caught him posing in a window or checking how he looked. Vlad once asked him why he did it. Janus said, "in case there were any cameras around that might catch me." Janus looked at my practice target.

"Not bad," he said. "I bet I can shoot better than that." Ranko being a friend and faithful to the team, said, "Vlad is the captain of the team, and the best shot."

"Are you the captain because you're the best shot?"

"The team voted me captain."

"Then it is an honorary title?"

"Let's see what you can do." Vlad said, handing him the rifle. He sent a target down to the far end of the firing line and looked over the rifle very quickly. "Your sights are a bit off, but I think I can compensate for it." After he had shot, Janus pulled back his target, the bull's-eye was in shreds, five shots through the center, it was that clean; there were no other holes.

"You always shoot like that?" Vlad asked.

"Always," he said, his voice betraying a supreme confidence in his abilities. There was another awkward silence then he said, "let's shoot again!" Because they had nothing else in common they shot all afternoon, feeling each other out, discovering their strengths and weaknesses on the field of competition, and that was how it always ended. Vlad shot well; Janus shot better, perfect.

The sun was getting higher in the morning sky. Soon the hunger would return, but he also knew the hunger would go away. Of more concern was the craving for a cigarette. He hadn't had one in almost three days now. He hoped today would be the day Janus would return to his sniper's lair. Vlad didn't know how much longer he could hold out against the cravings, against the elements, against the boredom.

Vlad raised his head just enough to see a larger view of his surroundings. Buildings methodically bombed by artillery, then ransacked by militias and burned, left for ruins and sniper's nests. He hoped Janus hadn't detected his stalking and had changed positions, or he wasn't now in Janus' cross hairs at this moment. Vlad lowered his head back down to the sights, and to his memories.

Over the years Vlad and Janus became best friends vacationing with each other's families. One vacation, Vlad went to Janus' family cabin in the woods. It was a typical wooden hunting lodge—rustic, rough-hewn furnishings, hunting trophies on the walls, an ornately carved wooden cabinet filled with rifles, and stairs that led to the bedrooms. The railings were made of tree branches or made to look like them. There was a big living room table, and big overstuffed leather couches in a sunken living room near the fireplace. Janus' parents were well off.

Janus' father was older, in his late 50's or early 60's with gray hair, and a neatly trimmed mustache. He was an anachronism, he looked like he was plucked out of an old sepia tinged black and white photograph and dropped into the modern world. It was made clear that dinner would be formal, jacket and tie. Luckily, Janus had forewarned Vlad, and Vlad had brought along a white button-down shirt, tie, and his team blazer. He hoped this would pass muster with Janus' father. When Vlad went downstairs Janus' father was already sitting stiffly at the head of the table, which was set with a white tablecloth, china, and crystal goblets. Janus came downstairs wearing his usual white shirt and leather jacket.

"Janus," his father said sternly, "go back upstairs and dress in the proper attire for dinner."

"But this is going to be my trademark, so people will remember me after I'm dead."

"It's easy to die when you're young and immortal," his father grumbled. "People will remember you for your deeds, not your clothes. And as for dying, that's not going to happen any time soon, is it?"

"Probably not."

"Very good. Now, since we're in agreement when you're at the dinner table you will wear a proper coat and tie like your friend here. Mr. Smirtonev knows how to dress for dinner. Please go change." Janus went back upstairs to change. Janus' father smiled wanly at Vlad, he seemed embarrassed. "So, Mr. Smirtonev, how do you like being the captain of the shooting team?"

"It is a great honor the others have bestowed upon me." Which was the stiff formal answer the coaches demanded if he was ever asked the question.

"Good answer. That attitude will take you far in life." There was another awkward silence, Vlad didn't know what else to say. Janus' father and the boys inhabited two different worlds, only briefly sharing the same space and time.

Janus and the shooting team were the extent of what they had in common. Finally, Janus came back downstairs dressed as his father had decreed and took his place at the table.

"There, that wasn't so bad, was it? Why do we have to go through this every time Janus?" It was a rhetorical question. The battle lines of their war had long ago been drawn and each knew the stakes, life and death. They were both combatant and casualty, and both abided by the status quo. Janus sat there glumly, but his posture was erect, and he had a sly smile on his face. He wasn't beaten. He'd lost a battle in the war with his father, but somehow, he knew he'd win the war.

"I only dressed this way for Vlad." His father raised his glass in a toast. Vlad and Janus followed suit. "To my son. The only pleasure he has brought me in life is when he made the national shooting team."

The next day, Vlad was sitting on the front porch of the cabin reading and smoking, enjoying the afternoon. The cabin was far out in the woods. There was no road to speak of, just two worn tire tracks in the dirt. It was early fall. There was just a little chill in the air. The trees were all burnt with gold and red, the grasses brown, and the woods only about a hundred feet from the stone and wood cabin. When Janus came back, walking up the dirt path towards the cabin holding up two pheasants by their limp necks, he smiled and yelled, "dinner!"

"How did you catch so many?" Vlad asked, as he walked up the stone steps of the porch.

"The smart hunter lets them come to him," he said. "You should hunt, you'd enjoy it walking around in the fresh air."

"And kill living things."

"Come on, we have to kill to live. We're both marksmen, man is a predator. We have the right to hunt, we're at the top of the food chain."

"Who says we're at the top of the food chain?"

"No other creatures hunt us."

"But it's not on equal terms. You go out into the woods with a rifle and a scope, and your prey doesn't even see you, doesn't even know you're there. Maybe if you approached nature on its own terms. If you went out into the wild with only a knife or a spear, then you'd discover who is at the top of the food chain."

"You mean like hanging from a tree limb in a loincloth with a knife clenched between my teeth, like Tarzan?"

"Come on, be serious," Vlad said.

"Seriously, you should hunt, you'd enjoy it."

"I don't like to kill."

"What do you shoot for?"

"For the art of it, for the sport, as a challenge."

"The sport of it is hunting."

"It's something I do well. I like being the best."

"I'm the best." Janus chided, laughing. "Besides, I do not expect the hunted to understand the hunter. Everything kills. It is the natural order of things. There is no innocence."

"Animals kill for survival, to eat, to protect their young, to live. Only man kills for sport. Once you justify the killing of one creature, no matter how small and insignificant, you can justify the killing of any other creature. It's an illusion."

"What's the illusion?"

"Your imagined power over life and death."

"What are you, a bleeding heart?"

Janus looked towards the woods and saw a rabbit hopping along the tree line. "Here, watch." He pointed the rifle at the rabbit and shot in front of the animal. Panicked, the rabbit turned and ran in the opposite direction. Janus jerked the rifle fast.

"Don't shoot!" Vlad yelled. Janus shot in front of the rabbit again, the bullet kicking up dirt right in front of its nose. The animal froze in fear not knowing where its attacker was.

"Jesus, leave the poor creature alone." Vlad said.

"You can save it."

"How?"

"Stop me." Vlad didn't know if Janus was trying to provoke him or not. Maybe this was his idea of a joke? Or maybe Vlad had pushed him farther down this path than he had intended?

"Don't shoot!" Vlad said again.

"That's what you said before, and it didn't stop me." Vlad looked at Janus, then the rabbit, still frozen in fear, breathing hard, and too frightened to move. Vlad saw Janus' finger edging its way towards the trigger. Vlad steeled himself and grabbed the barrel as roughly as he could. Vlad felt the resistance against the force, Janus was stronger. Vlad could see the veins in Janus' arm popping. The barrel bounced off target momentarily, as Janus lost his aim, but he was ready, his grip tight on the gun and he easily pulled the gun back into place. Janus smiled a bit. Vlad let go. Vlad didn't know how to stop him. He walked back towards the cabin door—Janus, tired of playing with the animal, took his time sighting it.

"The coaches are right about one thing." Janus said.

"What's that?"

"You think too much about the shot." With one fluid stroke of a finger, Janus ended the rabbit's life. "I'll make a hunter of you yet," he said, leaving the rabbit where it died. Vlad dropped his head. It felt like a failure.

Thereafter, Janus and Vlad agreed to disagree. Although, thinking back, maybe it was a trait he shouldn't have tolerated in a friend. It's easier to stop a boulder before it rolls down a mountain, then after it has started rolling. Maybe it would have made a difference, maybe it wouldn't have. But that's not the way kids think. Janus was his friend and that's all Vlad understood. Over the years Janus and Vlad would debate it many times over, neither conceding nor conceiving an argument to convert the other.

The sun started arcing higher in the sky over Vlad's lair, the shadows getting longer like a sundial of death. A few people scurried by on the street trying to accomplish whatever errands they needed to do to survive without getting caught in the war.

As time went on, Janus led them in adventure. He was a true rebel. Our rebellion had so far been silent, Janus made our rebellion an open rebellion. He stood up against the coaches, and not in our petulant schoolboy manner, he did it to their face, he was our hero. Janus became our leader, he was the mastermind of their 'commando' raid and escaped from being under the scrutiny of the coaches at all times, at least for a night. Their days were regimented right up until the moment they went to sleep. Their dreams were their freedom. Vlad was asleep in the dormitory when he felt a hand slap him and Janus' voice, softly whispered, "Vlad." Vlad looked around at the rows of bunk beds, and the moonlight shining in, reflecting up a dark light off the highly waxed linoleum floor. The moon's light and the surrounding woods filled the dorm with a blue, gothic, eerie light. Janus stood there dressed in black, carrying a flashlight. Obviously, he'd been planning this. The blue and black light across his face looked like pieces of a jigsaw puzzle.

"Wha?" He mumbled sleepily. "What's going on?"

"Shh…" Janus hushed him.

"Where's the coach?"

"Asleep in the room behind his office. Now be quiet and wake up sleepy head. Life is moving on without us, and we have a commando raid to accomplish."

"A what?"

"A commando raid on that roadhouse about two kilometers down the road."

"What time is it?"

"About eleven."

"We'll get in trouble."

"Only if we stand around here debating it. It'll be easy, we sneak out of here, walk down the road, have a couple of beers, play a couple of songs on the jukebox, dance with any girls there, and hopefully not get into a scuffle with their boyfriends. And we come back with an adventure, and a story, all without anyone knowing." Janus then leaned down and woke Ranko in the bunk below, and then the others until they were all awake and dressed.

They climbed out one of the dormitory windows, ran across the wet grass as stealthily as they could, jumped a fence and soon they were walking down the road to the roadhouse.

The roadhouse was straight down the road and when they saw it, it was a welcoming site, warm lights pouring out into the darkness. When they walked into the bar it was a surreal moment. Everything stopped, like something out of a movie, and everyone there was looking at them. They looked out of place, young, most of us dressed in dark clothes for the 'commando' mission. Everyone in the bar knew who they were and where they were from and that they weren't supposed to be there. They walked into the bar, and everything returned to normal. They ordered beers, played darts, played songs on the jukebox, and there were a few girls to talk to.

After a few beers and songs from the jukebox the front door burst open, and the head coach walked in with the local police. Out of habit they all stopped doing what they were doing, except Janus who sat coolly at the bar drinking his beer, ignoring the intrusion. "Line up boys," the coach bellowed. We all did, except Janus who stayed seated on his barstool facing the coach.

"I thought I'd find you boys here," he said, pacing up and down the loose line of the team. "Don't we have a match tomorrow?" he asked rhetorically. "Aren't you supposed to be resting so you can do your best at the meet? You boys have the potential to be the finest marksmen in all of Yugoslavia, maybe the world, yet you insist on not being serious in your avocation. If you don't improve your discipline, we can always put you in the military. I'm sure they'll know how to improve your discipline there. Now, any of you want to tell me whose idea this was?" There was silence. Then he walked right up to Janus, "but that would be an unnecessary exercise, wouldn't it? You think you can get away with murder because you're the best shot in Yugoslavia?" A smile curled at the edges of Janus' mouth. "You better get that smug smile off your face. You know at one time I was considered the best marksman in all of Yugoslavia, what do you think of that?"

"Not much," Janus answered.

"You have all the answers, do you? Someday with that attitude…well, we'll see the hand life deals you. In the meantime, these gentlemen from the local militia will escort you back to the dormitory." They all started to file out of the roadhouse looking defeated except Janus, he held his head up high as he walked past the coach, who grabbed him roughly by the arm.

"If you lose the competition tomorrow, I will personally throw you off the team."

The next day at the shooting match Janus won. Vlad could still hear the announcer's voice over the public address system "another perfect set for Janus Trimako, team Yugoslavia wins the event." Afterwards, Janus walked up to the head coach and said, "I guess I can get away with murder."

It was the summer after this that that the team won gold medals at the Olympics. Vlad could still see Janus standing on the victory dais in the first-place position. A gold medal around his neck, and Vlad in the second position wearing a silver medal. In third place their teammate Ranko with the bronze medal. Their heads bowed in salute as they played the national anthem. In the films and pictures of that moment, Vlad saw himself smiling.

The team flew back to Yugoslavia arriving in the middle of the night.

There were a couple of limousines waiting for them and they were whisked away into the night. The limousines pulled up to a gymnasium in the middle of the city. The gymnasium was empty and dark, there were only five lights on in the center of the gym that reflected off the lacquered hardwood floor. At the end of the lights was a gun case. A government official stood dressed in the uniform of all government officials, a dark suit and tie.

"Come in boys," he said, "line up in the middle of the room." Outside the penumbra of the lights, it was dark. Sounds echoed wildly off the hidden walls, bleachers and equipment in the darkened gymnasium. They did as they were told. "Good," he said, "stand at attention and wait here." He walked off into the darkness, his shoes echoing ominously off the cold hard surfaces. They didn't know what to do, not even Janus. They all stood there at attention, waiting, listening to the rain splattering on the skylight above, every once-in-a-while seeing a far-off flash of lightning. Vlad recognized the guns in the case. They were Mausers, a rare German rifle that had been handmade during World War II.

Suddenly, one of the gymnasium doors opened with a pneumatic whoosh, and some of the pressure rushed out of the room. Some government officials entered the room and talked amongst themselves. Finally, one of them came forward and said, "gentlemen, in honour of your outstanding victory for Yugoslavia, General Tito himself will personally award you a medal and a ceremonial rifle. When he approaches you, extend your hand to shake his. If he speaks to you, be brief and polite." They were going to be awarded a Mauser by Tito himself!

A cadre of old men entered the gymnasium surrounding Tito, who was dressed in his most martial finery, his jacket was filled with more candy coloured, striped ribbons and awards than could been won in any one war, or lifetime. He moved down the line, followed by two aides, shaking each boy's hand and mumbling a perfunctory, "good work young man, Yugoslavia is proud of your accomplishment." One of the aides trailing behind Tito handed him a medal which he pinned to the breast of each boy's blazer. The other aide handed him a rifle which he presented to each boy, who in turn replied, "thank you, sir," until he came to Janus.

The old man looked over Janus, standing there in his leather jacket and white shirt. One of the aides whispered in the old man's ear. Janus shifted in his place, the only time I've seen him even a little nervous. Tito said, "so, you're the rebel, eh?" Janus didn't say anything. He didn't know what to say, no one did. No one knew what the Grand Marshall was going to say. Nobody could anticipate the mercurial mood of the dictator. Would he be amused by Janus? Or outraged?

"You'll either be a great leader or in prison." Then the old man chuckled as he walked away, swallowed up by the aides, and soon they were again alone in the gym with the coaches.

To celebrate the team's victory at the Olympics, Janus' father let them use his cabin for a celebratory party. Janus and Vlad were sitting on the front porch having a beer next to the keg. The door to the cabin was open, and loud music was blaring from the stereo system. The rest of the team was running around with their new rifles in one hand and a beer in the other. Janus and Vlad were talking about their futures.

"So, what're you going to do now?" Vlad asked.

"I don't know, I'm going to see where this talent can take me. We're famous now, you know. Heroes. We can do whatever we want. What about you?"

"I'm going to university to study electronics," they sipped at their beers and shared an easy silence that good friends can share.

"Hey Janus!" The rest of our teammates ran over, "that was pretty brave of you wearing your white shirt and leather jacket for Tito."

"It's my trademark," he said. "Besides, I thought I'd give the old man a thrill."

"Did you smell him?" Krystof asked. "He smelled like dust."

"And his hand felt like old leather," Ranko threw in. Tomko was looking at his rifle, opening and closing the bolt, checking the sights, pointing it down range.

"So, what's so special about these rifles?"

"They're Mausers," Janus said. "The Germans made them during World War II. They're all individually hand crafted, and when they're fired, they have a very distinctive sound, a sharp powerful report. It is said that your target will hear the shot before it kills them."

"Did they do that on purpose?" Krystof asked.

"Sounds like an old wives tale to me." Ranko said.

"No, it's real. The Nazis built the Stuka fighter planes to have a 'screaming' sound when it dived, to instill terror in people. So, of course they intended people to hear the shot that kills them."

"How do you know so much about it?"

"I read it in a book. Our boy Vlad here isn't the only one who can read."

"Is that all?" Krystof asked, sounding drunk, fumbling around with the rifle. "Looks like any old rifle to me. Those old communists probably just told us they're valuable. They lie about everything else. They're probably cheap factory-made rifles. They probably have warehouses filled with them."

"They're real," Janus said. "The Germans made them easy and fast to load. They're for snipers." Janus pulled out a bullet, loaded his gun and aimed it down range. "And now for the best part, listen."

Janus squeezed off the trigger and the gun thundered out the round, and it echoed through the woods. "That's the sound you'll hear before you're killed by this rifle. Well, now that I've properly gained your attention," Janus said, "I would like all of you to come inside for a minor induction ceremony."

"I thought we were done with ceremonies?" Ranko asked.

"Hardly, my boy, hardly. It's only the beginning. We have a future to look forward to that are filled with ceremonies! Awards, accolades, plaudits, decorations, graduation ceremonies, marriage ceremonies, all to come! Now follow me inside." They all dutifully followed Janus. He stood in front of the rifle cabinet, while the others stood in semi-circle around him. "Now, everybody, quiet! Befitting the solemnity of the occasion of this award."

"Not to mention raiding your fathers' liquor cabinet." There was laughter all around.

"Quiet. Now, as I was saying, the solemnity of the occasion. This rifle," Janus held the Mauser above his head, "that has been awarded to me by Tito himself! Will be placed among my father's prized rifles!" With all the mock pomp and circumstance, he could muster, Janus reached up and took the key off the top of the cabinet, opened it and placed the Mauser in an empty receptacle.

"Let's stop playing with those silly guns," Ranko said, "and let's get another beer!"

Later that night, they were all very drunk, but most of their energy had drained out of them. They were draped over the leather couches in the conversation pit. There was a fire burning in the fireplace and the music was quietly playing in the background. Everybody was quiet, sedate, almost relaxed, and reflective. Perhaps they sensed this might be the last time they'd be together as a team and as friends.

"So, what do we do now?" Ranko asked.

"You mean, now that we're done with the shooting team, and have adult life in front us?" Tomko said.

"I don't know I…" Krystof stammered out.

"I'm going to school," Vlad said, "meet a pretty girl, marry her and maybe have a kid or two, maybe open a shop."

"Always the dreamer." Ranko said. "What pretty girl is going to look at you?"

"What kind of shop?" Tomko asked.

"Computers of course," Janus said.

"The future's just a tomorrow away."

"I don't want to be a shopkeeper," Janus said. "I don't want a job, I'm an artist."

"Since when?" Vlad asked.

"I'm an artist with a gun."

"Well, off to the military for you then," Krystof said, more laughter.

"No, I don't want to take orders from those fat old men anymore. War is an old man's game fought by kids, and I'm sick of taking orders and coaches yelling at me, using my talents for their glorification and advancement. I want to be remembered. I don't want to be swallowed up by life."

"I'm tired of them yelling at me too," Tomko said. "'Squeeze the trigger, don't jerk it.' They can jerk this!" He said, grabbing his groin with his hand.

"How about coaching?" Krystof asked. "The government pays the coaches well enough."

"No coaches here!" Ranko yelled out.

"Ahh, you might as well. Now that we're disbanded, they have to field a new team."

"No, I want to be a player in life and death," Janus said.

"Taking yourself a bit seriously, aren't you?" Vlad asked.

"You're drunk!" Ranko bellowed at Janus. "Get used to being anonymous in the streets, it'll do you good."

"Who wants to be anonymous in the streets? Just because you're already used to it. I'm the star of this team." They all laughed again. Janus got up and left the room.

"I don't know, I was asking you guys," Ranko said, "hoping to get some ideas." They all laughed. Ranko and the others looked up and behind Vlad, their faces suddenly turned serious, their laughter was gone. Vlad turned to see Janus pointing the Mauser at him. He cocked the rifle, "BANG! You're dead!"

Vlad dropped his beer.

"What the hell are you doing?!"

"Just a little demonstration. I could kill you! All of you and you'd never know it! You think you're better than all the rest of us because you're not a hunter." Janus was slowly circling the group as he was talking. Most of the boys were immobilized. One or two said softly, "put it down," Tomko flinched as if he was going to grab the gun, but Janus saw the movement and pointed the gun at him.

"I never said that." Vlad said.

"You never had to. Acting our moral center, never saying anything, but judging, always judging. Our little watcher, spying for the communists?"

"He's drunk," Krystoff said.

Then suddenly Janus was mad, yelling, "All of you! I made you famous! You lived off me, you won because of me, I made you!" Janus pulled the trigger again. There was the hollow SNAP! of the empty chamber. Ranko threw himself out of his chair tackling Janus, the others jumped on them, until Ranko wrestled the rifle away from Janus.

"What're you trying to do ruin our last night together?" Then Janus was laughing hysterically.

"It's a joke, I'm just trying to have a little fun."

"It wasn't funny." It was then that Vlad saw they were on different paths, paths that were leading them away from each other.

II

A car pulled up in front of the safehouse. Vlad looked down the sights of his Mauser. A man got out of the car, he looked around, surveying the area, they were being careful. Vlad watched through the scope. The man tapped the top of the car. Another got out of the backseat, on the far side, closest to the house, and walked straight to the door. Vlad relaxed. It wasn't Janus. He wasn't wearing a leather jacket and bright white shirt. Vlad knew Janus would never give up that affectation, he'd fought too many battles for it.

Undoubtedly, the man was a sniper. They could all well be snipers, but it didn't matter. They were unimportant. Janus was the one who could kill with impunity from a great distance. Janus was the truly dangerous one.

"It has to be today! He has to come today!" raged in Vlad's mind. He knew he couldn't take much more of the waiting. He hadn't changed position in three days. He looked at the sky. He couldn't tell what time it was, except that it was afternoon. The sun had arched high in the sky. Janus had told them the Mauser's had been handmade during World War II, with a distinctive sound among guns, a sharp powerful report, where often the victim heard the shot a split second before it killed them. If it was true, then when the time came, Janus would know who killed him. "There's nothing more to do than wait." Vlad reminded himself. Resigned, he returned to his memories.

After the Olympics came adulthood. Janus and Vlad moved off in different directions. Vlad went to university. The first day he walked onto the campus was like walking into a new world. The campus was full of colour, trees lined the pathways, with open grassy areas where students walked about as freely as they wished and talked with whom they liked. It was as far from the regimented existence he had led up until then as could be. Although some things did remind him of his previous life, the crenellated walls and towers of the university reminded him of the confined and cloistered existence he had led.

It had been a year since they'd won the Olympics and Vlad had grown up. He walked with more confidence in his stride as he lived the life of a college student, registering for classes, living in a dorm room, attending classes, working on computers, talking with peers, none of whom knew who he was. He didn't have to be captain of anything. He didn't have to be a leader; he was responsible only for himself. Anonymity gave him the freedom to be himself. Vlad had managed to get through to the spring of my first year before it was discovered who he was.

One day a reporter for the student newspaper went up to him and asked, "you're Vlad Smirtonev, aren't you?" Vlad was totally unprepared but guessed it would have happened sooner or later. He was fatalistic about it. He answered the only way he could in the moment, truthfully.

"Yes, I am."

"The Olympic shooting team captain?"

"Yes, and who are you?" The reporter started talking fast, making his pitch.

"I'm with the school newspaper, and I was wondering if I could do an interview with you? And maybe we could take a couple of pictures for the article too?"

"I don't think so, I left that behind a long time ago."

"It wasn't all that long ago, and people would really like to know that a national hero goes to the school." Vlad hesitated. Maybe it was his vanity. The reporter sensed the indecision and pushed his advantage.

"Look, the photographer is right over there, and we can take the pictures right now." He waved over to someone on the sidewalk behind them to come over. Vlad turned, and he saw her for the first time, Kaja, the woman who would become his wife. She was beautiful, a round face and long blond hair cascading down her back, falling around the camera hanging around her neck. She walked over, smiling. Her face shone in the sunlight, or maybe the light emanated from her. The reporter kept talking as Vlad watched her walking up to them, "and then go to a coffee shop and do the interview before your next class."

"Yeah, sure, whatever you want," Vlad said, distracted.

"How have you managed to remain anonymous?"

When she walked up, Vlad asked, "you're the photographer?"

"Yes," she said simply. The reporter noticed Vlad noticing the photographer.

"This is Kaja," he said, knowing he had Vlad.

"Well…," this time Vlad feigned indecision, "I guess I could talk to you."

"Great!" The reporter said, "let's do the pictures." He stepped out of the way and Vlad smiled at Kaja as she aimed the camera, and with the bright flashes of light the pictures were taken, leaving him only the image of her face, burned into his memory, and the interview washed out of his mind.

That night Vlad was at a party thinking about her when coincidence, synchronicity or just plain fate intervened. The house was jammed with people. Vlad was off talking in the living room with a group of his friends, when from across the room he saw Kaja come in the front door. She was dressed in a white peasant blouse and black jeans. He kept his eye on her the whole time she talked with her friends, until finally she was off by herself, and he could pry himself away from his friends.

"It looks like we were destined to meet again," Vlad said.

"Or you're following me."

"I could say the same about you, I was here first." She giggled. Looking into her gray eyes he could see forever. He could see the future, their future. Her smile was the sun that brightened the room, and for the first time in his life, he was filled with hope.

"You're the gun enthusiast, right?"

"Well, it's a little more than that."

"I know, I'm just teasing a little. Mikal is a big fan, and when he found out you were at the school, he made it his mission in life to hunt you down. So, you were on the Olympic shooting team?"

"I was the captain of the team."

"Does that mean you're the best?"

"One of the best. Not many people in the world can shoot better than me."

"What made you so good?"

"A lot of natural ability, good hand eye coordination, a lot of practice and a father who was glad I was good at any sport."

"Do you still shoot?"

"I thought I did the interview this afternoon?"

"Well, you didn't answer the question."

"No, I put that part of my life away after the Olympics. I thought it was time to do something else with my life. It was something I was good at, but not my life."

"So, at the risk of asking a clichéd question, what's your major?"

"Computers. They're the future, and I want to be part of the future."

"And you couldn't be in shooting?"

"I guess I could be a coach, but it's a lot of politics, and I had six years of politics and politicians on the national team."

"What're you going to do after graduation? Design computers?"

"No, I don't think I'm smart enough for that. I guess I used all my natural ability on shooting. But I'm good with my hands so I can fix them, maybe have a shop and sell them."

"When are you going to open your shop?"

"After graduation. For my services to the state, I got a scholarship for university and a small stipend to get me started in life."

"You gave better answers to me than to Mikal."

"I didn't want to talk to him. I only agreed to the interview when I saw you." She smiled, she was clearly impressed and flattered by what he had said.

"What about you?" Vlad asked, "are you going to be a photographer?"

"Sure!" She said, confidently, "Kaja Valorc, girl photographer! Sounds like it comes straight out of a comic book." They both laughed, as only two people can who are sharing a private joke, a private language that lovers speak. "It's maybe not as ambitious as you, but I could see myself working on a newspaper or magazine."

They spent the rest of the night talking only to each other, looking only into each other's eyes. As the night slowly progressed, the party thinned out and they found themselves sitting on the couch in the living room, talking and holding hands until they were the only two left. About two or three in the morning the hostess came in, she wasn't angry. She only smiled tiredly at them.

"Kaja, I'm going to bed. If you two leave, can you lock the door on the way out?"

"Sure," Kaja said, "we're only going to stay a little while longer anyway."

"Or you can stay the night." She turned out the light in the other room, and they were bathed in a soft light and everything that followed seemed to happen in a gauzy impressionistic film. They talked until they couldn't talk anymore, the night seemed to take them out of themselves, out of time; they became immortal, at least for a little while. Later when Vlad told her of this feeling, he said, "I know it's a silly idea." She replied, "it doesn't mean the feeling really didn't exist." They stretched out on the couch holding hands until they fell asleep. The next morning, they awoke still holding hands. It was the most beautiful night of Vlad's life.

When he awoke, she was still asleep. In the morning light you see things with eyes opened, everything is new and fresh—you can see everything the way it was meant to be, without judgement, and without the film of your prejudices. He watched her sleep, the evenness of her breathing. It was amazing, like having captured a wild animal that trusts you enough to sleep in your arms, its life literally in your hands. The little makeup she had on was gone, it had only enhanced the beauty that was there. Vlad could see himself waking to her every morning.

Vlad soon graduated from university. The auditorium was decorated with colourful bunting and frills for graduation and filled with people there to witness the event. He and all the other graduates stood on a stage, dressed in their graduation garb, robes and black mortar board caps with crimson tassels. Traditional music added to the pomp and circumstance of the ceremony. When Vlad heard his name called over the loudspeaker, it seemed a larger and more satisfying moment than hearing his name over stadium speakers at the Olympics.

He and Kaja were married soon after graduation. All their family and friends were there except for the shooting team. By that time their lives had moved off to different directions, and they had lost touch with each other. Vlad remembered standing at the altar in his tuxedo as Kaja came down the aisle, a vision in white that seemed to float towards me, and then those momentous and solemn words "Vlad do you take Kaja as your wife?"

"I do."

"Kaja, do you take Vlad as your husband?"

"I do."

"I now pronounce you man and wife."

They had their wedding reception in Vlad's new electronics shop which he called 'Olympic Electronics.' He supposed trading a little on his past wouldn't hurt. They had a little ceremony in front of the store, the wedding party still dressed in their wedding clothes, holding a flute of champagne while Kaja cut a ribbon officially opening the store. Vlad carried her over the threshold, inside the shop, the shelves were gleaming white and filled with computers, bulky CRT's, keyboards, and processors. Everything looked shiny, immaculate and new. Vlad's Mauser was laying on a glass display case. He had one last ceremony planned.

"May the good fortune that allowed me to win this," he said, holding up the Mauser for all to see, "follow us all of our years together." He kissed Kaja and then put the Mauser on the gun rack on the wall behind the counter, as everyone cheered. "I want to thank all of our family and friends for being here, and to comrades," his voice faltered and cracked a little at the thought, "my former teammates, wherever life has taken them, I hope they're as happy as we are."

They had a little apartment above the store. It was nearly barren of furniture, and what was there was basic and utilitarian, except the bed. Kaja had bought a big four poster bed with a deep mattress and down pillows and covers. The covers felt cool and crisp against his skin. When Kaja got in the bed, he could feel the warmth of her body near him. He pulled her closer and wrapped the big down covers over them. He felt his body relax and they fell asleep, satisfied.

As his business grew, so did their life. Kaja and Vlad could soon afford a house and they painted it with bright colours. Kaja filled it with beautiful furniture and plants when they moved in. It felt warm and alive. One evening Vlad was sitting around reading a newspaper when Kaja came in acting unusually coy.

"Do you think I should quit my job?"

"Why?" He asked.

"Well, you said that once we had enough money saved for a house, and enough money saved for a baby..." Vlad was preoccupied with other matters, blindly oblivious to the obvious hint.

"Don't you like your job anymore?"

"It's not that," she answered, even more coyly. "I guess I could work, and you could stay at home with the baby."

"A baby?" He said as it finally dawned on him. He jumped out of the chair and hugged her.

"So, what do you want? A boy or a girl?"

"A boy." Then he thought for a second, "no, no, no. Every guy wants a boy. How about a girl?"

"Well, those are the choices." Soon enough they were blessed with a daughter, Trina. She grew up quickly.

✳

Like the coming of spirits and hauntings there are precursors to war. Vlad had lost all track of Janus. He assumed Janus had done the same.

One afternoon as Vlad stepped out into the swarming afternoon street, as the usual lunchtime crowd rushed to get their lunch and back to work in their allotted time. He strolled towards his usual café. He wasn't paying attention and collided with a man. They started apologizing and as Vlad saw the man's face, he realized it was Janus. He almost hadn't recognized his old friend. He looked older than he should have. Janus was the same age as Vlad. When they were young Janus had been a little soft, but there was nothing soft about him now. He looked ten years older than Vlad, his body hardened and lean, his face—a hardened mask of the boy Vlad once knew. He seemed feral. Janus was, of course, dressed in his trademark black leather jacket and bright white shirt, now minus the wide lapels. Janus looked at Vlad and seemed to recognize him immediately.

"You haven't changed much." He said.

"Me!" Vlad exclaimed, "how about you with that jacket!" They both laughed, and Vlad invited Janus to dinner that night.

Because Janus was a special guest, Kaja broke out the china and silverware for the first time. She served a roast, potatoes, vegetables, rolls. All through dinner Kaja and their daughter Trina mostly listened as Janus and Vlad told their war stories of the shooting team, their adventures, and their misadventures, which were the more interesting stories. Everybody was laughing and having a good time. Neither Janus nor Vlad talked about their present lives. Maybe they were afraid of what the other would say. After dinner they sat around smiling at each other, satisfied with the meal and the company.

"That's the best meal I've had in a long time," Janus said.

"Well, it's not often we have one of Vlad's old friends over," Kaja replied.

"Oh, have you had any of our teammates over?"

"No, I haven't seen them in years, although, Kaja and I ran into Ranko a couple of years ago."

"More than a couple now," Kaja said, "Trina was still a baby."

"Really?"

"Can you believe he's the coach of the national team now?"

"That explains how come they haven't placed very high lately." Janus said.

"So, what have you been doing with yourself all these years? Have you been married?"

"No," Janus said, lighting a cigarette. "I haven't been as lucky as you. I've been traveling a lot, making a living exhibiting my skills."

"How's your father?" Vlad asked.

"He died years ago."

"I'm sorry."

"That's ok, you know what kind of relationship we had."

"I remember," Vlad said. After a moment of an uncomfortable silence or maybe a short requiem for Janus' father. "So, are you visiting, or have you come back to stay?"

"To stay. I'm looking to settle down and see what opportunities present themselves. I don't know about a family, but we'll see." He smiled weakly at the thought.

"You should find yourself a woman who isn't impressed by the fact that you were on the shooting team." Kaja said.

"That isn't as easy for me as it was for Vlad."

"Why not?"

"First of all because that's who I am, that's what I am." Janus looked at Vlad. "You didn't tell her?"

"Tell her?" Vlad asked, truly perplexed.

"What?" Kaja asked, her eyes desperately moving from Janus to me and back, as if trying to discover some great truth or to decipher some great mystery.

"He didn't tell you I was the best?"

"It doesn't matter who the best shot was." Kaja said.

"You didn't want to know who the best man was?"

"It wasn't important, I just know Vlad was the best man for me."

"How about you? Have you seen any of the others from the team since you're back?" Vlad asked, trying to change the subject.

"I've run into a few of them." It sounded like there was a menacing undertone to his voice when he said it, but Vlad was unsure if he had really heard it. Trina got out of her chair and ran up to Janus and asked, "do you like to play?"

"It looks like you have a young admirer," Vlad said. "Why don't we go down to the basement, and we can relax."

After dinner, Janus played with Trina, hide n' seek, flying her around the room, stealing her nose, all the games that would make a child fall in love with you. And he fell in love with Trina. Vlad had a videotape camera set up in the basement for taping Trina, he had it on for his friends visit.

"The daughter I never had." Janus said, a pall of regret crossed his face, "probably never will have."

"Come on!" Vlad encouraged, "sure you will, you're still young!"

After Trina and Kaja went to bed, Janus and Vlad talked. "So, Janus what have you really been up to? The decorations and awards?"

"Are you gloating?"

"No, I...."

"Not as many as I thought."

"I'm sorry Janus, that it didn't go the way you thought it would."

"That's all the past, have you heard?" Janus asked.

"What?"

"War, Milosevic says we need our lands back to remain a nation, and we need to take it back."

"I don't follow politics much, my family..."

"Well," Janus said, leaning in furtively, as if to pull Vlad into some conspiracy or perhaps he imagined another one of our 'commando raids.' "Soon we'll have the opportunity to shoot at something more interesting than targets and prey a little smarter than birds or rabbits." Vlad started a little at the mention of the rabbit and Janus' barb.

"What are you talking about?" Vlad asked, even more perplexed than at dinner.

"The ultimate quarry. People. They become the targets. It's the ultimate actualization of our art. Wouldn't you say?"

Vlad was horrified! "No! How did you get this so twisted in your mind? That's even a perversion of hunting! What kind of a man have you become?"

"A man just like you," he said.

"No, not like me." Vlad said disdainfully. "I live in a civilized nation of laws not lawlessness."

"The only law is the law of survival. If we don't extinguish them, they will most certainly eliminate us. Our talents will be very much in demand."

"What do you mean them?" Vlad had a sick feeling in his stomach. "Since when do you have any political belief?"

"I don't."

"Religious belief?"

"None."

"Ethnic identity?"

"Never."

"Then why get involved in the war?"

"I want to hunt people."

"You're going to be a soldier?"

"We don't have to be."

"What are you talking about?"

"Our talents raise us above mere soldiers. We'd be snipers, our talents would go to the highest bidder."

"You really haven't changed much in the past fifteen years, have you?" Vlad asked. "You're still going after quarry that doesn't know it's being hunted. You still don't hunt on an even playing field. You shoot safe, unseen, and our skills far exceed the ordinary."

"I represent the future." Janus said.

"The only future you're progressing towards is death."

"If I want to be able to kill, I can kill what I want, and I'll be the most unremorseful killer of all. Man is not defenseless."

"You're a coward. Killing by rifle is impersonal. You don't get involved with your prey. Why don't you make a commitment to killing? Go out in the field, be a soldier."

"What...?"

"But you can't, can you? It would be an even match your skills wouldn't be superior. But at least you'd see the effects of your handiwork." Janus glowered at Vlad.

"What ordinary dreams you've settled for Vlad. I expected as much from the others, but you? You had some vision. You could see beyond the horizon. It's too bad you were washed up at seventeen."

"And what has it left you? You sought the quick and easy route to what you thought would be fame and glory. What has it left you? Impoverished, desperate." Vlad felt bad at having taken Janus' bait, attacking instead of listening. "Why are you telling me this about the war?"

"Because I'm giving you the chance to escape. I can even help you to safety."

"I'm not leaving my home."

"Then stay out of it. After the war starts, you'll hear things, maybe about me. Just stay out of it."

"Why? Are you afraid?"

"Of you? No, I know you're not man enough. The only thing you've ever killed is a paper target. Let me ask you this." Janus said. "What did you think those targets we shot at represented?" Vlad knew Janus was right; he had never thought of what those human shaped targets represented. He just shot for the highest score, not that those paper figures represented a human being. Vlad knew he was right. Vlad couldn't stop him. He could never kill a man.

Janus looked at Vlad with a faraway look, a look Vlad hadn't seen in Janus in a long time, the friend he once knew. "My offer was sincere. If you want to get out, I can get you out." They looked at each other without saying anything for a long moment and Vlad knew it would be the last time Janus and he would see each other as friends, if ever again. Then Janus turned and left through the basement door into the night. It was then that Vlad realized even though we grew up together, shared each other's secrets, he was saddened by the gaps that had widened and put them on these separate paths. It was like they could only see each other from afar and the distance between them was too great to reach each other anymore. Everything was on videotape; how many times had Vlad watched it since that night?

It was a few weeks later that the war broke out. Kaja and Vlad were in a movie theater watching an American war movie of all things. They were in the darkened theater. His arm around her, sharing a popcorn when the theater was rocked by an explosion. At first Vlad thought it was part of the movie, but it didn't match the action on the screen, and it had rocked the whole building.

"That wasn't the movie," he said to Kaja. Then the lights went on in the auditorium and the manager of the theater came rushing in.

"The war has started!" He yelled, as people started to scream and madly scrambled to the doors. Vlad grabbed Kaja and pulled her close and they hurriedly left the theater. Outside the world had taken on a surreal aspect. The neon lights of the theater shone in the night, as cars raced up and down the streets and people blindly running in all directions. Vlad was trying to get to their car when there was a BOOM! And they could see the far-off glow of newly started fires from the explosion, the glow made eerie, reflecting off the clouds. Vlad grabbed a man as he raced by.

"What's happening?" He asked, desperately.

"They've been shelling the far end of the city everybody is trying to get out!" The man pulled away from Vlad in a panic. That was the beginning.

Vlad didn't remember how long after that he started hearing rumors of a sniper who could shoot unbelievable distances, a sniper that never missed. Vlad thought them to be the exaggerations of war. Life during war takes on its own sense of normalcy. Chaos becomes expected, safety uncertain, existing only moment to moment. Innocents are killed, houses and buildings bombed, refugees pour out of the city. Most people who are affected by war aren't the active participants, but those surrounding it, those that must adjust and adapt to find a normalcy amidst the chaos and live a life by keeping their heads down, not attracting attention, and praying you get through the day, any day, every day, even when what was once considered extraordinary becomes ordinary. New moralities are created every day.

III

Out of the snipers' house came the men that had gone in a few hours before. They congregated around the car again, talking. Talking about what? Vlad wondered, where to lunch? Maybe with their families? As though their lives were normal. Perhaps lunch with their children, their sons and daughters, their daughters. Vlad sighted one of the men. All he had to do was pull the trigger and this would be all over, a probable sniper dead. Then he wouldn't have to lay in this rubble, trying not to move, trying not to breathe, his muscles cramping, no more rats scurrying over him, and he could go to lunch with his daughter again.

Vlad had lived with the uneasy compromises of survival until one day. He went to lunch with his daughter. Before then, the war had been an abstract idea. He knew it existed, but it didn't affect him, until one afternoon, when he was pulled into it, and it became his war.

Vlad had an enjoyable lunch with Trina. They had talked about everything and anything, nothing out of the ordinary. She told him about school, he told her how nice she looked. As they walked out of the restaurant, Vlad was holding her hand as they crossed the street. He remembered asking her, "what did you learn in school today?"

"We learned about history."

"That sounds very exciting. Did you like your lunch?"

"Yes, the hamburger was very good." Just at that moment there was a sharp crack of a shot. People around them scattered, screaming, off to all directions, ducking behind any obstruction they could find. Vlad was frozen with shock. He had recognized the report of the gun. It was a Mauser. Trina was pulling on his hand, yelling.

"C'mon daddy! C'mon daddy!" All Vlad could do was stare in disbelief in the direction the bullet had come from, as if it could ward off the fear of what he had suspected. The crack of the second shot ricocheted off the ground behind Trina. She ran to Vlad wrapping her arms around his legs, sobbing into his pants. The crack of the third shot, the bullet bounced off the ground in front of them, closer, trying to scare him into bolting in fear. He felt his daughter's body wanting to tear away in the opposite direction. He held onto her. The fourth shot was behind them, but closer still. Vlad knelt down and whispered to her.

"Ok, now walk that way," he ordered, pointing in the direction of the last bullet, "walk! Now, let's go." He held her hand as if they were out on a Sunday stroll. When they got close to a truck, they dove behind it. Vlad knew the gun that had shot at them was a Mauser.

"It's him!" Vlad raged. "It can only be him!"

"Who?" Kaja asked after Vlad told her what happened on the street. They were among the safety of the cups and clapboards of their kitchen, and it occurred to Vlad she was the last beautiful thing in Sarajevo. The war hadn't taken her looks, yet.

"Janus! There were only five Mausers, all given to the shooting team, only given to my friends!"

"How do you know it's him? Maybe he gave it to somebody. Maybe he's dead and somebody else has it."

"No, he would never give it to anybody else. It meant too much to him, to all of us. He was playing with me, like he played with that rabbit, shooting in front of it, behind it, trying to frighten me into accepting the inevitable. There's no escape before he pulls the trigger."

"The rabbit?! The one he killed almost twenty years ago?! How can that make any difference now?"

"The rabbit lost its life because of me. I could've saved that rabbit, knocked Janus' aim off, taken the rifle from him. I should have stopped him then. Maybe if I'd stopped him then this wouldn't be happening now."

"Janus is responsible for killing the rabbit, and if he's the sniper, he's responsible for killing people, not you."

"I knew beforehand."

"How?"

"The night he came to dinner he told me his plans after you and Trina went to bed. If I don't stop him now, a lot of people will die because of me. If Janus is killed, I will have saved many futures. There will be some people alive who won't be if Janus lives. They still won't have the advantage, but at least the shooter may be more prone to miss after the first shot when chaos is reigning, and people are scattering. He wanted me to know it's him, he's playing with me the same way he played with the rabbit. He wants me to know that he can get to me and my family any time he wants, and there's nothing I can do about it."

"He said he would leave you alone if you left him alone. What changed?"

"How do you know that?"

"I saw the video you made that night."

"He knows I'm the only one who can stop him, and he's tying up his loose ends, eliminating those who can threaten him or even identify him."

"How do you know?"

"I checked. Ranko has disappeared. Chrystof and Tomko are dead."

"Why do you have to do it?"

"Because no one else can. I'm the only one as good as him."

"Or is there something else you want? Maybe something you need?" She asked.

"What?"

"To prove you are the best, that in the end you are as good as he is, and on his terms. Somewhere, you think he's right, that you can't prove you are a man until you kill."

"No." Vlad said, quietly. "I've thought about that too, and I can say without a doubt I'm not doing this out of jealousy or trying to prove anything. I'm the only one who knows his habits, and I'm the only one equal to his abilities. There is no one else. I wish there was. If there was, I would pass this cup to them. I wish it would be true. Then I could deny my motives and not commit the crime I know I have to commit."

"Why? What will it get you? There still won't be any peace."

"Sometimes all it takes is one bullet to end a war."

"Janus' death won't end the war."

"It will save lives of many who will otherwise die."

Vlad had found the snipers' safehouse. It wasn't difficult, everyone knew where they were. It was fear that kept them safe. Vlad spent his last day doing things he enjoyed. He spent time with Trina talking and playing with her. Kaja and Vlad were a different story. She knew and understood what he needed to do, what needed to be done, but wished he wasn't the one who had to do it. She found him in the living room on the couch watching over and over the tape of Janus playing with Trina the night he visited, a half bottle of whiskey cradled in his hands.

Vlad had one last look around his shop, standing in the doorway surveying what was left. The war had taken its toll on his business, most of the shelves were empty, what merchandise he had left had a thin layer of dust on them that he couldn't get rid of, the war was sucking the colour out of their lives. There was nothing left. He turned off the lights.

The next morning Vlad woke up early and started making breakfast. Soon the smell of bacon filled the room and reminded him of better times, of times when life was simple and easy, when he and Kaja were first married;

and going back further, of his childhood, his mother making breakfast in the kitchen, and the smell waking him up. It gave him a sense of a gentle domesticity. It made Vlad feel like there was still some normalcy left in life. The wafting smells and clatter must have woken Kaja because she soon came into the kitchen.

"I would've made you breakfast…"

"That's ok, I'm not hungry. It's for you and Trina. I was hoping it would make me feel…normal."

"Why do you have to go Vlad?"

"Maybe I've been stalking Janus all my life. Maybe Providence put me here to study him, someone to know his habits, his traits, his idiosyncrasies, to be the balance to his counterbalance. And because no one else can. I'm the only one as good as him and there will be some people alive who won't be if Janus lives."

"And what of the next sniper that comes along?"

"I don't know, but at least I've done what I could."

Kaja fell into his arms crying. "Don't go, please don't go, please don't go."

Vlad left their house, his Mauser packed in a carrying case. As he walked through the neighborhood, he could hear the sounds of a normal day through the open windows, radios on, bacon frying. He wished he didn't know about any of this, that he could be innocent and not know what he knew. As he passed the diner in town, he noticed a woman in a battered dress, a dress that used to be white, but was now dirty from constant wear. She was sitting at a table eating a huge piece of white cake with white frosting. He smiled weakly and walked on to the train station.

On the train he sat watching the scenery pass him by. He could occasionally see his reflection in the glass of the window. He was lost in thought, but he didn't recall thinking about anything in particular. The city flew past. Signs at first read Nord and the city was relatively untouched by the war, but when the signs started reading Sud, the area was rougher. It was war torn and scarred, with bombed out buildings and ravaged people.

Vlad found a bar to sit in until night fall. It was a workingman's bar, a place where men come to drink after a hard day's work, or to find a haven from the war. Vlad looked like any of the other patrons, dressed in jeans and a dark shirt, and black jacket. The only thing that looked out of place was the Mauser in its leather case at his feet. The bartender brought him another beer.

"It's going to be dark soon," the bartender said. Vlad was distracted, he wasn't paying attention. He heard him as if from some far-off distance or through a fog, but finally managed to say, "I know."

"People from around here know that a lot of the war comes around here after dark."

"Thanks for the advice."

"Were you at the shooting club?"

"What?" Vlad asked through the fog.

"Were you at the shooting club?"

"Yes, I did some shooting today."

"How'd you do?"

"What?"

"Did you shoot well?"

"Yes, I always shoot well."

"Have you shot long?"

"Since childhood."

The bartender stood close and almost whispered, "you better be careful; the shooting club was bombed the first week of the war." Suddenly Vlad was concerned what the bartender might think he knew. Maybe he was part of a local militia. He might even know Janus.

"You won't mention seeing me to anyone."

"I haven't seen or heard anything since the war started," he said, wearily.

"Where's the washroom?"

The bartender jerked his thumb backwards, "in the back." Vlad got up, taking the bag with him to the washroom. He came back out dressed in camouflage. The bartender looked shocked, as if Vlad was his worst nightmare.

"Remember," Vlad said, "don't mention seeing me to anyone." Vlad left all his money on the bar.

"When you're done with whatever it is you're going to do and you live, don't bring your troubles back in here."

When the bar's door closed behind Vlad, he was alone. There was nothing around, no light, no colour, no people, just the enveloping darkness of the night. He walked down the street. Everyone tried to avoid the night because like the bartender said, a lot of the war came around at night. Vlad looked around one last time. If someone was watching him, they would've thought him suspicious. He slipped into the bombed-out building across from the safe house and climbed to what had been the top floor of the building. He knelt down and took out the Mauser, set it up, laid down in the rubble, becoming part of it. As he waited, the sun passed over him three times. The world turned without him. He was alone with his thoughts and memories, his lips parched, his skin cracked, his eyes teared and he waited.

A car pulled up, pulling Vlad from the mantra of his memories. A shoulder in a black leather jacket emerged from the car. Vlad's heart started pounding in his chest. Everything was moving in slow motion. The man stood, his back to Vlad. The hair was the right colour for Janus. The man walked towards the house. Vlad had to wait until the man turned around. He had to be sure it was Janus. He was walking straight to the house. It didn't seem like he was going to turn around. The man paused, something had made him hesitate on the grass, and then he turned very slowly. The man was wearing a dazzling white shirt. Vlad looked through the scope and held his breath. It was Janus. He remembered the boy he first met at thirteen, how innocent he looked, the friend he lived with, competed with, loved.

Vlad pulled the trigger. Janus' body twisted to the sound of the shot. Vlad saw a plume of blood appear on the brilliant white shirt. One clear, clean shot through the heart. Janus clasped a hand to his chest and brought his blood covered hand up, looking at it as if it weren't his. Janus looked in the direction of the report, and smiled, as he recognized the sound of the rifle. Janus knew who had killed him as he slumped to the ground.

Vlad wept.

ACKNOWLEDGEMENTS

The two Connie's, first my mother who read to me as a kid, acting out all the parts and putting the pictures in my head. My sister Connie, for her support, technical advice, proofreading and early sounding board of my ideas from the roughest of drafts on up.

Ms. Karen Hermann for her encouragement and support and usually being the first reader of these stories and offering a frank and honest opinion.

Charles and Barbara Post for all their friendship, support and encouragement throughout the years.

Mr. Jovan Thomas, budding Hollywood director. When Jordan Peele was looking for stories for his *Twilight Zone* reboot, Jovan knew that I wrote science-fiction or had read something I wrote and asked if I'd be interested in writing a spec story for the project. He sent me a 600 word start of a screenplay that was rife with possibilities and provided the backbone of the stories *Judgement Night* and *Judgement Night-Redemption*. I wrote a story that he liked parts of but we had the old "artistic differences" in the direction to take the story, but he was cool enough to let me carry me on with the story and use it. What he didn't know was that I was coming off an experience where I had to dump an 84.000 word manuscript and I was bummed out about it. Thanks to Jovan he got me writing again, and because I had *Judgement Night* and a couple other short stories I decided to write what would become *The Lion Communique*. I'm looking forward to seeing his first feature film.

Mr. Tom Schlak who read primitive, jejune, tyro stories of mine a lifetime ago and thought they were good, being one of the first with encouragement and giving me the courage to show my work to others.

Ms. Salli Stevenson who provided input on some of the early versions of some of these stories.

Mr. Paul Levinson for accepting *Godwired* (and convincing me it was the better title) for his anthology *Touching the Face of the Cosmos*.

Jay Jeff Jones for his sage advice in literary matters, as well as turning me on to some writers I might have otherwise missed.

Mr. Jack Preston King who read early versions of these stories on Medium and offered constructive critiques.

Rich Weidman, a kindred soul in rock n' roll.

Mr. Cyrus Wraith Walker for an extraordinary cover and advice and technical support in getting the book together for publication. My thanks to him for guiding me through the labyrinth of self-publication.

The Doors for providing an inspiration and a soundtrack to my writing, their energy still goes on.

No animals were harmed in the writing of these stories, nor are they meant to encourage, condone, glorify or romanticize killing of them either, and are not meant to be advocating for or romanticizing big game hunting. They are allegories and are meant to be read as such.

The song in Judgement Night (& Redemption) is a verse from *Me and the Devil Blues* by Robert Johnson.

In Memoriam: Ms. Sally Stevens who never read any of these stories but offered support and input on the 60's L.A. scene and who died to early, she is missed.

ABOUT JIM CHERRY

JIM CHERRY was born in Chicago in 1960. Although, he missed out on all the cool things. He read his grandmother's book of first editions of Twain, Dickens, Conrad, Conan-Doyle and having backyard adventures of his own. At 12 to he decided be a writer, in college he went to school for filmmaking but realized it was just an excuse to write. He's lived in Los Angeles, visited New Orleans, Mexico, France and Germany, usually when he didn't have the money. He's written the novels *Becoming Angel, The Last Stage*, a book of short stories, *Stranger Souls*, and a compilation of articles *The Doors Examined*. If you want to know more about him, you can find him in-between the lines of his stories.

Printed in the USA
CPSIA information can be obtained
at www.ICGtesting.com
JSHW021019240124
55891JS00001B/53